Praise for

Or Be Reconciled

Or Be Reconciled is a well-written story of love and marriage, and a strong apologetic for faithfulness to the marriage covenant, even when confronted with an unfaithful partner.

—Mark and Cindy Fox
Mark and Cindy pastor Antioch Community Church in Elon, NC. Mark is an instructor at the School of Communications, Elon University, a columnist, and an author.

Or Be Reconciled is a lovely book. Ruth Johnson has created an engaging and uplifting read, written with grace and tenderness.

—Lori Borgman
Syndicated columnist, author and speaker

Or Be Reconciled

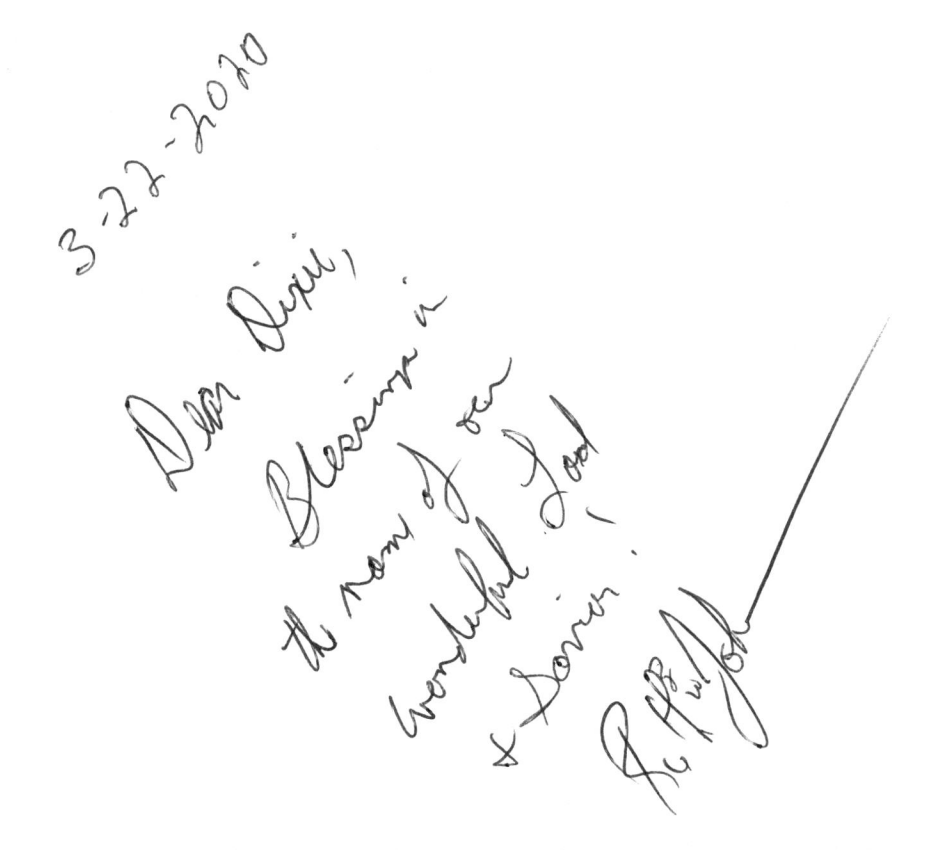

Or Be Reconciled

1 Corinthians 7:11

Ruth Z. W. Johnson

TATE PUBLISHING
AND ENTERPRISES, LLC

Or Be Reconciled
Copyright © 2013 by Ruth Z.W. Johnson. All rights reserved.

No part of this publication may be reproduced, stored in a retrieval system or transmitted in any way by any means, electronic, mechanical, photocopy, recording or otherwise without the prior permission of the author except as provided by USA copyright law.

Scripture quotations marked (kjv) are taken from the *Holy Bible, King James Version*, Cambridge, 1769. Used by permission. All rights reserved.

The opinions expressed by the author are not necessarily those of Tate Publishing, LLC.

Published by Tate Publishing & Enterprises, LLC
127 E. Trade Center Terrace | Mustang, Oklahoma 73064 USA
1.888.361.9473 | www.tatepublishing.com

Tate Publishing is committed to excellence in the publishing industry. The company reflects the philosophy established by the founders, based on Psalm 68:11,
"The Lord gave the word and great was the company of those who published it."

Book design copyright © 2013 by Tate Publishing, LLC. All rights reserved.
Cover design by Jan Sunday Quilaquil
Interior design by Joana Quilantang

Published in the United States of America
ISBN: 978-1-62510-897-5
Fiction / Christian / General
16.08.16

From the Author

I clearly remember the morning—over fourteen years ago—when I awoke from a vivid dream about a young widow falling in love with a charming man who happened to be divorced. I sat down at my computer and two thousand words later, I had the synopsis for *Or Be Reconciled*. Since that morning, I packed our family's belongings and returned home to North Carolina from Brooklyn, New York, where we had served as urban missionaries for ten years. I spent five years taking care of my elderly father (until his death from Alzheimer's at age ninety-one); assisted my husband in founding Vision India, a missions organization that provides support for native ministers and 120 orphans in Odisha, India; celebrated the marriages of my four children; received a diploma in nursing and worked as a nurse in long-term care settings for seven years; welcomed fifteen grandchildren into the world; observed my thirty-ninth wedding anniversary; completely renovated (with my husband) our almost-one-hundred-year-old home; and finally, after many promptings by that still, quiet voice, completed this story.

I was pleasantly surprised when Stacy Baker of Tate Publishing responded to my proposal with a phone call. She asked, "What do you want to be the result of publishing this book?" My response—marriages will be reconciled. She followed up with an e-mail: "I hope this works out; this is a passion of mine; may God bless the work of your hands."

My heart has always been broken by the breakup of what was once a happy family. I grew up in a loving, Christian home and never gave divorce much thought. Divorce was very rare in the fifties. As a young adult, I began to encounter friends from broken homes, and as I grew older and divorce became more prevalent, my life was touched—though not intimately—by the effects of shattered marriages.

My husband became a minister, and I was called upon to assist him in teaching, counseling, etc. We met so many couples with troubled marriages who often chose the path of divorce and remarriage. Times were changing, but in my heart, I knew God's word had not changed. "What therefore God has joined together, let not man put asunder" (Matthew 19:6). My husband and I took a stand that marriage was for life; he did not perform weddings if either party had been divorced. Some people got angry at us. Some said they appreciated our position. Satan began throwing fiery darts at our own marriage. We went through some very challenging times, but we determined that we would set an example for our children by working on, not giving up on, our marriage. Today, all four of our children are committed to their marriages. It is interesting to me that God sent us four wonderful children-in-law, each one from a broken home. Their experiences have taught me a great deal about the heartbreak children endure when their families are not intact. My prayer is that the example my husband and I have set—not of a perfect marriage, but a committed one—will see them through any difficult times.

Well, enough of my story. It is time to read the story of Jillian and Matt and Shannon, and by doing so, I pray that one or two or many more husbands and wives who have an open door of marital reconciliation in front of them will let go of bitterness, choose forgiveness, and *be reconciled*.

Acknowledgment

I want to express my thanks and love to…

My Lord and Savior Jesus Christ; you are my all in all.

My husband, Randy—through it all, baby!

Our children, their spouses, and our grandchildren—Benjamin, Jessica, Caleb, Joshua, and Blaise Johnson; Steve, Rachel, Talise, Jada, Aria, Geilia, Nelani, Lahela, and Ezra Zachary Diaz; Hoyt III, Amy, Hoyt IV, Aiden, and Meia Tigerlily Stone; Steven, Emily, Emma Grace, and Izabella Edwards—"I have no greater joy than to hear that my children walk in truth" (3 John 1:4).

My precious parents, J. Boyd and Olive Wright (home in heaven).

My sisters, Elizabeth, Rodema (home in heaven), Rachel, and Anna and their families.

All my in-laws in Oklahoma and my sweet mother-in-law Bernita (home in heaven).

Our "family" in India.

Pastor and Marilyn Thompson and my church family, especially the ladies in Sunday school class.

Mona, thank you for being a friend!

Cher, my "little sister" and fellow author.

Cindy, my friend for life.

All of you who have encouraged me through the years to keep writing.

The Tate Publishing family.

Contents

1 A New Start --------------------------------------- 15
2 The New Neighbor ------------------------------ 28
3 The New Church --------------------------------- 38
4 New School/Job ---------------------------------- 44
5 Settling In --- 50
6 Memories -- 54
7 Life Goes On -------------------------------------- 58
8 Not Just a Cookout ------------------------------ 63
9 New Feelings ------------------------------------- 68
10 Seeking --- 74
11 So That's Shannon ----------------------------- 81
12 Now What? -------------------------------------- 95
13 Reminiscing ------------------------------------ 102
14 Love Thy Neighbor --------------------------- 107

15 What If?	114
16 Dream a Little Dream	121
17 Dreams Can Come True	129
18 I Feel Giddy	133
19 We Are Family	137
20 Love Is in the Air	148
21 Be Careful Not to Fall	154
22 Merry Christmas!	161
23 A Time To Grieve	170
24 Oops!	184
25 All in the Family	188
26 Ringing in the New Year	193
27 Full Disclosure	201
28 Where Do We Go from Here?	221
29 Alone	232
30 Troubled	240
31 Cancer	245
32 Letting Go	250
33 The Kiss	259
34 Worse than Expected	262
35 Breaking the News	267
36 Things Are Not Always as They Seem	274
37 Till Death Do Us Part	291
38 Prayer Changes Things	302
Epilogue	309
Study Questions	315

Chapter 1

A New Start

Father, I don't know where to begin this morning. I am grateful to you for leading us to Lakeview and for opening new doors for us to walk through. I am thankful we don't have to take those steps by ourselves. It is so comforting to know you are with us. Even through the difficult times of the past several years, I have felt your presence, and I know you love me and my children. Help us to love you as we should.

Bless Bryan's friends for giving up their Saturday to move us to our new home. Thank you that the kids are happy and excited about the move. Lord, help them adjust well to our surroundings, especially their new school. Please bless them with Christian teachers and friends. Thank you for my job at the hospital. Use me to share your love with those who are sick and hurting and lonely…and dying. I am anxious, but I trust you to help me adapt quickly.

Take care of Mom and Dad and all the kids at the orphanage and the workers who help them. Be with Grandma and Grandpa Hamilton. Help Molly, Joshua, Caleb, and me to stay close to you and guide us in all we do. Keep your loving arms around my children, Lord…and me too! In Jesus's name.

Jillian threw the covers back as soon as she whispered, "Amen." Resolutely, she completed her routine stretching exercises before her feet hit the floor. She loved the sensation of the cool hardwoods beneath her feet. They were a stark contrast to the plush carpet in the master bedroom she and Bryan had shared in their home in Richmond.

Just another reminder that everything has changed, she acknowledged wistfully while pulling back the filmy bedroom curtain at the eastward-facing window. She opened the faux wood blinds to let in the morning sunshine. Across the narrow side yard, she could barely make out a figure standing at what she supposed was a kitchen window. Quickly, she pulled the blinds closed.

"Oh well, views inside your neighbor's house are definitely not a benefit of a cul-de-sac," Jillian grumbled audibly, realizing the neighbors would be able to see inside her house as well.

Yesterday, Mrs. Cecil, the elderly neighbor on the west side, had stopped by to introduce herself. Curious to meet her other next-door neighbors, she was disappointed that no one appeared to be home. Now she had caught her first glimpse of the man of the house. *Lord, help them to be nice and not the nosey type*, she prayed silently as she chose an outfit from her ample walk-in closet.

"It's not as large as in some master suites of houses this size," the stylish realtor had advised, "but since you're not married, it should do fine."

At that time, Jillian had refrained from acknowledging that awkward assessment. *Yes, it will do fine since I'm not married*, Jillian now assured herself with only a hint of melancholy.

Walking on the smooth oak floorboards brought back long-ago memories of summer mornings at her childhood home, memories that produced serenity in her spirit. *I wish Mom and Dad were close by now.* The longing passed fleetingly as she stuck her head out of her bedroom door and called to her children.

"Joshua! Caleb! Molly! Time to get up, sleepyheads. It's Sunday morning, and we don't want to be late at the new church."

"Mommy...Mommy...come here, Mommy."

It was Molly's plaintive voice, and Jillian knew instinctively what was wrong. Sighing, she paused briefly before walking the few steps down the hall to her daughter's room.

"Are you okay, sweetie?" she asked tenderly.

"Mommy, I'm sorry. I did it again," Molly whimpered as she sat on the edge of her twin-sized bed, the brand-new fairy princess sheets soaking wet from the accident.

"It's okay, Molly. I know you didn't mean to," Jillian comforted as she began unmaking the bed. "As soon as I get these in the washer, I'll run some bath water for you. Why don't you run on in the bathroom and wait for me?"

"Thank you, Mommy," Molly responded gratefully before standing on her tiptoes and adding a kiss for good measure.

Jillian's heart melted at the combination of her five-year-old daughter's sweet words and sweeter kiss. She believed that of all her children, Molly had been least affected by Bryan's death. Only three years old when he died, at first Molly appeared to have hardly noticed her father's absence. When she started wetting the bed, her pediatrician had suggested Molly might be reacting to Jillian's palpable grief, rather than her own feelings of loss. Dutifully, Jillian made a brave attempt to hide all evidence of her grief from her children, but Molly had continued to wet the bed from time to time. She assumed this occurrence was a result of their move.

"Mom, where are our clothes?" Joshua's shouted question brought Jillian back to the task at hand—getting to church on time.

"I'll be there as soon as I take these sheets to the laundry room," she called back, immediately regretting sharing Molly's secret with her big brother.

"Did Molly-pee-wee wet the bed again?" Joshua smirked as Jillian passed by the boys' door on her way to the laundry room.

Jillian ignored his smart mouth, aware that he already knew the answer. As soon as she had stuffed the sheets into the washer, she remembered the plumber wasn't scheduled to hook up the machine until tomorrow. *If Bryan were here, he would have got the washing machine up and running last night.* She sighed and once again reminded herself to stop thinking of everything in terms of "if Bryan."

Hurrying back to the boys' room, Jillian gave both of her sons a quick pat on their shoulders. Joshua, going on adolescence at eleven, flinched, reminding her that in so many ways he was like his father. Neither was outwardly affectionate. Independent, they seemed to resent assistance unless they had personally asked for help, which they rarely did. Bryan and Joshua shared common physical traits as well—thick, straight, sandy blonde hair and blue eyes; tall, muscular physique. Since kindergarten, Joshua had enjoyed being the tallest boy in his class. It was hard for Jillian to believe he would be in the sixth grade this year.

Caleb, her nearly perfect eight-year-old, was rather opposite of his big brother. He responded to her touch with an affable hug. Like his mother, he was loving, obliging, and thoughtful. Obviously, he had also inherited Jillian's flashing green eyes and ash-brown, naturally wavy hair. And unlike his big brother, when Caleb gauged himself by the charts in the pediatrician's office, he ranked in the lower percentiles in height and higher percentiles in weight. *Poor Caleb, he's going to be pudgy like me*, Jillian had often lamented. Though she was only five-feet, four inches tall, she was not actually pudgy. Neither was she slender. "If only I had lived during an earlier time when curves were appreciated" was her routine self-consolation.

When Jillian and Bryan met in high school, his hair was unkempt and as long as his dad would allow. On their first date, she had told him that he reminded her of a shaggy puppy. He kept that style during college, but his priorities changed after graduation. Before his first interview with the police department, he chose a modified military style that was cropped close on the sides and spiked on top. When Joshua and Caleb were old enough to sit in the barber chair, Bryan had chosen the same classic style for them. To honor him, Jillian continued to take the boys to the barber once each month for their "daddy cuts."

"Did you guys sleep okay last night?" Jillian asked while rearranging the stack of moving boxes she had been too tired to unpack last night.

"Okay, I guess," was Joshua's apathetic reply.

"I slept really well!" Caleb responded heartily. "I was tired after moving all day."

"What did you do besides play with Molly while I helped Dad's friends actually carry things?" Joshua attempted to provoke his younger brother.

Why does Joshua have to be so contrary? Jillian considered before speaking preemptively. "I think we were all tired. You both worked hard, and I appreciate it. Maybe we can take a nap this afternoon," Jillian offered, thinking how much she would love to do just that.

"I don't want to take a nap. I'm not a little kid," Joshua shot back.

"People of all ages need plenty of rest," she acknowledged before changing the subject to avoid a needless debate. "Here you go." From the box labeled Clothes Needed Right Away, she pulled out a pair of jeans and a shirt for each of the boys. "They might have a few wrinkles, but they'll be fine."

"Why didn't you hang them up last night?" Joshua complained.

"Why didn't you hang them up last night?" Jillian reacted, not expecting or receiving an answer.

"Mine will be fine," Caleb assured as he gave his mom a knowing smile.

"Mommy, I'm cold!" Molly's plea sounded from the bathroom.

"I'm on my way!" Jillian called, stopping in the hallway to grab some towels and washcloths from the box labeled Kids' Bathroom.

After a quick bath, Molly ran to her room and dressed herself in a new denim jumper with a matching blue and white-striped T-shirt. A quick brush through her almost-shoulder-length curly, blonde-streaked hair was all that was required for a polished look. Her green-blue eyes sparkled, and her rosy cheeks appeared as if they had just been lovingly pinched.

"Mommy, where's my shoes?"

Stepping into her room, Jillian replied, "Molly, honey, I put your sandals on the floor in your closet."

"I like my new room, Mommy. It's pretty and the closet is *big*!" Molly's exaggerated pronunciation conveyed her enthusiasm as she pulled open the folding doors.

"I'm glad you like it, Molly. I think we're going to be very happy in our new home."

Jillian rushed to her bathroom and plugged in the curling iron. While she waited for it to heat up, she brushed some minerals on her warm, ivory complexion and swiped her naturally long eyelashes with dark brown mascara. She had always considered her green eyes her best facial feature. Although considered attractive by others, her cheekbones were not as prominent as she would like, and her nose exhibited an unusual curve that made it a little less than perfect. Bryan occasionally told her she looked pretty, but he had never made her feel truly beautiful.

Intricately placed blush, to define the wanting cheekbones, and a swipe of not-too-red lip gloss completed her casual look. The sleeveless white cotton blouse and the knee-length navy skirt seemed a good choice for church. She liked the way the skirt fit, sliding smoothly over her curvy hips and falling gracefully with a flirty, but not too wide, swing.

Not that I'll be flirting with anyone, she laughed to herself. At this stage in her life—the two-year observance of widowhood—she had yet to meet a man that would reawaken that inclination. Wrapping the curling iron around handfuls of her chin-length mousy-brown hair produced just enough soft curls to give her a satisfactory look. She touched up the bright red polish on her toes before slipping her bare feet into her dressy navy sandals. She would have preferred flats for comfort but appreciated the extra two inches in height the wedged heels provided. Looking at herself in the full-length mirror on the inside of her closet door, she concluded, "It'll do."

Turning for a side view, she did not dwell on the less-than-impeccable image looking back at her. *It really doesn't matter... who cares what I look like anyway?* she mused.

Since Bryan's death, Jillian had been known to throw an occasional pity party. Usually, it was when she was exhausted or feeling overwhelmed. Always, she felt guilty and would scold herself, acknowledging that even through the worst of times, God had always been there to sustain her. Now, considering all she had been through, she marveled that, for the most part, she was carrying on a normal life—lonely, but normal for a widow with young children. The two-year milestone had induced her to make a conscious decision to get on with her life. She decided the best way was to make a new start in a new location where, she hoped, the unpleasant memories would not be as vivid.

It was an article in a nursing magazine that had caught her attention and introduced her to Lakeview, a former resort town that was now an emerging suburb of the state capital. A new state-of-the-art community hospital had just been completed, and the review touted the many positive aspects of small-town living.

Growing up, Jillian and her parents had lived in metropolitan areas. In high school, she read a book about a family that lived in a small town that offered "idyllic country charm with city convenience." It became her goal, along with marrying her Prince Charming and starting a family, to someday find that picture-perfect place. Although her family makeup was no longer perfect, she wondered if Lakeview could still be the perfect location she had dreamed about for so long.

When she went online to check out opportunities for employment at this new hospital, she was pleasantly surprised to find several openings for nurses with her credentials and experience. She wasted no time in completing an online application.

Then, just for fun, she decided to check out the nearby real estate offerings. Even if she didn't get a job offer, she considered there was no harm in daydreaming. After being overwhelmed by the prices of new homes in a gated community, she was drawn to a listing for a "turn-of-the-century charmer with refinished oak hardwoods on a family-friendly cul-de-sac; photo not yet available." This house was in her price range.

An e-mail from the hospital's human resources department landed in her inbox while she was still perusing Lakeview's real estate.

"Could you come for an interview next week?" The prompt response was from the human resources director at Lakeview Medical Center.

Amazed at the opportunity before her, Jillian had quickly replied in the affirmative.

Lakeview was just a three-hour drive from her home in Richmond—not too close, not too far. Four days later, Mona, a neighbor and good friend, watched the kids so she could pursue a new direction in life. The lack of heavy traffic and the sunny, summer day created a calming atmosphere as Jillian set the cruise control for the interstate's speed limit and popped her favorite CD into the player. The miles flew by on the smooth, gently winding pavement. She had no trouble finding her destination, which was visible from the exit ramp. As soon as she had pulled into the parking lot of the ultramodern hospital campus, butterflies erupted in her stomach. Her scheduled appointment with human resources was still thirty minutes away. She grabbed her Bible from the seat beside her and opened it to Psalms. After reading a few chapters, she breathed an earnest prayer, asking God that his will be done, and stepped out of the car into a new phase of her life.

Marie Milkalski, the human resources director, put Jillian immediately at ease with her pleasant smile and cordial manner. When she asked Jillian why she wanted to move to Lakeview, Jillian was forthcoming and related a little more information than was necessary. However, that led to a friendly conversation in which both women shared rudiments of a more personal nature.

Mrs. Milkalski mentioned that her husband was the pastor of a nearby church. "We'd love to have you visit us sometime if you decide to move to Lakeview," she invited warmly.

"My dad was a pastor. I admire you. Being the pastor's wife can be challenging," Jillian replied. "And, yes, if we have the opportunity to move here, I would love to visit your church."

With their interview completed, Marie accompanied Jillian to the office of the director of nursing for another lengthy session. This time, there were more technical questions regarding Jillian's education and experience as a nurse. Before leaving the director's office, she had received and accepted a job offer—on her terms—pending satisfactory reference results. Jillian was not the least concerned. She believed the references would confirm to Mrs. Milkalski and the director of nursing that they had made the right decision by offering her the position. As she walked to the parking lot, she felt both thrilled and terrified.

It was only two o'clock. She had promised Mona she would be home by seven. True to her spontaneous nature, a notion struck her. If she hurried, she would have time to stop by the realty office that had listed the turn-of-the-century house to see if a photo was now available. She had placed the address of the office in her purse as she rushed out of her house that morning. She asked the security guard at the parking lot exit for directions.

Jillian felt positive about the steps she was taking in her pursuit of a new life for her family. In her heart, she had that peace that was difficult to explain, the peace that she knew came only from following God's leading.

"Oh, I can do better than that!" the female realty agent had gushed when Jillian asked if a photo was now available of the turn-of-the-century house. "Let's go see the house in person. I have the keys!" She stood up from behind her mahogany desk and flashed a jangling set of keys, almost in Jillian's face.

Uh-oh. She's the pushy type, Jillian contemplated, beginning to have second thoughts about taking such a big step so quickly and without having someone else with her. Reminding herself that she had accepted the position at the hospital and that her family would need a place to live, she hesitated only a few seconds before agreeing to look at the house.

However, she insisted on driving her own car, not wanting to be stuck with the realtor and forced into an extended tour of homes. Besides, hunger pangs were beginning to distract her, and she realized she had not eaten since her morning bowl of oatmeal.

The realtor handed her a packet of papers containing information about the house, including a map with directions taped to the outside. Without opening the envelope, she threw it in the passenger seat and followed the marked route on the map, hoping she would find a decent place to grab a quick bite to eat on the way. Bingo! She spied a familiar beckoning sign. A step up from the usual fast-food places, the restaurant offered a drive-thru and some reasonably healthy choices. After picking up her veggie wrap and a fresh lemonade from the window, she pulled into a parking space and tried not to eat too fast.

At first disappointed—the turn-of-the-century house was built in 2003, not the early 1900s—she was won over by the charming bungalow style and immaculate condition, including the just refinished hardwoods.

"The former owner had a big dog," the realtor explained.

Jillian was relieved that she did not observe any other evidence of the previous four-legged occupant. In fact, she considered the house was a perfect fit for her family. There were three bedrooms, two baths, and a laundry room with an entrance from the two-car garage. A wood-burning fireplace anchored a large family room at the front of the house. From the family room one could enter either the formal dining room or the large, well-appointed kitchen. With a granite-topped island, an adequate pantry, and a corner banquette, Jillian knew she had found a keeper. The rocking-chair front porch and convenient entryway were icing on the cake.

"Being a widow, I think you will be happier with this newer home in move-in condition." The fashionable realtor twisted several huge baubles on her ring finger as she offered her opinion in response to Jillian's initial disappointment at discovering this wasn't the older home she was expecting. "Low upkeep," she further explained as if Jillian had not understood her inference.

"Oh, I guess it doesn't matter that you're a widow. I can't get my husband to do anything around the house anyway," she continued, sounding more inappropriate with each attempt to say the right thing.

Jillian was used to the nervous babble into which people occasionally tumbled when they attempted to address her widowhood. She reminded herself to stop revealing her marital status unless it was essential and quickly changed the subject.

"I like most everything about the house," Jillian commented without betraying her actual enthusiasm. She was, after all, going to make an offer below the asking price.

"Oh, that's great!" The realtor's zeal made up for Jillian's indifference. "And you would have nice neighbors. I sold the houses on either side of you. On your left is a sweet little old widow lady …oh, I'm sorry."

Jillian just smiled pleasantly.

"She downsized after her husband passed away three years ago, just like…" the realtor stopped mid-sentence. "I mean, she is just so sweet and look at her beautiful flowers. She certainly has a green thumb!"

She paused briefly before making a grand gesture toward the other house. "Oh, what was his name? Martin? Something like that…anyway he teaches at the local elementary school. I'm not sure about his family. I didn't get to meet them, but you know, teachers usually make good neighbors."

"Well, thank you so much for the tour and the helpful information. I do have to get back to Richmond tonight—"

"Oh, you're going already?" The realtor's disappointment was apparent.

"Just as soon as I make an offer," Jillian replied coolly.

The realtor's expression immediately changed from one of distress to surprise. "Without looking at any other houses? I mean, that's okay with me, but most of my clients want to look at least at several properties, you know, for comparison."

Jillian just knew this house, and the neighborhood, was right for her family. The hospital was less than a mile away. A school was even closer. Anyway, there was no one else to consult. Her parents were halfway around the world in India. Her in-laws were in Florida, and she really would not feel comfortable asking their opinion anyway. She had asked God to lead her, and she believed he had. "No, this is the right house for me and my family," she stated confidently.

Therefore, the blueprint for her new life had transpired just a month ago. Now she was here, commencing what she believed was going to be a promising future for her and her children. Above all, she determined to make her relationship with Jesus her number one priority. She had already experienced the way he gently touched her grief with his comfort when she drew close to him. She constantly reminded herself—as did her friends and family—that her life had purpose beyond being Bryan's wife. Still, she struggled with the reality that half of what she had been was gone and was never coming back.

Chapter 2

The New Neighbor

Our Father in heaven, be with us as we go to our new church today. Please help Joshua and Caleb and Molly to be on their best behavior.

Jillian was praying over their breakfast of instant oatmeal, toast, and milk.

"And help Molly not to pee in her pants," Joshua taunted in a spirit unrelated to the compassionate one Jillian had endeavored to instill in her children.

"Totally out of place and unkind!" Jillian stated matter-of-factly as she gave Joshua the look that served to wipe the mischievous grin right off of his face.

Turning her attention to Molly, Jillian recognized the pitiful I'm-going-to-burst-into-tears-any-second-now expression on her little girl's face and knew she had to take immediate action to rescue their first Sunday morning in Lakeview.

"Molly, when I was your age, I used to wet the bed too. You'll grow out of it just like I did," Jillian overstated. She could barely remember the one or two times she had nighttime accidents.

"You did, Mommy?"

"Yes, I did. Just ask Grammy the next time we e-mail her. Okay, now let's finish our morning prayer…without any more interruptions, please.

"Thank you for the privilege of going to church. Many people around the world do not have the opportunities that we have. Help us to be grateful and help us to be kind. In Jesus's name, amen."

She wanted to address Joshua more directly, but Molly seemed to have forgotten his rude big-brother comment. *Choose your battles!* Jillian reminded herself as she made a mental note to pray more diligently for Joshua as he entered the wonderful world of adolescence. She considered that his mouth had already arrived there.

As the foursome stepped out onto their front porch, Jillian relished the cool breezes and clear blue skies of the September morning. The kids ran ahead to their car. With the garage stacked with unpacked boxes, she had left the car parked in the driveway last night. Bryan's friends had offered to carry the remaining boxes into the house, but she preferred to leave them in the garage until she could unpack in an orderly manner. They would be off to school and work Monday morning, and she anticipated not having the time or the energy to tackle the heavy-duty unpacking until the weekend.

She watched her eldest as he opened the passenger door. Since Bryan's death, he had always insisted on riding in front with her.

Dutifully, Caleb assisted his little sister as they climbed into the back seat.

An aura of tranquility swathed Jillian as she moseyed to the car, admiring the colorful blooms in Mrs. Cecil's flowerbed and the well-manicured yards of her neighbors. God had blessed her family with this charming little house in a charming little neighborhood in a charming little town. And she was going to enjoy life.

"Uh-oh."

Jillian had just positioned herself comfortably in the driver's seat when Joshua's exclamation caught her attention. From the tone of his voice, Jillian knew immediately that he had done something he shouldn't have.

"What now?" she asked in a slightly annoyed tone.

"You won't believe this," he began.

"Oh yes, I probably will," she replied too quickly, irritation continuing to creep into her voice.

"You know when I came out last night to look for my iPod? I had to turn the overhead lights on to find it. I must have left them on. Do you think it hurt anything?" he asked with just a hint of apprehension.

"Well, there's one way to find out," Jillian countered as she put the key in the ignition. Breathing a prayer, she turned the key. Again. And again. Nothing. Not even a whimper.

"I guess it did hurt something." Jillian sighed, not daring to turn and look at Joshua.

"It was an accident, Mom. I didn't mean to—" Joshua justified, and Jillian didn't miss the opportunity to make a point.

"Yes, Joshua, accidents do happen," she spoke deliberately. "I know you didn't do it on purpose. But you have to be responsible. Accidents have consequences."

Even she heard the sarcasm in her voice, necessitating a smooth over. "It'll be okay, Joshua. We are just going to be late for church…if we get there at all."

Jillian felt beads of perspiration forming on her forehead. Unable to lower the electric windows, she threw her door wide open to let in the breeze. She didn't have a clue what to do next. *Why didn't I have Bryan teach me about dead batteries and flat tires and all the other things a woman has to do by herself when her husband dies?* she asked herself for the umpteenth time, already knowing the answer. *You don't make plans to be a widow*, sounded over and over in her head like a broken record, until…

"Good morning. Is everything okay here?"

Jillian was startled by the friendly, male voice. In her brooding, she had paid no attention to the man who had approached from the neighboring driveway.

"I'm not trying to be nosey, but I noticed you all sitting here, and it appeared you were trying to start your car without any luck."

What a brilliant deduction! Jillian wanted to respond to the analysis provided by the man standing outside her car. Instead, she turned toward the voice, catching her first glimpse of Matthew Morgan.

"Good morning…yes…it does seem the car won't start," she managed to fumble out the words, feeling silly that the sight and sound of this man could fluster her so.

As Jillian stepped out of the car, her next-door neighbor introduced himself. "I'm Matt Morgan, and it seems we're going to be neighbors, or actually already are," he greeted while extending his hand.

She thought he sounded just a little self-conscious but couldn't imagine why. His appearance was impeccable. The descriptive phrase "tall, dark, and handsome" was surely composed just for him. His chestnut hair was impeccably tousled; his smile was straight from a toothpaste commercial.

"I'm Jillian Hamilton. It's nice to meet you," she replied as stoically as she could without sounding rude. "Yes, we just moved in yesterday."

"Sorry I wasn't here to help, but I had an out-of-town soccer match," he apologized.

That helps to explain the athletic physique and glowing suntan, Jillian thought. "No problem. My husband's…my late husband's friends were here and actually did most of the work for us. They're policeman, big and strong, you know," she divulged and immediately regretted being so chatty.

"I'm glad you had help. Uh, sorry for your loss," Matt Morgan offered somewhat awkwardly.

"Thank you," was Jillian's controlled reply. She didn't want to go there.

"So the car won't start?" Matthew Morgan had regained his composure.

"No, the interior light was accidentally left on last night." She chose her words carefully as Joshua walked around from his side of the car. She didn't want to embarrass him in front of their new neighbor.

"And who's this young man?" Matt didn't miss a beat as he stretched out his hand to Joshua.

"I'm Josh Hamilton," he replied coolly as he shook Matt's hand.

Jillian continued, "Joshua's my oldest, and I have two more in the back seat—Caleb and Molly."

Matt leaned over and gave a friendly wave through the back window. "Hi, guys!" *It must be tough raising three kids without a husband.* Such was the empathetic thought that coursed through his mind as he warmly greeted the children. "Welcome to the neighborhood."

Shyly but courteously, Molly and Caleb smiled and waved at their new neighbor.

"Your kids are…they're really cute."

Jillian sensed a trace of sympathy in his tone.

"Cute?" the disapproval in Joshua's voice was evident.

"Not you, of course, Josh." Matt turned his attention to the eleven-year-old. "I was referring to your younger siblings. You, my man, I would never describe as cute."

Jillian watched in awe as Joshua laughed and returned Matt's high five. Matt did not allow her the luxury of contemplating the scenario that had just taken place.

"Well, if it's just your battery, that shouldn't be a problem. I'll get my cables and give you a jump."

"I don't want to trouble you, but I would really appreciate your help. We don't want to be late for church," Jillian blurted. *There you go again, Jillian. Just say what needs to be said.*

"No trouble at all. Be right back." Matt was already striding toward his garage, seemingly indifferent about Jillian's intended destination.

"Joshua, get back in. We'll be going soon," Jillian directed but decided she would wait outside the car for her helpful neighbor to return. She was just reaching inside to pull the latch to release the hood when Matt approached, and no cables were anywhere in sight.

"Man, I am so sorry, Jill...it is Jill?" Matt asked.

"Jillian. She doesn't like to be called Jill," Joshua answered for her as he ambled very slowly back to the passenger side of the car. Jillian shot a quick look his way. "Joshua, I told you to get back in the car. Anyway, you call me Mom," she added to temper her response.

"Jill's fine. I'm just used to Jillian," she explained to her neighbor, trying to sound as if it didn't matter.

"Then Jillian it will be...and Jillian, I hate to tell you this, but I forgot that I loaned my cables out last week to one of the other teachers."

"Oh, that's okay. I really appreciate your wanting to help," Jillian spoke the appropriate words but still felt a keen disappointment that this man was not going to be her knight in shining armor this morning.

"Why don't I give you and the kids a ride to church? Are you going to Family Fellowship?" Matt asked, assuming the largest church in Lakeview was their destination.

"Well, actually, no. We're going to the New Life Center. I know the pastor's wife, Mrs. Milkalski...well, not really *know*... but Mrs. Milkalski is the human resources director at Community Hospital where I'll be working. She invited me to attend their church," Jillian stumbled through the unnecessary explanation, once again divulging way more information than was obligatory.

"No problem. Isn't that the small church about a mile from here on Conover Road?"

"Yes, that's it," Jillian confirmed, wondering why her neighbor considered the church *small*.

"Thought so. One of the other teachers goes there. It's on the way to Family Fellowship where I go, so I can drop you off. Since you know the Milkalskis, I'm sure they can arrange for a ride home. I'll get my cables back and bring them over this afternoon and give you a jump.

Jillian felt a little uncomfortable about this whole situation. A strange—but remarkably handsome—man was offering to take her and her children to church. She didn't doubt he was her new next-door neighbor, but still...

Sensing her reluctance, Matt hastily devised a plan. "Mrs. Cecil, how are you this morning?" he called out as Jillian's other next-door neighbor meandered down her driveway to get her Sunday morning newspaper.

Jillian and the children had met Mrs. Cecil briefly yesterday. She was a frail but charming elderly lady and, as Mrs. Cecil had pointed out to Jillian, "a widow like you." Her short, curly grey hair was perfectly coifed, and she wore a blue and pink floral housecoat and blue vinyl slippers.

"Just great, young man. And how about you?" she replied in her singsong voice. "I see you've already met the young widow-lady," she crooned with a twinkle in her eye.

Oh, good grief! Jillian gasped under her breath. *What is Mrs. Cecil thinking to make such a comment!*

Or Be Reconciled

And for the first time since meeting Matt, Jillian considered the marital status of her new neighbor. Obviously, Mrs. Cecil would not have made that leading comment if Matt had a wife. Discreetly, Jill stole a glance at her new neighbor's ring finger. *Nada*.

Good-naturedly ignoring Mrs. Cecil's insinuation, Matt continued, "I was just wondering if you could provide a character reference for me, Mrs. Cecil. Jillian's car won't start, and I've offered her and the kids a ride to church, but since we just met, I thought she may feel more comfortable about accepting if you'd put in a good word for me."

"A good word for you, oh you know I will," Mrs. Cecil gushed as she leisurely walked the short distance to Jillian's driveway. "Jillian, dear, you could not ask for a kinder, more gentlemanly neighbor than this young man. Now, he's only lived here a little over a year, but the whole neighborhood wonders how we ever got along without him. He's a teacher and coach at the elementary school, and his students and the parents think he's the greatest. I do too," she added as she slipped her fair, fragile arm around his tanned, muscular one. "You and the children will be safe with him," she added with a wink.

"So are we ready to go?" Matt motioned toward his squeaky-clean, navy-blue minivan.

"Well, we'll have to get Molly's booster seat." There was just a tinge of apprehensiveness in Jillian's response. Still, it seemed more logical to accept Matt's offer, especially after Mrs. Cecil's glowing endorsement, than to make a big deal about rejecting it, and they did need a ride to church.

"Caleb and I can handle that, can't we, Caleb?" Matt was already assisting Molly out of the booster seat before unbuckling it from Jillian's car. "Caleb, how about bringing it over and we'll get it situated in my van?"

"Sure," Caleb responded, pleased that he had been asked to assist.

Jillian savored the moment when Matt opened the car door for her. It always surprised her how little things could invoke such poignant memories.

"So, where did you move from?" Matt asked as he backed the van out of the driveway. He followed up his question with a quick glance Jillian's way. She was slightly embarrassed that he had caught her staring at him.

"Richmond, Virginia," she replied, hoping her voice did not convey the nervousness she felt.

"Not too far away."

"No, I'm thankful for that. Still, moving is not much fun, well I mean, the process of moving."

"I understand. I moved here a year ago from Charlotte. This is a great neighborhood. I think you and the kids will enjoy living here. I have been impressed with the Lakeview schools, but of course, I teach at the elementary and middle school complex."

"Mrs. Cecil mentioned that..."

"Yeah, she did, didn't she? She's a sweet little lady. So you'll be working at the hospital?"

"That's right. I'm a nurse. I will be working in the emergency department."

"That should keep you on your toes."

For a few minutes, there was an uncomfortable silence, at least for Jillian. Matt appeared to be in deep thought. Just before they turned into the parking lot of the New Life Center, Matt reminded her that he would be over that afternoon to jump the battery and added as he handed her a business card, "Here's my cell phone number just in case you can't find a ride home."

She started to decline, having already decided that if no one offered a ride—but she was sure someone would—that she and the kids could walk home. There were sidewalks in their pedestrian-friendly neighborhood, and it would be a nice way to check out their new surroundings. Not wanting to appear rude, she placed the card in her purse.

"Thank you so much, Matt." She wanted to sound cordial without betraying the full extent of her gratitude.

He stopped the car under the covered entrance.

"Thank Mr. Morgan, kids," she prompted while unlatching her seat belt. As the mumbled thank-yous echoed from the back of the van, she conceded to herself that she was hoping her neighbor would open the door for her. "I really do appreciate your kindness," she reiterated as she stepped out of the van.

"Glad to help out my new neighbors," were Matt's last words before he drove off toward Family Fellowship.

She directed the kids toward the entry door and then suddenly remembered. "Molly's booster seat!" she called out as she turned and started after her neighbor who was almost at the exit.

Matt was looking at Jillian in his rearview mirror as he drove away. When she turned to run after him, he came to a sudden stop, screeching his brakes on the parking lot pavement. When he turned around to see what she was doing, he saw Molly's pink booster seat.

The driver-side door opened, and Matt leaned out, yelling in her direction, "I've still got your daughter's booster seat!"

Walking as fast as she could in her heeled sandals, she hurried to meet him. She was less than halfway to his van when he met her. "Let me carry it in the church for you," he offered.

Surely, Matt Morgan did not think she needed help carrying a booster seat. Jillian soundly refused his offer. "I appreciate it, but you're going to be blocking traffic soon. I can do it myself," she added, as an afterthought that she feared sounded ungracious.

"No problem. See you later." Mr. Morgan was nonchalant.

Men! Jillian mused to herself as she rejoined her children at the entrance of the church.

Women! Contemplated Matthew Morgan as he effortlessly jogged to his waiting van.

Chapter 3

The New Church

Father, thank you for sending our neighbor to help us out and bless him today as he attends his church. Help the children adjust to their new classes, and please help Joshua behave. Lord, I long to hear from you this morning. I love you, Lord.

Jillian and the children had arrived at New Life Center just as the Sunday school classes were convening. She disliked being late to anything, especially church, and especially on their first day. She knew that Marie Milkalski would have greeted her had they arrived early as she had planned before the car trouble. Nevertheless, today's greeters were very kind, and she appreciated that they spoke fluent English as well as their native Spanish.

Jillian had always enjoyed worshipping in culturally diverse churches, and if the assortment of faces she had seen so far was an indication, this was one. The wife of the greeter couple, Maribel, had accompanied her and the children to their classes. Joshua and Caleb joined a small group of like-age boys around a large round table in their classroom. Molly was only a little hesitant to join the group of preschool and kindergarten boys and girls in their brightly decorated room. Then Maribel took Jillian to the church parlor explaining, "This is a ladies-only class."

Jillian sat in the first available seat, an upholstered armchair that had seen better days, and she was praying silently when…

"We are so glad to have a new member of our class with us today." It was Mrs. Wilson, the teacher, breaking into Jillian's hushed prayer. "You must be Jillian." As she spoke, the matronly lady approached with outstretched hands.

"Yes, Jillian Hamilton," she responded cordially, a little surprised that the teacher already knew who she was.

"I assumed you were the young woman Marie described to me. You just look the part," Mrs. Wilson explained as she grasped both of Jillian's hands in her own.

What part is she referring to? Jillian wondered.

"Jillian and her three children just moved here from Richmond. From the big city to our nice, little town," Mrs. Wilson continued, eliciting pleasant laughter from the group of a dozen mostly middle-aged women.

"Our dear pastor's wife told me you might be here, Jillian, and I'm so glad you didn't disappoint us. She'll even be working at the hospital with Marie." After addressing this additional tidbit to the other women in the class, Mrs. Wilson again focused on Jillian. "We're so glad to have you, dear, and we hope you will be pleased with our church. Ladies, please make her welcome."

As Jillian glanced around the room, returning the smiles and greetings, she realized that at thirty-five, she was probably the youngest woman in the class. *Oh, great,* she thought. *Maribel must have considered me one of the older women.*

Mrs. Wilson cleared her throat after a moment, and the fellowship came to an abrupt halt. Teaching from the fifth chapter of 1 Peter, she listed the biblical qualifications of pastors and referred to the time, many years ago, when she and her husband had founded New Life Center.

"Lakeview was a different place back then," she lamented, "such a peaceful and picturesque community before the urban sprawl crept our way and shattered our innocence."

As Mrs. Wilson paused and appeared to be reminiscing about Lakeview's pristine years, Jillian noticed that several ladies exchanged amused glances.

"Yes, I've been a widow now for almost twenty years, so I understand what you're going through, Jillian dear."

The comment surprised and almost offended Jillian. It seemed to have been offered in genuine empathy, however, and Jillian consciously decided not to be bothered by her teacher's gratuitous comment.

As the lesson ended and the ladies made plans for their monthly get-together, Jillian skimmed the church bulletin. She was not emotionally ready to be included in the social life of this new church. She noted that, this being the first Sunday of the month, the children would remain in children's church, which allowed the adults to worship together in the sanctuary. Jillian conceded that she needed peace and quiet this morning and was thankful for this consideration.

Marie Milkalski came rushing into the parlor just as Mrs. Wilson dismissed the class. Marie apologized profusely for not being at the door to greet Jillian and her family. "I was so glad when Maribel told me you were here. Are you all settled?"

"No need to apologize. Everyone's been so kind, especially Maribel…" and she paused and added as an afterthought, "and Mrs. Wilson." Jillian felt obliged to include the woman who was

Or Be Reconciled

standing directly in front of her. "We're as settled as possible, considering we just moved in yesterday."

"Oh, you just arrived yesterday? And you're in church already? You are a faithful one!" Marie smiled broadly and looked to Mrs. Wilson for confirmation, but Jillian felt Mrs. Wilson's expression was one of condescension. She appeared to be scrutinizing Jillian, especially her sandaled feet and brightly colored toenails.

"I could move your orientation back a day or two if you'd like," Marie offered kindly, but Jillian was ready to get on with her new life.

"Oh, no, that won't be necessary. I'm prepared," Jillian replied candidly.

"Now don't be too sure of yourself. You know pride goeth before a fall," Mrs. Wilson interjected.

Jillian was stunned by the insensitive words.

Before she could reply, Marie shielded her. "As I was saying, I'm sorry I wasn't there to greet you this morning, but I had to be in our class early. We teach the couples' class, and we were taking registrations for an upcoming marriage seminar."

In her haste to change the subject, Marie had inadvertently mentioned another delicate topic.

"Well, that's something neither Jillian nor I will be attending!" Mrs. Wilson's awkward attempt to make light of the subject sounded almost sinister.

Several of the ladies from the class who had been waiting in uncomfortable silence seized the pause in conversation to greet Jillian. After the cordial introductions, Marie gently placed her hand on Jillian's arm and accompanied her to the foyer.

"Do you have all the documents you'll need tomorrow for orientation?" Marie asked.

"Everything's ready…including me." Jillian looked around to make sure Mrs. Wilson had not heard her make yet another affirmative statement. She did not think of her confidence as

41

being prideful. She trusted in the Lord to prepare her for this new job. Maybe she should have said that.

Sensing Jillian's thoughts, Marie whispered, "Don't worry about Mrs. Wilson's comment…sometimes…"

"It's okay," Jillian responded. She didn't want to appear overly sensitive to her new coworker.

"Personally, I'm glad to know you are ready to take on your new job. That's an attitude I would like to see more often at work," Marie reassured. "Go ahead and find yourself a seat. I'm going to the choir. Do you sing?"

"Only to my children when they were babies," Jillian responded with a gracious smile.

Jillian found an unoccupied aisle seat about halfway to the front in the quickly filling sanctuary. A few minutes later, Mrs. Wilson tapped her shoulder and asked in a louder-than-necessary voice, "Mind if I sit with you?"

Without answering, Jillian quickly scooted across the burgundy velvet cushioned pew to make room for her Sunday school teacher.

"I would have come with you, but I had to stop off at the little girls' room," Mrs. Wilson confided with a wink and a grin.

Jillian forced a smile in response, all the while thinking, *I'm not sure how to read this lady.*

The worship service began with an extended time of praise and worship. Jillian basked in the presence of the Lord, her hands lifted, an occasional tear spilling from her closed eyes. They were neither tears of sorrow nor of joy, but of surrender. This was her time to lay her soul at her Savior's feet and allow him to fill the emptiness that often resided there.

Pastor Milkalski's sermon, from the parable of the sower, was interesting, but did not address the longing in Jillian's heart as she had hoped it would.

What is the longing of my heart? Was a question she asked herself frequently. She knew she wanted to put God first in everything she did. She wanted more of him. Was there something else? As she contemplated her spiritual needs, a young couple ended the service by singing one of her favorite songs, "Beauty for Ashes." As she listened to the words—"He gives beauty for ashes, strength for fear, gladness for mourning, peace for despair"—tears flowed freely down her cheeks.

Mrs. Wilson handed her a tissue before putting her arm around her shoulder, patting her gently, and purring, "There, there, it's going to be all right. Jesus knows all about it."

Chapter 4

New School/Job

Father, thank you for this beautiful day! I praise you for your loving-kindness that is new every morning. As usual, Lord, I need your strength today...maybe a little more than usual. Help me adapt to my new position at the hospital and use me to minister words of comfort to my patients. I pray especially for Molly as she begins her first day of kindergarten. Be with the teachers and help them to be patient. Help Molly to behave well and not miss me too much. Help the boys as they adjust to their new school. I know it's a scary time, especially for Caleb, so I ask that you be with them and give them your peace. Help us to be kind to all those we encounter today, Jesus. Bless Pastor Milkalski and Marie, and Mrs. Cecil and uh...and

Bryan's parents and my mom and dad. Lord, continue to meet their needs as they serve you on the mission field. I commit this day to you, Lord. Amen.

Jillian felt distracted toward the end of her morning prayer. After she mentioned Mrs. Cecil's name, she almost prayed for Matthew Morgan, but although she wasn't sure why, she reconsidered. He had been right about someone from the New Life Center offering her a ride home after church yesterday. In fact, Pastor Milkalski and Marie invited them to their home for lunch, and her new pastor drove them home afterward. He also offered to jump her battery when she explained why they had needed a ride to church that morning. Even after she told him her neighbor had agreed to do it, he insisted, and Jillian reluctantly pulled the latch to release the hood. She had never been very good at turning down people's offers of help as she didn't want to offend anyone. Yet when she saw the expression on Matt Morgan's face when he came over later in the afternoon with his cables in hand, she felt as if she had offended—or annoyed—someone after all.

"Oh, I'm so sorry. Our pastor drove us home, and he went ahead and took care of it," Jillian had explained.

Matt appeared slightly frustrated but quickly recovered. "Well, I needed them back anyway. You never know when they'll come in handy." Before turning to leave, he added an abrupt, "I'll be next door if you need me."

Jillian had watched in silence as he strode naturally across her yard and entered his house through the garage, not looking back. She couldn't explain what she was feeling at that moment, but she recognized it as an emotion she had not experienced in some time. Later that evening, she was almost disappointed when the car started flawlessly as they left for the evening service at New Life Center.

Jillian stretched her arms over her head and forced her thoughts back to the present. She had rehearsed this day in her mind many times, and her mental preparation was helping her cope. She knew she had made the right decision to coordinate their move with the beginning of the new school year. Only once had she ever had to begin a new school in the middle of the year. She remembered what a difficult experience it had been and didn't want to put her kids through that, especially considering everything else they had experienced in their young lives.

Jillian had planned the morning schedule perfectly, and they arrived early at Lakeview's combined elementary and middle school. With Molly in tow, she escorted Caleb and then Joshua to their respective classrooms. She took time to introduce herself to their teachers. Without being overbearing, she planned to be as involved in their education as possible. Caleb had been assigned to Mr. Rogers's class. As she waited her turn behind two other mothers, she quickly sized him up. A middle-aged black man, he seemed quite in control of his classroom, but not too stern. She was thankful for that, considering Caleb's sensitive character.

"Mr. Rogers, I'm Jillian Hamilton, and this is my son…"

"Yes, Mrs. Hamilton and Caleb. Didn't I see you at church yesterday?" he greeted them warmly.

Not recalling his face among the many new ones she had seen at church, she blurted, "Oh, so you attend New Life Center?"

"Yes, ma'am, for many years. Welcome to Lakeview." He extended his hand to Caleb, who responded only after Jillian nudged his arm. "I'm looking forward to having you in my class, Caleb."

Caleb smiled shyly at Jillian before responding, "Thank you, Mr. Rogers."

"Nice name for a teacher." Jillian couldn't help but make the reference to another Mr. Rogers.

"Yes, ma'am, over the years, my name has served me well," Mr. Rogers replied with a big grin.

Joshua, whom she had stationed just outside the door with Molly, started yanking on her sleeve. With a quick wave to Caleb, Jillian excused herself.

"M-o-m," Joshua extended her title to three syllables in a way only he could. "You're going to make me late."

"Calm down, Joshua. I'm on schedule. School doesn't start for fifteen more minutes."

Jillian walked in silence down the hall with Molly holding her left hand and Joshua straggling a few feet behind. She wanted to turn and ask, "Now who's making us late?" but thought better.

She often reminded herself of a Scripture from Proverbs her mother had instilled in her as a young girl: "She opens her mouth with wisdom, and on her tongue is the law of kindness." Her thought was more wisecrack than wise and was certainly not kind. She appreciated that with God's help she had learned to avoid unkind, unwise words (at least most of the time), but he was still working on her thoughts.

Oh no! Jillian silently meditated on the exclamation when she saw the teacher standing in the doorway with "Ms. Antonio" in bold neon colors above it.

You're going to have your hands full with my son, Jillian allowed another one of her critical thoughts to flash through her brain. She couldn't imagine that Joshua was already at the age where he was noticing attractive females, but when he saw his teacher, he stood tall and took on the guise of a disciplined scholar.

"I'm Josh Hamilton. Nice to meet you," he spoke distinctly as he offered his hand to the twenty-something teacher who could have certainly found employment as a model.

Jillian couldn't tell if Ms. Antonio was impressed or amused as she reciprocated Joshua's warm welcome.

"It's nice to meet you too, Josh. Is this your mother and little sister?"

Joshua reminded Jillian of a quick-change artist as he instantly returned to her eleven-year-old, not very-interested-in-school son. "Yeah, that's them," he responded and headed toward the back of the room as soon as he read the message printed on the board: Please select your desk for the first six weeks!

Jillian smiled and greeted Ms. Antonio cordially, all the while thinking how much better it would have been if Joshua had Mr. Rogers and Caleb had Ms. Antonio for their teachers.

As she and Molly turned to leave, she was almost broadsided by a young boy—obviously a sports enthusiast—racing into the room.

"Whoa there, Carlson!" she heard the stern voice from just down the hall, and without looking, she knew it was Matthew Morgan who had issued the warning.

"Sorry, lady, I didn't want to be late," Joshua's new classmate mumbled before taking a seat beside Joshua at the back of the room.

Jillian was expecting Mr. Morgan to say something else, but he stayed put in the middle of the hall, about ten feet to her right. His arms were crossed over his chest, and he just shook his head from side to side, displaying the exact demeanor a middle school teacher and coach is supposed to exhibit on the first day of school.

Jillian gave a quick wave in his direction as she put her arm around Molly and turned left to go to Molly's class—although she knew she was taking a detour to avoid walking past Matthew Morgan.

By the time they got to the kindergarten class, she could feel Molly's little hand trembling in her own.

"Are you afraid, Molly?" She knelt down so she was at eye level.

"A little bit, Mommy, but I'm excited too."

"I know how you feel because Mommy's a little bit afraid and a little bit excited about starting her new job today."

"Is a job like going to school?" Molly's expression had turned from worried to just serious.

"A lot like it. We must both be brave, do our best, and be kind to everyone we meet today."

"I think I can do that, Mommy."

"I know you can, sweetheart."

Molly's teacher welcomed them with a big smile. Jillian thought, *What a portrait of a traditional, but not too elderly grandmother.* Molly transferred her little hand from Jillian's to her teacher's outstretched one without hesitation. At that moment, a new chapter of Jillian's life began: working, single mom. She was glad Molly had no idea how afraid she actually was.

Chapter 5

Settling In

"Lord, what a day!" Jillian wasn't sure if it was a prayer or an exclamation as she fell into bed just after ten-thirty. "Thank you, Lord, for helping me make it through another day at the hospital and being with the kids at school. Molly loves kindergarten, and her teacher, short, plump, beautiful, gray-haired Mrs. Ratterman is a doll! Thank you, thank you for that. So far, so good with the boys. I pray that continues. Bless Mom and Dad as they work with the orphanage and the native pastors. I miss them so much. Take care of them. Be with Mom and Dad Hamilton and help them be able to come see us soon. Take care of Pastor Milkalski and Marie and our church family, especially Mr. Rogers and his family and Mrs. Wilson."

"Oh yes, Lord, please help that woman."

Jillian was beginning to feel weary and knew her last request was not offered in a benevolent spirit. Attempting to be more serious, she asked God to take care of Mrs. Cecil and then, hesitated only a second before mentioning her other next-door neighbor, whose name she had just penciled in on her prayer list.

"Be with Mr. Morgan. Thank you, Jesus..." were her last words before she fell into a deep, restful sleep.

All of her adult life, Jillian wished she were one of those people who could wake up at the crack of dawn, raring to go; but it had always taken her awhile to adjust to the conscious world after the delightful world of slumber. With the exceptions of when the kids were newborns, the first few months after Bryan's death, and when she was really frazzled or excited, she had always been able to sleep soundly. Waking up alert was another story. Routinely, she set the alarm to go off fifteen minutes before she actually had to get up; eagerly she would hit the snooze button and steal a few more minutes of repose. Often she would use that time to pray or contemplate the day ahead.

This morning, though, she accidently hit the off button and fell back into a fretful sleep, consumed by a dream that was so vivid it was like watching a movie. Bryan was there, in his police uniform. Joshua, Caleb, and Molly had cameo appearances. She recognized the exterior of their former home, but it had been completely redecorated inside in a style she would have never chosen. Although their house had been a one-story ranch, in the dream it was two stories with a massive rotunda and an elegant staircase that lead to...nowhere. As she literally floated around the house, staring at the majestic stained glass windows, she felt as if she was a stranger in her own home. The children and Bryan were standing on the landing of the staircase to nowhere, laughing merrily. She came down from her flight of fancy, but when she landed beside them and they didn't seem to notice, she felt compelled to run away. Blithely she attempted to flee down the staircase when the front door suddenly burst wide open. Standing on the threshold with strong arms outstretched toward her was a beaming Matthew Morgan. In her dream, she screamed, and then she woke up with a start.

"Oh my goodness." She threw off the covers and grabbed her alarm clock from the bedside table. "Eight o'clock?" she shrieked in panic. As suddenly as her dream had ended, Jillian's mind came back to reality. She snuggled into her bed and drew the sunshine-yellow chenille comforter around her almost bare shoulders. *It's Saturday, Jillian*, she reassured herself. *You've made it through the first week.*

A flash of the dream she had just awakened from appeared in her mind's eye. For a moment, she tried to recall the ending of that dream, but it was gone.

She had promised the kids a pancake breakfast, something she knew she would never be able to pull off on weekdays. She let them sleep until nine, taking that hour for herself—enjoying a leisurely bath, shaving her legs, and giving herself a quick manicure. She even made herself a pot of tea and enjoyed the first cup in seclusion on their worthy-of-a-turn-of-the-twentieth-century front porch while she read her daily devotions. It was a beautiful day although a little cooler than usual for the first week in September. Before leaving her breezy sanctuary, she momentarily contemplated her lengthy Saturday to-do list.

"Great pancakes, Mom," Joshua remarked as he crammed the last bite of his stack of buttermilk pancakes, covered in blueberry syrup, into his mouth. He was still smacking his lips as he headed to his room to spend some quality time with his iPod.

"Not so fast, Joshua. We have chores to do. It's Saturday, remember?"

"Oh, Mom, we've been in school five days straight. Can't you give us a break?"

"You bet! As soon as your room is picked up, your laundry put away, and the garbage taken out, you can go out and mow the yard. Shouldn't take you an hour. Then you can take a long break."

Jillian tried to inject an element of accomplishment to which Joshua could aspire but still expected her firstborn to waste some valuable work time whining. Instead, he gave in unusually easily.

"Okay," was all he said as he slowed his pace and continued down the hall.

"What do you want me to do?" Caleb volunteered his services as he placed his empty plate on the counter.

"First, help Joshua with your room, and put away your laundry, and then you can help me finish unpacking the boxes in the garage. We'll break them down for recycling. How does that sound?"

"I like to do the boxes. When we finish, can I have a break too?"

"Sure, we'll all take a break."

"Good, because I want to go see Mr. Morgan. When he taught us PE this week, he said I could come over this Saturday and meet his son."

Jillian hoped that Caleb didn't see the surprised look on her face. "Oh," she thought aloud. "I didn't know Mr. Morgan had a son."

"He's the same age as me," Caleb added as he brushed her cheek with his before joining Joshua.

Molly was busy stabbing her last bite of pancake with her fork and swirling it in the puddle of syrup on her plate.

"Finish up, Molly. We've got a lot to do," Jillian instructed, but her mind was no longer on unpacking, dusting, or vacuuming. She was wondering how it came about that Matthew Morgan had an eight-year-old son…and where was his mother?

Chapter 6

Memories

Father, it's been awhile since I've come to you like this. You have helped me so much the past few years and especially this past week. Sometimes it's as if it was brand new, as if Bryan had just died yesterday. I thought I was getting over that agonizing ache. Please help me. I don't want the kids to see me like this again. Lord, I'm laying down my grief at your feet. Please, Lord, replace it with your comfort. Amen.

The morning had gone well. It was a breeze to clean their small home, especially since it had been spotless when they moved in. Caleb had gone beyond the call of duty, dutifully completing his own chores and hurrying to help her unpack the remaining

Or Be Reconciled

boxes. Molly had even cooperated by playing quietly with her dolls and tea set on a quilt Jillian had spread out in a corner of the garage. Then she opened the box marked Keepsakes. She had planned to store this box in the unfinished attic bonus room but got in a hurry and grabbed the box without looking at the label. In her haste, Jillian wielded the box cutter carelessly, gouging right through the center of the card that lay on the top of the stack of memories. Quickly, she rescued the card, but the damage had been done. It was the last anniversary card Bryan had given her before he was killed—a card in which he had once again tried to describe his love for her. It was just too much. She asked Caleb to keep an eye on Molly while she went to check on something in the house and barely made it to her bathroom before bursting into tears. She sat on the side of the tub with her face in her hands, sobbing and praying and praying and sobbing.

"Mommy, are you okay?" Caleb called softly from just outside her bedroom door.

"Caleb, you're supposed to be watching Molly." She tried to regain her composure.

"She's right here with me. I just thought you looked sick."

"Oh no, honey, I'm not sick," Jillian quickly pulled herself together. "I'm okay. Mommies do have to go to the bathroom sometimes, you know," she replied, hoping to inject a bit of humor in their conversation. "I'll be out in just a minute."

She splashed cold water on her face, gave her bangs a quick brush, and decided to dab a bit of make-up under her eyes.

Like two wooden soldiers, Caleb and Molly were standing solemnly in the hallway when she opened the door.

"I love you so much," she whispered while gathering them into a warm embrace.

Their kisses, hugs, and simultaneous, "We love you too, Mommy," were like a soothing balm applied to her aching heart.

The ring of the doorbell interrupted their spontaneous soirée. Caleb was quick to respond. "I'll get it. I bet it's Mr. Morgan!"

I hope not, Jillian thought, then stepped back into her bathroom and glanced in the mirror, just in case. She heard a man's voice, then the closing of the front door. Caleb was running down the hall.

"It was the mailman. Look! He brought a box from Grandma and Grandpa Hamilton."

She had never felt very close to her in-laws, even though they were kind and generous people. Elizabeth Hamilton, who had always insisted that Jillian call her Mom Hamilton, seemed preoccupied no matter what the circumstances. As long as she had known him, Jim Hamilton had always been devoted to his career as a financial planner. Bryan was an only child, just as she was. The Hamiltons were members of the church Jillian's father had been called to pastor when she was in high school. Mr. Hamilton was treasurer of the church board, and Mrs. Hamilton was active in women's ministries. No one seemed surprised when the Hamilton's son, the high school football team captain, fell for the new pastor's daughter. Anyway, Bryan had already broken the hearts of all the other girls in the youth group, or so she was informed by a few of the heartbroken.

"Hurry, Mom, open the box." Caleb was too excited to notice Jillian's mind was far away, but his plea brought her quickly back to the present.

"Can I help, Mommy?" Molly wanted to get in on this welcome surprise.

"Just a minute, I have to cut the tape. Fingers back!" Jillian directed as she used her box cutter—more carefully this time—to open the box and reveal the contents. "Oh, how nice!" Jillian unwrapped a framed photo of Mom and Dad Hamilton, taken in front of their Florida retirement home.

"I like the trees," Caleb affirmed as he pointed to the palms in the background.

Molly leaned forward and gave the picture two big, wet kisses. Jillian placed the frame on the dining table, then pulled out the other contents. There were several of the latest family DVDs, puzzles and books for the children, two boxes of Jillian's favorite gourmet tea, and what appeared to be a year's supply of sugarless gum. Letters written in longhand by Elizabeth, full of news of their latest travel adventures as well as a personal love note, were addressed to Jillian and each of the children.

"What are you doing?" Joshua asked breathlessly as he entered from the garage, sweat and grass clippings clinging to his arms and face.

"Josh, we got a surprise box from Grandma and Grandpa Hamilton!" Caleb squealed excitedly.

"Lots of good stuff," Molly added.

"And you opened it without me? Was my name on the box?" he replied, obviously riled.

"Joshua, the mailman delivered it a few minutes ago, and we just opened it. I'm sorry, I should have waited for you. Will you forgive me?" Jillian reached to put her arm around her older son's shoulder, but he shrugged her away and headed for the bathroom.

"I'm going to take a shower. Mowing makes me itch."

Chapter 7

Life Goes On

Lord, sometimes I feel like I'll never be able to be the parent Joshua needs. I honestly don't know how to deal with a young man his age. He's still such a boy, but longs to be the man of the house. Work in his heart, Lord. Help him to want to please you and serve you. Don't let him be bitter over losing his father. Show me what I need to do to be a better mother. Help our family to be a peaceful, happy one. Thank you, Jesus.

Jillian stood at the kitchen sink, praying silently, as Joshua hungrily devoured his pizza. Caleb and Molly chattered about the surprise box from their grandparents. Since all the chores had been completed, Caleb asked permission to go to Mr. Morgan's after he had played awhile.

Molly decided she wanted to take a nap and scooted happily off to her room after stopping to retrieve her favorite doll from the family room sofa. Jillian considered she was blessed indeed to have a daughter with such an accommodating disposition. She had never known another child who took self-imposed naps.

Joshua continued to eat with relish but only shrugged when Jillian asked what he would like to do with his free afternoon. Each day, it seemed more and more to Jillian that Joshua was growing away from, rather than closer to, her.

Several of her close friends back in Richmond had noticed the changes Joshua had gone through after Bryan died. One friend at church had encouraged Jillian to "find him a new father." That suggestion always struck Jillian as out of place although she knew her friend meant well. If there was to be a new man in their lives, and she was rather sure there would not be, it seemed proper to her that she should focus on finding a husband, not a father for her children.

Find a new husband? Jillian laughed out loud at the thought. She had just not come to the place where she could seriously consider such an idea. God was taking care of them. She was fine. She had her times, like earlier today, but she had tried to avoid dwelling on her loss and the grief that accompanied it. "Keep close to God and keep busy" was the advice another friend had given her, and it was her goal in this new chapter of her life to do both.

When she finished washing the dishes, Jillian walked Caleb next door, just to be sure he had been invited. Mr. Morgan and his son, a boy an inch or so taller and with a sturdier build than Caleb—athletic like his father, Jillian conceded—had greeted Caleb at the front door. Jillian, waiting on the top step, was casual.

"Just wanted to make sure it was okay for Caleb to come over."

"Yeah, sure. We've been expecting him. I wanted him to meet my son, Aiden."

"Hi, Aiden!" Jillian called and waved in his direction.

Aiden acknowledged her with a shrug of his head that propelled his shaggy blond hair across his right eye. The mom in her almost reached forward to push the straggles aside, but the three guys were already heading inside, and Matt closed the door behind them.

Jillian walked slowly back to her house, rehashing the scenario that had just taken place and considering that her first impression of Matthew Morgan—as a genuinely friendly person—was exaggerated. He was just another next-door neighbor who came through in times of trouble. As she pondered this observation, Molly opened the front door. "I'm ready to play now. Nap's all done!" she announced in her lilting voice that always made Jillian smile.

"World's shortest nap!" Jillian announced.

Jillian gathered several of Molly's favorite books as well as the new ones from Grandma Hamilton. The two of them, mother and daughter, snuggled comfortably on the overstuffed sofa, and Jillian read each of the books—two times—before Molly started to squirm and asked, "Can we do something else now?'

The next hour was spent coloring and cutting and pasting and singing and talking and laughing. Occasionally, Jillian heard exclamations of victory or defeat from behind Joshua's closed doors as he played his video games. She would much rather he be outside, or at least read, but she didn't have the energy today to talk him into an activity other than his chosen one.

Jillian had just begun to think about what she could prepare for supper when Caleb burst through the front door breathlessly and exclaimed, "Mr. Morgan's having a cookout, and he wants us to come!"

She had a perfect view of the front door from the dining table where she and Molly had been sitting. She looked up to see an

Or Be Reconciled

excited Caleb, a smiling Aiden, and what appeared to be an even-more-excited Mr. Morgan.

"Come on, guys. I have everything ready—hamburgers, hot dogs, and all the fixings...except I'm out of mustard. Do you have some you could bring, Jillian?" he asked as if the arrangements had already been discussed and agreed to. For an instant, Jillian resented his bravado but quickly reconsidered. She used to wish Bryan could be more spontaneous. He never wanted to do things spur-of-the-moment.

Uncharacteristically, she almost jumped up from the table, hastily opened the refrigerator door and a second later held up a large yellow squeeze bottle. "I'm ready if you are," she responded with eagerness.

"Yes!" was Mr. Morgan's response as the boys exited as quickly as they had entered. Jillian was still holding the mustard in the air, staring at the front door, when Mr. Morgan stuck his head back in. "See you in a few!" he called, with a smile and a wink. Jillian only smiled in returned. She was glad no one could see the butterflies dancing in her stomach!

"What's all the noise about?" Joshua was standing in his barely open bedroom door.

"Mr. Morgan has invited us over for a cookout," Jillian replied matter-of-factly, trying to hide the anticipation she felt.

"I'm not hungry," Joshua droned as he closed his door behind him.

Jillian sat back down at the table where Molly was still coloring and cutting and pasting. "What am I thinking?" she considered aloud.

Molly looked at her curiously. Silently she contemplated. *I hadn't given another thought to Mrs. Morgan because it didn't matter. Now he's invited us over to his house, and I accepted—rather eagerly at that—and I have no idea if he is married or divorced or widowed. Surely if he was widowed he would have told me that...maybe*

I should just go over and say we can't come because Joshua isn't feeling like eating...but Caleb would be disappointed.

"Mommy, I want a hot dog. Can we go now?"

"Try to talk your big brother into going with us. We can't leave him here alone." Jillian thought Molly might have better luck with Joshua than she would, and if she didn't, then Jillian would have a good excuse to withdraw her acceptance to her neighbor's invitation.

A few minutes later, Molly playfully dragged a not-too-reluctant Joshua from his room.

"Okay guys, let's go!" Jillian tried to sound blasé. Yes, she wanted to go. She was already thinking of how she could find out her neighbor's marital status without sounding too nosey. Holding the bottle of mustard in one hand, she pulled the front door closed with the other.

Chapter 8

Not Just a Cookout

Dear Jesus, please give me the right words to ask Mr. Morgan about his marital status. I feel very uncomfortable being here with him and not knowing. He seems so nice, but this is rather strange for me. I don't want to be a nosey neighbor, but for my own peace of mind—is that really what I'm seeking? Anyway, Lord, I need to know. Guide my words.

Jillian was reclining in a much too comfortable lounge chair on her neighbor's deck. Her stomach was full, and she felt a sense of pleasure, but the question of her neighbor's marital status still whirled in her mind. Not only had Mr. Morgan provided hamburgers and hot dogs with all the trimmings, but also a delicious pasta salad. For dessert, he scooped up bowls of rocky road ice cream. The menu seemed much too extravagant to have been thrown together at the last minute. She wondered if he had planned the evening, taking for granted that she would come. On the other hand, maybe he just did this for his son and invited them as an afterthought. Nevertheless, there had been plenty for all of them. She watched as Matt played lawn darts with the children, coaching the boys and being very patient with Molly. She liked his fathering style. She was also impressed with his style—as in his appearance. Once again, his hair was impeccably tousled, his tanned skin the appropriate background for a white T-shirt and khaki shorts that fell loosely at his knees. His toned calves revealed the hours he spent enjoying his athletic pursuits. And that slightly crooked smile that revealed a perfect set of teeth…

Stop it, Jillian, she scolded herself. *You still don't know anything about Mrs. Morgan.* As if on cue, the man she had been admiring told the kids they could play one more game without him, then walked over and fell back into the matching lounge chair beside her.

"You've got some great kids, Jillian."

"Thank you, Mr. Morgan. Aiden's a very nice young man too."

"Mr. Morgan? Mr. Morgan? Please, I'm your next-door neighbor. Call me Matt."

Jillian just smiled in response and quickly realized that this was the opportunity for which she had been waiting. "Okay, Matt. No more Mr. Morgan if you'll just clue me in on one thing."

"Let me guess…you want to know if there is a Mrs. Morgan?"

She could only muster a shy smile in return. He definitely was being presumptuous, but he was right. He continued, seemingly oblivious of her palpitating heart and dry mouth.

"I really should have mentioned something to you sooner, especially since I did invite you over, and it could have been a little awkward if I had been hiding Mrs. Morgan in the closet." He chuckled at his attempt to make light of his saga. Averting his

Or Be Reconciled

eyes from hers, he looked toward the kids playing in the yard. Now it was his turn to express—ever so slightly—his own discomfort.

"There is no Mrs. Morgan. She took back her maiden name after the divorce. She had an affair with her boss, a rich lawyer almost old enough to be her father, and after seven years of wedded bliss—or was it mess?" He paused briefly, looking in her direction, then quickly away. "She left me to be with him. She took Aiden except for one weekend a month and alternate holidays. This is my one weekend a month, and we always celebrate."

And she thought she provided too much information when responding to a question! Jillian could not think of an appropriate reply. Matt's account seemed cold and calculating, as if he had rehearsed it. There was that fleeting thought that produced a sense of relief—*he's not married*—but any joy this revelation may have generated was stifled by the pain she thought she detected in his voice as he shared his intensely personal story.

Finally, Matt broke the silence. "Hey, it's okay. What can I say? Obviously, someone that treats you like that—unfaithfully—I'm better off without her. The only bad part is losing all that time with Aiden. However, I'm saving up for a good lawyer, and we'll go back to court and see what we can do. Until then, I appreciate every moment I have with my son and try not to look back."

"I'm sorry." It was insufficient, but Matt didn't seem to think so.

"Thank you, but don't be. Like I said, I'm better off."

Chirping crickets and children's laughter made up the soundtrack as the young widow and the young abandoned husband sat side by side, watching the sun go down, each absorbed in their own thoughts of what had been, what could have been different, and what the future would still hold.

Jillian surprised herself when she eventually spoke. "Matt, you know, I've always believed that God works in everything that happens to us to bring about what's best. Sometimes bad things happen when people make their own choices without considering the consequence. But ultimately, we are in God's hands, and he will take care of us."

Matt turned to look directly at Jillian, and for a moment she thought she had upset him, and he was going to object to her sermonette.

Instead, he grew pensive. "Jillian, I grew up in church, but once I became a teenager, it didn't seem important anymore. I know I disappointed my parents, especially since I was their only child. My dad died suddenly the year after I graduated from high school, and Mom passed away five years later, probably from loneliness. The last time I saw her she told me her prayer was that I would find God. I never really had a personal relationship with Jesus Christ until after the divorce. I looked for him when I had no other place to turn. He has been there for me, and though I'm by no means a saint, I am trying to learn what it means to let him be the Lord of my life. But I got to tell you, Jill, I haven't been able to understand how good could come out of this mess. I'm sorry. I called you Jill, didn't I?"

"That's okay, Matt."

"Joshua said you prefer Jillian."

She just smiled as she thought how interesting that he would have remembered that from the morning they first met, or maybe Caleb had mentioned it this afternoon.

"Mommy, Mommy, look at the moon!" Molly squealed with delight as a bank of fluffy clouds broke, revealing a breathtaking full moon that illuminated the late summer sky and cast intriguing shadows across the backyard.

Molly climbed into her mother's arms. Matt remarked that they would make a lovely picture. Jillian thought that her very first impression of her neighbor had been right after all.

As soon as Matt made the request, the boys worked together to quickly replace the lawn darts into the storage container. There were thank-yous and high fives and laughter as the Hamiltons said their good-byes to the Morgans. As Jillian and her children crossed their neighbor's yard to their own, Matt called her name, and she turned eagerly to hear what he had to say.

"Would it be okay if we went to church with you tomorrow? Aiden doesn't know anyone at our church, and it is so big, well actually we both feel a little lost. And I've heard some really good comments from the other teachers about Pastor Milkalski, and the church is closer…"

"Okay, okay," Jillian responded with amusement as Matt continued to make his case. "That will be fine."

"Great!" Matt and Aiden's faces lit up as they voiced their affirmation.

"I'll pick you up at nine sharp…if that's okay?" Matt offered.

"We'll be waiting for you," Jillian assured.

"See you in the morning, Aiden!" Caleb called.

"See ya!" Aiden shouted back.

"Good night, Jillian," Matt's simple adieu resonated like a memorable movie line to Jillian. Her only response was her from-the-heart smile before she turned and strolled across the yard to her new home and what was becoming her new life.

Chapter 9

New Feelings

My mind is racing, Lord. Thank you for blessing the kids tonight with such a good time. Even Joshua seemed to enjoy himself. I don't know how to pray for Matt and Aiden…only for your perfect will Lord. I know they are both hurting after the divorce.

Divorce. The word stung. It always brought back unpleasant memories of her teenage years when there was that awful split in her dad's church-the only church she had ever known until then. Even in that terrible situation, God brought good. If they had not moved, she would have never met Bryan or known the joy of mothering Joshua and Caleb and Molly. As she consoled herself with that thought, sleep began to overtake her. "Lord, help me keep my eyes on you…"

Jillian viewed the morning sun from her kitchen window and knew this would be a lovely Sunday. Molly's bed was dry as it had been since that first Sunday morning in Lakeview. Joshua wasn't complaining, and Caleb could not contain his excitement at having a friend to go to church with him. Jillian was also looking forward to going to church with a friend. The Hamiltons were dressed and were waiting patiently at five minutes to nine in their neighbor's driveway when Aiden poked his head out the front door.

"We're coming," he shouted. "Dad can't get his hair to do right."

Jillian laughed out loud. She couldn't imagine Matt, with his dark, good looks and disheveled style having a bad-hair day.

A minute later, the two Morgan men came out to greet them. When Matt opened the front passenger door, Aiden scooted in. "No, son, we let the lady sit up front," he admonished.

When Jillian saw the questioning look on Aiden's face, she quickly intervened. "That's fine, Matt. I'll sit back here with Molly so I can fasten her booster seat," she spoke decisively and was already climbing inside before he had a chance to reply. She didn't want Matt's son to resent her.

"Well, okay. Women rule I suppose," Matt responded good-naturedly.

Jillian immediately regretted usurping Matt's authority with his son and promised herself she would be more careful in similar situations. As was often her tendency, Jillian replayed the encounter in her mind, imagining how she could have responded differently.

I could be sitting up there by that handsome guy just now, she pondered. As she fantasized about that possibility, she chided herself. *What am I doing?* Suddenly, Jillian was alarmed at the visions playing out in her mind. She began questioning her feelings and motives. This whole situation was awkward in some ways; she told herself this was just a neighborly thing—next-door neighbors going to church together. No big deal. Period. Then a thought from left field would come crashing through her mind. *He is such a kind man, a good father.* She immediately tried to redirect her thoughts, but time and time again her mind's platonic relationship declarations were quickly followed by the what ifs.

Matt engaged the kids in a quick game of "I spy something," and before she had time to complete a decent daydream, they were pulling into the church parking lot.

"Which entry door do you use?" Matt turned and asked Jillian. As their eyes met, he added, "Jillian, you look lovely today."

She had chosen a colorful print top because of the way it skimmed over her upper body, hiding her perceived imperfections. Almost sleeveless, there were actually two fabric petals at the shoulder seam that overlapped when she was still, but provided a peak of her lightly tanned and toned upper arms when she moved. The navy slacks were tailored, a design style that elongated her legs. She had been pleased at the woman that smiled back at her from her full-length mirror this morning and was more than happy to have Matt agree. Still, she didn't want her reply to focus on her looks.

"You're having a pretty good hair day, yourself," she responded to keep the atmosphere light.

Matt rolled his eyes and shook his head as he replied, "Well, I wanted to make a good first impression on the pastor."

Jillian directed Matt to the side entrance where Pastor Milkalski greeted the two families, with what Jillian thought was a look of just a little surprise. When one of the ushers started to direct Matt and Jillian to the young marrieds' class, Pastor Milkalski quickly intervened. "Matt, we have a great men's class that meets in the pastor's study. May I show you the way?"

"I go to the ladies' class," Jillian hastily informed Matt. "I'll meet you in the sanctuary after Sunday school."

―――――― Or Be Reconciled ――――――

As Matt walked beside the pastor down the long carpeted hallway, he couldn't help but think this church must be a little backward to separate men and women. He was used to attending the huge single's class at his church, which he readily admitted was more like a social club than a Sunday school class. He wasn't too sure about this. Then again, he was seeking to grow spiritually. All those years away from church had robbed him of the Christian maturity he now longed for to help him deal with being a single father. Maybe God had brought him here for that purpose.

Mrs. Wilson's lesson was appropriately about keeping one's eyes on Jesus. Jillian enjoyed the way she interjected personal stories into the Bible-based lesson. *Maybe I was wrong about her, or maybe Jesus is answering my prayers,* Jillian reflected as she soaked up her teacher's words of wisdom.

"I'm so glad you're back," Mrs. Wilson greeted Jillian with a hug after class. "We have lost a few of our younger people to that big church on the highway. They say there are so many activities for all the family members."

"I was right at home last Sunday and feel this is where God wants us," Jillian reassured, stretching the truth only enough to overlook Mrs. Wilson's hurtful comments. As they walked toward the sanctuary, Jillian decided to offer more kind words. "And your teaching is excellent, just what I need."

Mrs. Wilson seemed both pleased and surprised; her cheeks grew rosy. Jillian almost added that she had brought two visitors from "that big church on the highway" today but felt cautioned in her spirit to leave well enough alone.

"Well, I do try to let God direct me," the gray-haired lady replied with an air of humbleness. "Now, dear, shall we find our seats in the sanctuary?"

"Oh." Jillian considered her situation, then thought she had made the wrong decision by not telling Mrs. Wilson about her guests. "That will be fine, but we need to find an empty pew. Our next door-neighbor and his son came with us this morning."

Mrs. Wilson's countenance changed to one of suspicion. "Is he a widower?"

"No." *How am I going to put this?* Jillian considered, resenting the question. "No, he's not," was all she said, feeling pleased at her restraint and at the same time disappointed that Mrs. Wilson had asked that question.

"Jillian, I'm so glad I came today." It was either perfect or terrible timing when Matt approached the two ladies enthusiastically. "The men's class was so encouraging. They are a great group of guys, and I've met a few of them before. I'm looking forward to being a part of the class. I think I'll learn a lot that will help me be a better dad to Aiden."

Matt had obviously enjoyed himself, but Jillian found herself in the awkward position of introducing him to Mrs. Wilson. She didn't get a chance. "So you must be Jillian's neighbor she was telling me all about," Mrs. Wilson overstated as the thrust her hand into Matt's.

"Yes, ma'am, Jillian and I are next-door neighbors," Matt replied comfortably as he vigorously shook her hand.

"Hold on, young man," she not-so-gently scolded. "That's a rough handshake for an old lady with arthritis."

Jillian was perplexed at Mrs. Wilson's response.

Matt's apology was amusingly charming. "I'm so sorry. I had no idea you had arthritis, and I *certainly* didn't consider you an old lady."

Mrs. Wilson was only slightly moved by Matt's defense. She made a half-hearted attempt to downplay her rude behavior. "That's okay, sir. Just go easier on me if you come back again."

Matt looked questioningly at Jillian, who was once again stunned by her teacher's remarks. She considered Mrs. Wilson might have a medical problem.

Fortunately, the children appeared from their classes with perfect timing, thrusting Sunday school papers toward their parents. As Jillian and Matt were caught up in the ritual of giving approval, Mrs. Wilson left the group and found a seat at the end of an almost-full pew.

Chapter 10

Seeking

Jesus, Jesus, Jesus.

Those were the only words Jillian uttered as she knelt at the prayer altar, seeking solace. So many concerns were tumbling through her mind: qualms about Mrs. Wilson's strange behavior, continued anxieties about her children's well-being and her new job, and now, apprehensions about her budding relationship with Matt—how or even if it should be evolving.

"Cast all your cares on him." Jillian heard the words of her pastor as he gently placed his hand on her shoulder.

Yes, Lord, I do put all my cares in your hands. The tension seemed to leave her body, and she rested in the arms of her Savior.

Pastor Milkalski's sermon had been taken from the fifth chapter of Matthew, the Sermon on the Mount. "Blessed are they that mourn, for they shall be comforted." She knew Matt had turned toward her when Pastor Milkalski spoke those words; she saw from the corner of her eye but did not dare return the glance. She considered that both she and Matt had gone through their time of mourning and wondered if their being brought together was God's way of providing comfort. The sermon had so ministered to her that when Pastor Milkalski gave the invitation for "anyone needing to hear from the Lord to come to the altar and seek him" Jillian immediately responded.

She had knelt on the prayer bench, sobbing her heart out, only occasionally aware of her fellow Christians joining her in prayer. Eventually she heard the congregation singing "search my heart, make me clean." Sometimes those words were difficult for Jillian to sing. Did she really want God to search her heart? She opened her eyes and realized she was the only one still praying. Slowly, she stood and took several baby steps backward. When she felt the edge of the pew cushion against the back of her knee, she sat down, looking straight ahead. She sang along softly until the end of the chorus: *"Do what you will, I belong to you."* Standing when Pastor Milkalski led the benediction, she then fulfilled the obligatory hugs and handshakes as she made her way to the pew, almost halfway to the back, where the children and Matt were waiting for her.

"Are you okay, Mommy?" Molly asked as she watched Jillian dab at her eyes with a tissue.

"Oh, yes, baby. Mommy just needed some prayer time."

Jillian embraced her precious daughter, holding her curly-haired head close to her heart. She closed her eyes and took a deep breath, inhaling the scent of Molly's cotton candy–scented shampoo. When she opened her eyes, Matt was staring at her. She wasn't sure what the expression on his face meant. Did he think that her crying and praying at the altar was strange? He probably had not seen much of that at his former church. He smiled a tender smile that erased her fears. In what seemed to her the most natural response, she continued holding Molly with her right arm and held out her left hand to Matt. He wrapped his strong hand gently around hers.

"Don't worry, I don't have arthritis yet," she reassured.

Matt responded by tightening his clasp on her hand. Jillian turned around to see if Mrs. Wilson was close by; she felt relieved when she did not see her. Thinking of Mrs. Wilson caused a momentary flashback. Did someone place their hands on her shoulders in a less than gentle manner while she was at the altar? Vaguely, she remembered the grasp and the voice. What were the words she used? *Keep this woman from adultery? No…no one would have prayed that*, she reconsidered. *Surely not.*

This time, as they got in the car, Aiden readily climbed in the back seat beside Caleb. Matt whispered, "That's my boy," as he motioned her toward the passenger side, grandly opening the door for her. Before pulling out of the parking lot, he suggested they go out to eat—his treat. Much to her children's dismay, she declined, declaring that Matt had done too much for them already this weekend.

"I'm exhausted. I could really use a long nap this afternoon. It's back to work and school tomorrow."

"Don't remind me," Matt moaned. "So why don't you let the kids come over for leftovers? Aiden would love the company, and you could go home and have that nap you're longing for."

Her kids heard the invitation and pleaded for her to agree. How could she say no?

"Are you sure you want the kids without me?" she meant to imply he might need her to watch her own kids, but she was concerned that's not how he took her question.

"Well, certainly I'd rather have *you* and the kids. But I understand your need for rest. It's been a busy week. Moving and starting a new job can drain you. I remember what it was like for me last year." For just a second, Matt's thoughts seemed to travel far away; they quickly returned. "And you probably don't often get a chance for an uninterrupted Sunday afternoon nap. Can I bring you something to eat?"

She was intrigued by his apparent concern for her well-being. *A nap? Nourishment?*

"That's really sweet of you. The nap I'll take. I'll get something to eat later."

She fell asleep almost as soon as her head hit the pillow. It was three o'clock when the kids returned home. They wasted no time waking her from a peaceful slumber.

"Mr. Morgan was sad you didn't come," Molly declared with a pouty expression on her face.

"Oh, how do you know that?"

"Cause when he brought us home, he said he enjoyed having us over, but it wasn't the same without our mommy."

"Oh well, maybe next time," Jillian murmured nonchalantly, not wanting to divulge to her children the pleasure she felt knowing that Matt had missed her.

Anticipating that he just might suggest returning to church with them for the evening service, she positioned herself discreetly on the front porch for over an hour. She didn't even catch a glimpse of him. Consoling herself with the thought that Family Fellowship did not have Sunday evening services, she was determined not to take it personally. Then she began to worry, just a bit, that her refusal to go out for lunch had put him off.

"It really doesn't matter," she told but did not convince herself. As she considered her only interest in Matt was her need for adult companionship, she knew she was not being honest.

Still, that was a real need of single mothers. Since Bryan had died, she felt awkward socializing with married couples. She thought the wives either felt sorry for her or suspicious of her intentions. Maybe a friendship with Matt was just what she needed. They had the same interests, and he was a Christian. Even though he had only recently given his life to Christ, she sensed in him a hunger to grow in the Lord. Maybe she could even encourage his Christian walk. Yes! Matt Morgan could be a very good friend. She told herself that was all. A friend. A good Christian friend. Nothing more. Heavens, no! That thought seemed utterly ridiculous to her. Besides, to her point of view, Matt already had a wife, even though they were divorced. *Till death us do part.* Those were the vows. She could never get seriously involved with a man who was divorced. Since she was a young girl, her parents had instilled the philosophy in her that marriage was for life. She would never forget the furor that erupted at her childhood church when her dad declined to perform the wedding ceremony of a deacon's daughter because her fiancée was divorced. The ensuing church split, and her dad's resignation was one of her worst memories. No. A romantic relationship with Matt was unthinkable. Yet she knew she had experienced some feelings during the last few days that she had not been aware of for some time.

Jillian sat alone at the Sunday evening service, a situation she had grown used to since Bryan's death, but one she still did not relish. The children had their own service, and Mrs. Wilson was not present. She tried her best to concentrate as Pastor Milkalski delivered an inspirational sermon on the importance of one-on-one time with God.

Afterward, she hurried home with the kids and prepared grilled cheese sandwiches before bedtime. As they ate, she tried to peruse the local Sunday paper, but her mind was too jumbled. She knew the week ahead would be a busy one. The kids seemed to be adjusting well in school, but Caleb, especially, needed her help with homework every night. Several times, Joshua had mentioned the unsavory antics of some of his classmates. Praying he would not get involved with the wrong crowd, she made a mental note to ask Matt to keep an eye on him. He was, after all, a teacher at Joshua's school.

The first week in her new position had been spent mostly in orientation. This week, her preceptor would allow her to begin to move out on her own. Slowly but surely, her nursing knowledge and skills were being reactivated. After earning her bachelor's degree in nursing before she and Bryan were married, she had worked two years in a hospital emergency room, retiring when Joshua was born. She had been scared to death to take the state boards in North Carolina for her nursing license. After investing a few hundred dollars for a classroom/clinical refresher course, she passed the exam on her first try.

Since Bryan died, she and the children had been living on his generous insurance proceeds and monthly benefits from his police pension. Mortgage insurance had paid off their house in Richmond, and she sold at a profit, enabling her to pay cash for her new downsized home. Her father-in-law had given her wise investment advice when she received Bryan's death settlement. They may have been able to squeak by without her working, but she felt responsible for taking over her husband's role of provider. With all three kids in school, she couldn't imagine staying home all day.

Last week she had fallen asleep easily almost every night because she was exhausted. On nights past, occasional flashbacks of the evening Bryan died would invade her mind, and she had to pray herself to sleep. As much as she tried, she had never been able to completely get that dreadful scene out of her mind, the one on the local news the night Bryan was killed. He was off duty, on his way home, when he heard the call and rushed to the scene of an armed robbery in progress at a convenience store. He saw the robber fleeing the store and pulled his patrol car behind the waiting vehicle to block an escape. A lapse of judgment...not enough time to think—whatever happened that evening, Bryan stood between the two cars as he pulled his gun. He had not seen the getaway driver already in place. As the robber fired once as he ran for the passenger side, Bryan returned fire before ducking down behind the car. The driver hit reverse, pinning Bryan between the two cars. The autopsy had determined death was instantaneous.

On that tragic evening, Jillian had been wondering why Bryan was so late for dinner. He had called her from the station when he got off duty, as had become his habit, and he should have been home. She experienced an anxious thought or two, but instead of dwelling on what was making him late, she turned on the television to watch the news while she waited. Just as the anchor reported that a police officer had been killed while a video of a crushed patrol car was being shown, her doorbell rang. The police chief and chaplain had arrived to tell her Bryan was dead.

Tonight her flashbacks were of a very different nature. Pleasant memories of the recent weekend filled her thoughts. Jillian's mind would continue the illusory glimpses and nurture them into what-if scenarios. She tried to catch herself and redirect her thoughts, but a few times, she let the imagined events continue until she and Matt were staring longingly at each other.

Chapter 11

So That's Shannon

Lord, I bless you. I praise your name. You are worthy to be praised.

"Mommy, Mommy, I can't find my Sunday shoes!"

This was becoming a habit for which Jillian considered she should be thankful—no more wet bed, always lost shoes. "Molly, you're going to have to take responsibility for finding your own shoes. I told you to put them away in the closet when you take them off."

Molly's appeal for help had brought Jillian's morning prayer time to an abrupt halt. She had already prayed through the ever-growing tattered list folded inside her devotional Bible. Sometime soon, she needed to update it. Many of the prayer requests had been answered, and new ones should be added.

It was hard to believe another week in Lakeview had already passed by. Her days at the hospital had been tiring as she took on more responsibility. However, most of her coworkers were helpful, and there had been no major issues.

Molly loved Mrs. Ratterman and kindergarten. Mr. Rogers seemed to have lightened the work load for his third-grade class, and Caleb was sailing through his homework. On Thursday, Joshua reluctantly brought home a note from Ms. Antonio noting he had not completed his assignments the night before. He had used attending church as an excuse, and the note seemed to indicate that Ms. Antonio thought schoolwork much more important than church.

To Jillian, the most disheartening part of the week was not seeing Matt. Oh, he did wave from his yard a couple of times when they were coming or going, but that interaction had not been nearly enough for Jillian.

Therefore, she was more than pleasantly surprised when she answered the doorbell last night and found her handsome neighbor standing breathlessly in jogging shorts and a perspiration-soaked T-shirt. Strands of wet hair, usually gelled in rumpled formation, appeared glued to his forehead. She caught a whiff of manly sweat and smiled, remembering that aroma that always clung to Bryan after a workout.

"Hi, Jillian, how was your week?"

She invited him in, but he declined, noting he was sweaty, as if she hadn't noticed. She stepped out on the porch, and they sat across from each other on the matching wicker rocking chairs. His face and arms glowed with beads of perspiration. She wished she looked that good when she was sweating.

"What a busy week. After your kids ate lunch with us last Sunday, I had to take Aiden back to his mom's, and I got back too late to go to church."

Or Be Reconciled

All that time she sat on the porch last Sunday, waiting for him to appear, she had thought his car was in the garage. "You don't owe me an explanation, but I appreciate your thoughtfulness. We missed you at church." She should have said *I* missed you; she didn't think the kids had even mentioned him this week although Caleb had asked if she knew when Aiden would be back.

"Did you say hello to that old lady for me?"

"That old lady has a name," she scolded, only partly in jest.

"Yeah, but she made a point of telling me she was an old lady."

She rolled her eyes at him.

"You like her, don't you?"

"She's a good teacher…sometimes she says things that don't seem appropriate."

"You're very generous with your appraisal of people."

"Actually, I try not to *appraise* people, but if I am called on to do so, I do try to be generous."

Matt enjoyed talking to Jillian. She was clever, and he could tell she really listened to what he said. Taking the towel from around his neck and wiping the sweat from his face, he decided to change the subject.

"This week really flew by…getting back into the routine of teaching and coaching…whew. It doesn't leave me much free time to socialize."

"We had a busy week too," Jillian agreed even as she thought, *But you shouldn't be too busy to at least say hello to the woman who lives next door.* She did not dare verbalize her thoughts.

"So I just thought I'd come over and see if you want me to drive you and the kids to church in the morning," and then he added before she could respond, "Of course, if you'd rather go by yourself?"

"No, no, let's go together," Jillian heard herself say, with a tad more enthusiasm than she had meant to convey. "So you've decided to give New Life Church another try?"

"I really liked it…even though that lady-friend of yours—"

"Now that's a little better than 'that old lady.'"

"I'm trying to be generous."

"Her name is Mrs. Wilson."

"Mrs. Wilson didn't seem too thrilled about my being with you."

"I haven't quite figured her out. It's just that her teaching conveys one message, and when she talks to you one-on-one, she comes across…"

"Isn't that what they call pharisaical?"

"I'm impressed." Jillian really didn't want to discuss Mrs. Wilson's character, and she was surprised that Matt used a biblical term to describe her. "Don't judge New Life Church by just one person." Jillian realized as she spoke that her motive was to encourage Matt to continue attending church with her and the kids. Of course, she had been hoping he would, especially after he mentioned the singles' class he had been attending at his church.

"How about if that person is you?"

"That depends…does that make you want to go?"

"Well, the honest answer to that question is *yes*."

"Good. I think it's sweetly old-fashioned for neighbors to attend church together."

"Well, if you don't mind having me tag along, I'd love to go to church with you and the kids. Weekends can be rather lonely without Aiden."

Jillian's heart ached for Matt. She couldn't imagine sharing her kids with an estranged mate, especially one that had been unfaithful.

"I think it's a fine idea, and…" Jillian began to speak before she had thought through her plans. "You can have lunch with us here after church. I owe you one." Immediately, she wished she had not extended that invitation, not because she would not enjoy preparing lunch for her neighbor, but she worried that Matt may read too much into her offer. His reply caught her off guard.

Or Be Reconciled

"Thanks, Jillian, but as much as I'd love to, I'll have to decline this time. Shannon—that's Aiden's mom—will be here at one o'clock tomorrow with some documents I need to look over regarding our custody arrangements. She just called this afternoon…took me by surprise. I suggested she mail them, but she insisted."

"Oh, sure, that's fine," Jillian had replied, surprised at the disappointment she felt. "We'll do it some other time."

"Look, Mommy, I found them," Molly stood at the bedroom door, holding up her white sandals.

"Good for you. Next time don't lose them," Jillian reminded her.

Molly's appearance put an end to Jillian's' recollections. The past few days, she had been peculiarly preoccupied with thoughts of Matt…and his ex-wife. Oh, how she disliked that label. She could not help but wonder what she looked like. Now, she might catch a glimpse of her today. Matt was certainly a handsome man. Although a mental picture of Shannon had not yet developed in Jillian's mind, she was sure that the woman Matt married was as beautiful as he was handsome.

Okay, Jillian girl, she scolded herself. *Get a grip. Turn your thoughts toward Jesus. And get ready for church. You don't want to be late.*

Matt was waiting by his van and hurried to open the passenger side door for Jillian when she and the kids walked out the front door at nine o'clock sharp. Greeting the children warmly, he bent down to receive Molly's hug, being careful not to disturb her blonde curls.

"You're sure looking pretty today, Molly," he complemented as she scooted in beside her brothers.

"Thanks…so are you, Mista' Morgan."

Matt and Jillian exchanged knowing grins. "And so is your mother," Matt added as he caught Jillian's glance just long enough to produce a scattering of goose bumps all up and down her arms.

Caleb and Joshua engaged Matt in a conversation about soccer before he was out of the driveway. Their sports talk allowed Jillian to silently bask in the glow of Matt's charming words and enchanting gaze. She closed her eyes, pressing both into the special memories section of her heart.

When Matt saw how crowded the parking lot was, he offered to let Jillian and the kids out at the entrance. "Wow, there are a lot of people here today."

Matt's observation nudged Jillian's memory, and for a moment, she felt a sense of dread.

"Yes, there was a seminar here this weekend, and the speakers stayed over for today's services," she now recalled the announcement Mrs. Wilson had made last week.

As soon as she stepped inside the church and saw the tables with resource materials set up for the marriage seminar, her first concern was for Matt. *I hope this won't be awkward for him,* she contemplated.

Soon he was by her side. Either he hadn't paid any attention to the displays or wasn't bothered by them. As the usher directed them to the sanctuary, where all the classes were meeting together, he asked expectantly, "Hey, we get to go to class together this week?"

"It appears that way."

Jillian was sure that from the corner of her eye, she saw Mrs. Wilson cast a disapproving look her way as she and Matt walked down the aisle. *She is probably just disappointed that she won't be teaching this morning,* Jillian considered in an attempt to assuage her concerns. At least she hoped Mrs. Wilson didn't have a problem with Matt and her attending church together.

Jillian slipped into the pew, leaving plenty of room for Matt; however, when he sat down beside her, he left no space between them. Ever so slightly, Jillian repositioned herself. She did not at all mind the closeness of Matt next to her, but she didn't want to give Mrs. Wilson any ammunition for a smug remark.

The first hour, both Reverend and Mrs. Brown shared stories from their experiences conducting marriage seminars for over twenty years. Much of the information they presented was depressing to Jillian. Statistics of divorce in the church, the affects of divorce on children, obstacles faced by blended families— Jillian could only imagine how Matt must be feeling as he sat silently beside her. Reverend Brown's closing comments helped put her mind at ease.

"We're not here to point a finger at anyone who has suffered through a divorce," he reassured. "We want to encourage each of you to seek God, whatever your circumstances may be. He is a gracious, forgiving, and most of all, a loving God."

"It's good to hear divorce being condemned from the pulpit, isn't it, Jillian?" Mrs. Wilson declared with conviction as she approached Jillian and Matt during the break before the worship service.

Jillian was speechless. She looked at the floor, wanting to disappear. Then she heard Matt's controlled, kind voice.

"Well, I don't think I've ever heard a minister endorse divorce from the pulpit," Matt stated, emphasizing the word *endorse* in contrast to Mrs. Wilson's assertion. "But we live in a sinful world, and sometimes really bad things like divorce happen to people who love God. I appreciated Reverend and Mrs. Brown's non-judgmental attitude toward those who are divorced."

Yes, what a great reply! Jillian thought and looked up to see if Mrs. Wilson would concur with Matt's summation. She watched in disbelief as the expression on Mrs. Wilson's face changed from one of self-righteousness to disdain.

"God hates divorce, young man. Don't you ever forget that!" the gray-haired lady spoke sternly, without a hint of Christian compassion. She turned away abruptly and marched indignantly toward the exit.

"Okay…so did she forget to put sugar on her oatmeal this morning or what?" an exasperated Matt asked a little too loudly.

Jillian shushed him but immediately regretted doing so. "Matt, I am so sorry. This is not the same woman who teaches the Sunday school class. I don't have a clue why she said that."

Mrs. Wilson did not return to the sanctuary for the morning worship service. The program noted that the guest speaker's message was "One Man, One Woman…for Life."

"Of course, that is God's perfect plan for marriage," Reverend Brown spoke authoritatively. "But look around us, church. The divorce rate in the church is almost the same as the divorce rate outside the church. Yes, almost half of all Christian marriages end in divorce. How can this be? What are we missing? God's word is clear—from Genesis 2:24 to Matthew 19:5 to Mark 10:7. The word of God declares, 'For this cause shall a man leave his father and mother, and cleave to his wife, and they twain shall be one flesh: so then they are no more twain, but one flesh. What therefore God hath joined together, let not man put asunder.'"

Reverend Brown paused and looked out across the congregation. Jillian recognized his demeanor change to the one her dad often displayed when he was preaching; Reverend Brown was about to share something that wasn't in his sermon notes.

"You know, my wife and I live in a state with a far different reputation than North Carolina. Not as conservative, some people may say. Recently our state legislature has been embroiled in a controversy over something that I never imagined in my almost sixty years would ever be a controversy. I'm sure you are aware of those in our government and society who would like to diabolically change the definition of marriage—from a God-ordained and God-honoring institution to something I can only describe as an abomination. Our local newspapers have been deluged with letters to the editors, the writers advocating for their side of this issue. I read most of those letters, and recently, I have noticed a trend. Those who support unscriptural marital unions are using the Bible to justify their cause. How is this possible? Because they point at the church today and say, 'Look, you don't obey what the Bible says about marriage. You pick and choose the Scriptures you want to live by. You say marriage is between a man and a woman, but uh-uh, the Bible also says marriage is for life—no divorce—and you just completely ignore that aspect of God's word.' Church, we have to take a stand. Our enemy would like nothing more than to destroy Christian marriages because there are so many negative side effects that last for generations. We need to be the generation that says, 'No more.' Our grandparents knew that marriage is a commitment that lasts through wealth and want, sickness and health, till death us do part. Today, marriage seems more a trial run that lasts until 'I'm not happy anymore.' Marriage is so much, so much more than that.

"We are all aware of God's standard for marriage. Existing in a sinful world, we do not always live up to those standards. If you are here today and you have gone through a divorce, I want you to know that God loves you. Whether or not you wanted the divorce or even if you caused the divorce, God still loves you. Maybe you are remarried, and you feel guilty because your former spouse wanted to be reconciled and you refused. On the other hand, maybe you are happily remarried and ask yourself how your situation fits in with God's blueprint for marriage. Even though broken marriages break our Lord's heart, he remains a God of grace and forgiveness and reconciliation. When we turn to him and confess our sins, he is faithful to forgive us and restore what the enemy has taken from us. He can take the really big messes we have made of our lives and bring restoration, turning them into something beautiful.

"It would take me much more time than I have with you today to tell you the many, many stories that husbands, wives, and yes, even children of divorce have shared with me and my wife over the years. Some are heart-wrenching. Some have happy endings. But they all remind us that when we stray from God's plan, there is a price to pay, there are tears along the way."

The sanctuary was almost hushed. Jillian thought she heard someone nearby sobbing softly. Matt had barely moved since Reverend Brown had begun his sermon. Jillian wondered how he had construed the message. She wished her dad could have heard it. Mrs. Brown sat at the piano and accompanied herself as she sang, "Something beautiful, something good, all my confusion, he understood."

The conversation on the way home revolved around the next week's events at school as Matt and the children exchanged questions and answers. Neither she nor Matt mentioned the sermon.

"Mista' Morgan, you sure know a lot," Molly gushed.

Matt looked at Jillian, hoping she would concur with Molly's assessment.

"Yes, Molly, Mr. Morgan is a very smart man," she replied while still gazing at Matt's striking features. She considered that he had the most handsome profile of any man she had ever known. His nose was perfectly formed, and his cheekbones and chin appeared to be chiseled by a master sculptor. She was glad he didn't know how much she loved to ride in the car with him because she could stare at him while he had to keep his eyes on the road.

She wanted to tell Matt how proud she had been at the way he had initially responded to Mrs. Wilson after Sunday school, but then she remembered the glib remark he had made after she stomped off and decided to say nothing.

Matt looked nervously at his watch. "Well, almost time for the…" She wasn't sure what he had planned to say but deduced from the pause before he completed his statement that at the last second he had changed his mind. "For Aiden's mother to arrive… in all her glory," he added a little too sarcastically.

"Sorry." He didn't want Jillian to perceive the bitterness he felt toward Shannon, but he was *not* sorry for the way he felt about his ex-wife.

"Well, I hope all goes well this afternoon," Jillian responded when she could think of nothing else to say.

"Me too, but I can't imagine that it will." Matt's words left her wondering what he was expecting.

Jillian threw together a quick lunch for her children—sliced leftover meatloaf on sandwich buns, instant mashed potatoes, and a mixed green salad.

"That was good, but what's for dessert?" Joshua inquired as he swallowed the last bite of his second sandwich.

"I really hadn't planned anything special, but there's some fresh fruit in the bowl on the dining room table."

"Not exactly what I had in mind, Mom. How about some chocolate chip cookies?"

"Yes!" Caleb chimed in.

"Can I help you, Mom? Please?" Molly pleaded.

Jillian looked at their three persuasive faces and thought she wouldn't mind having a few warm, gooey cookies with an afternoon cup of tea, and then she considered an opportunity sweeter than from-the-oven cookies.

I could take a plate of cookies over to our next-door neighbor to repay him for his kindness. As she mulled this thought over—intertwined with reasons why she should and shouldn't—she heard herself give in to the kids' pleas and her own inclinations.

"Sounds like a good idea to me!"

All four of the Hamiltons had big smiles on their faces as they anticipated their afternoon treat.

Following Jillian's instructions, the kids hurried off to their rooms to prepare their book bags and clothes for tomorrow's return to school. Jillian noticed it was now one o'clock; *she* should be arriving. What if she just dropped off the papers and left? She almost ran to the family room window for a view of Matt's driveway. It was empty.

If I hurry, maybe I'll catch a glimpse of her. That thought quickened her steps as she began gathering ingredients for the cookies.

Molly returned to the kitchen in time to help spoon the dough onto the baking pan. As soon as the first batch was in the oven, Jillian stepped into her bathroom to check her hair and makeup. She added a dab of lip gloss and rescrunched the curls at the nape of her neck. She considered that the new shorter, curly style she had adopted just before their move was somewhat flattering to her oval face. All the while, she attempted to ignore that inner voice asking, "Why are you doing this?"

The kids quickly inhaled the first batch of the gooey confections. Jillian hurriedly refilled the pan with mounds of cookie dough and put it back in the oven. Again, she took a peak out the window. A late-model, striking, red sports car now sat in Matt's driveway. She paced nervously, waiting for the timer to go off. Fortunately, the kids had gone out back to play in the yard and weren't there to see their mom model a silly schoolgirl with a crush.

"*Buzz.*"

Jillian pulled the oven door open, almost burning her forearm in the process. Taking a deep breath, she told herself to slow down, but that's hard to do in the middle of an adrenalin rush. *What if she leaves before I get over there?*

Almost in panic mode, she picked up the feature section of the Sunday newspaper and briskly fanned the cookies, willing them to cool quickly so she could remove them from the pan. After a few minutes, she placed her perfectly soft-baked delicacies on a serving plate and covered them with a napkin. She almost ran out the front door.

It seemed an eternity after she rang the doorbell before Matt opened the door. He looked surprised. She tried to act nonchalant.

Or Be Reconciled

"The kids and I just baked some cookies, so I thought I'd do the neighborly thing, and…"

Before she could finish, an attractive, but older than she had expected female peaked over Matt's shoulder. Matt stepped back to make way for Jillian to enter his home. Inwardly, Jillian jumped for joy! The ex-wife wasn't nearly as striking as Jillian had imagined.

"How thoughtful," she gushed, a little too artificially for Jillian's taste. Removing the napkin, she helped herself to a cookie. "Mmm, still warm!"

Matt appeared only somewhat stunned by what was happening. "Uh, Jillian, I'd like you to meet my mother…uh…my former mother-in-law, Margaret Stewart."

Jillian's heart crashed to her feet. Though she tried to prevent it, she was sure her countenance had as well. *Why haven't I learned to listen to those inner promptings and not make a fool of myself?* As she awkwardly offered her hand to Mrs. Stewart, her attention was grabbed by the blonde bombshell walking out of Matt's kitchen.

"Matthew, you have nothing but junk food in your fridge," she mockingly complained before noticing there was another guest in the house. "Oh, hello, who are you?" she inquired of Jillian as she plopped onto the sofa and pulled her long, bare legs to her chest, hugging them with long, bare arms; her jean shorts and white tank top were way too revealing; her French-manicured fingernails must have been an inch long.

"Shannon, this is Jillian, my next-door neighbor. She just brought some cookies over."

Shannon threw her head back and erupted in giggles. "Oh, how quaint. I didn't realize people still did that," she purred.

With every passing second, Jillian's regret increased. Then Matt came to her rescue—and unbeknown to her, she to his. Ever so slowly and gently, he slid his strong arm around her waist and smiled broadly at his former wife as he spoke, "Jillian is one in a million. Not many single men are blessed to have a neighbor like her!"

Jillian could feel herself blush. She could not believe Matt had actually spoken those words. Shannon looked dumbstruck. Mrs. Stewart glared disapprovingly at Matt.

Somehow, Jillian gathered her composure. For a giddy instant, she sensed that Matt wanted Shannon to read more into their relationship than was there, and she was more than willing to play along. Turning toward Matt, she gave him a quick and playful hug with her free arm.

"No, Matt, I'm the blessed one," she responded affectionately, believing she could purr as persuasively as any blonde could—when she needed to.

Not wanting to wait for a negative or any response from Shannon or her mother, it was Jill's turn to take control.

"Gotta go now!" she called out as she thrust the plate of cookies into Matt's hands. "Nice meeting you, ladies," sounded like an afterthought as she opened the front door. "I'll see you later, Matt!" expressed more sentiment as she smiled directly into her neighbor's appreciative eyes and flashed the most flirtatious wink of which she was capable.

Chapter 12

Now What?

Father, please forgive me for making such a fool of myself. My motives were not pure. I wanted to get a look at Matt's wife—former wife—and I did, Lord, and now I feel so stupid. I'm so ashamed for acting the way I did. I feel so mixed up right now. I don't want to act like a child. Lord, I want my words and actions and even my thoughts, Lord…I want them to be pleasing in your sight.

Jillian offered her desperate prayer silently as she lay sprawled on her bed. She had hurried straight to her bedroom when she returned from Matt's, locked the door, and plopped down, emotionally exhausted. She berated herself for her lack of self-control. What had she been thinking? Why did she have to be so stupid? She closed her eyes, but the snapshots kept flashing in her mind: Shannon's gorgeous, perfectly toned legs; Shannon's perfectly straight, long blonde hair; the mother-in-law attractive enough to be mistaken for an overly sunned thirty-something; Matt reaching out for her and placing his arm around her waist. *That* was the view she tried to focus on.

"Mom, Mr. Morgan's here! Mom, Mr. Morgan's here to see you!" Joshua repeated as he banged on the bedroom door. It was almost two o'clock. Her first thought was to stay hidden away in her sanctuary, but she knew she would have to face him sooner or later.

"I'll be right out, Joshua. Tell him I'm coming." She didn't bother to check her makeup or hair in the mirror. Just a couple of slow, deep breaths and she turned the lock on her door.

She didn't care that she looked disheveled; her appearance would match her emotions. Still, she wasn't ready for Matt's reaction.

"You were great, absolutely great!" Matt exclaimed as she walked across the family room toward him. He was standing by the front door with a huge smile on his face. "Thank you, Jillian!"

"So you liked the cookies?" she asked, pretending she did not realize his gratitude had nothing to do with cookies. She still could not believe her silly performance in front of Shannon had won his approval.

"Oh, Jillian, the cookies were delicious, but I'm talking about the way you handled Shannon and her mother. It was brilliant! I couldn't have scripted it any better."

Jillian had not noticed her children until now. All three were sitting on the sofa, perfectly still and taking in every word. She hoped they had no idea what was going on, and she planned to keep it that way.

"Kids, I didn't even see you. You were being so quiet." She tried to sound calm. "Have you gotten everything ready for school tomorrow so we can go to church tonight?"

"You're just trying to change the subject, Mom," Joshua accused.

Looking in Matt's direction, she rolled her eyes, and he immediately realized he should have been more discrete.

There was a momentary, uneasy silence, which was broken by Caleb. "That's probably because this is adult stuff and not for us to hear, right, Mom?"

Jillian was still not sure how to respond; thankfully she didn't have to.

"Well, are you ready for school tomorrow? Because I was thinking if we left early, we could grab some burgers and eat at the park across the street from the church before service. It's beautiful out there this afternoon, and the days aren't getting any longer. And I've got some good news I want to share with all of you." Matt's exuberance continued.

If Joshua realized Matt was also trying to change the subject, he didn't acknowledge it. "All right!" he exclaimed, and Caleb and Molly joined in.

"Well, guys, we just ate lunch a couple of hours ago." Jillian was regaining her composure.

"So what would be a good time for you? Five o'clock? Should I come back then?

"That will be good," Jillian agreed. She was already anticipating the impromptu picnic, but even more, she wanted to hear what good news Matt had to share.

"Mom, why do you have to mess up things?" Joshua complained.

"Joshua, that's no way to talk to your mom. She's right. Now would be too soon after lunch."

She was surprised, but not put off that Matt would take up for her. What really surprised her was Joshua's reply.

"Yes, sir."

I could get used to having this man around, she considered as she stood at the front door, watching Matt jog back to his house. Jillian realized she no longer felt stupid about their performance earlier at his house. In fact, as she replayed it in her mind, she smiled and almost laughed out loud, recalling the stunned expressions on the faces of Shannon and her mother.

Jillian changed into her favorite summer outfit: sky-blue eyelet capris and matching sleeveless shirt. She slipped her feet into her most flattering sandals. The wedge heels tightened her calf muscles without adding too much height, although she didn't have to worry about that. At six feet, Matt had a good six inches on her. With autumn on its way, she knew she wouldn't be able to wear this outfit much longer, and it seemed perfect for a picnic in the park before church.

Matt pulled into the drive-thru at the Burger Palace and announced that he was treating everyone. There was laughter and confusion as each ordered their favorite burgers—cheese and bacon for the boys, cheese and lettuce for Molly, a veggie burger for Jillian, and a double with everything for Matt.

"We need lots of napkins 'cause we're going to church after our picnic and we don't want to mess up our clothes," Matt informed the girl at the window. She responded with a stack that was more than adequate. "You must think we really do look like messy folks," he joked.

"Oh no, sir, I was just thinking what a lovely family you have," she replied candidly.

Matt glanced at Jillian for her reaction. She smiled and shrugged as if to imply there was no need to correct the young lady's assumption. "Thank you!" Matt replied.

Jillian considered the impression they had just made at the window and allowed herself to mull over the possibilities. Each time she began daydreaming about pursuing a relationship with Matt, subtle warnings flashed in the background. She knew she should talk this over with her parents, but each week when they emailed, she avoided it, afraid of the caveat she was almost sure she would receive. In her heart, she knew she had never even considered dating someone who was divorced, but then again, she had never been presented with a prospect, and such a good prospect at that.

"Here we are!" Matt declared as he pulled into the parking area. The kids responded with excited squeals. Those were the first words he had uttered since they left the drive-thru, and Jillian wondered if he had been as deep in thought about the cashier's "lovely family" comment as she had.

"There's a really nice spot just over that hill, beside the stream," Matt directed the kids. "You go ahead, just don't fall in, and your Mom and I will bring the food."

The children needed no encouragement. Joshua and Caleb were already well on their way, and Molly was earnestly trying to catch up.

Jillian started to open the car door, but Matt placed his hand on her shoulder. "Wait."

Jillian released the latch and turned to look into his face, anticipating his words. "I sent the kids ahead because I wanted a moment alone." His tone was serious.

She knew he was going to say something about the "lovely family" comment and decided she would just brush the whole issue off as if she had hardly noticed.

"Shannon wants Aiden to live with me for a while." His announcement caught her off guard. She felt silly, once again, for daydreaming about their future when that was probably the furthest thing from Matt's mind.

"Matt, I know you must be thrilled!" she exaggerated her response.

"Mostly I was shocked. She fought so hard for him during the divorce—for show I suppose. Now she and her husband-to-be—yes, he's proposed—will be traveling overseas for an extended period, and as she put it, 'Aiden would probably be bored with international travel.' What she really meant was his presence would cramp their international lifestyle."

"Even so, Aiden will be with you, and I know how much you've wanted that."

"I worry that he'll feel rejected by his mother. He's only eight years old. I know he'll miss her. He's crazy about her. He might not even want to stay with me. She didn't bring him today because he said he would rather stay and play with a friend."

"Oh, you know how kids are when it comes to playing," Jillian offered. "I'm sure he'll adjust well. He also adores his father, and you've always been concerned about his living with them. Are they getting married before they leave?"

"Shannon said they would wait until they return because she wanted Aiden to be there…yeah, be there at the wedding, but not in their lives."

"Matt, are you upset because Shannon is getting married?" Jillian ventured into territory she felt only slightly was her business, but Matt didn't seem to mind.

"You know, I really thought I was over her—well, of course, I am—but when she told me what's-his-name had proposed, I got to admit, it was like stabbing me in the back. Don't get me wrong. I don't love her anymore. I have to force myself not to hate her, but it was a weird feeling, something I've never experienced before," he expressed himself awkwardly. "You know, when you get married, you don't think about your wife leaving you for someone else."

An uncomfortable hush hung over the next few moments until Matt broke through with a strong, resilient voice. "I am so glad I will have my son with me again. Let's go tell your kids the good news."

Matt gave no explanations to the children except that it was his turn to have Aiden for a while. Caleb was beside himself with excitement. Joshua seemed a little jealous that he would have to share his newfound adult friend with his own son. Molly shared Caleb's joy, but she didn't understand why a kid would live with only one parent.

"Mommy, if Daddy were still here, would I live with both of you?" Her innocent question surprised Jillian.

Jillian considered an apt response without having to go into detail. "Yes, sweetie, if Daddy were still alive, we would all be living together."

"But then we couldn't do things with Mista' Morgan, could we?"

Jillian was amused by Molly's naïveté. "I'm sure your daddy would have found Mr. Morgan to be as good of a neighbor as we have. Now we better eat our burgers so we won't be late for church."

Chapter 13

Reminiscing

Father in heaven, I praise you for another day of life and joy and for knowing you are with me even when I do silly, childish things. Bless Joshua and Caleb and Molly in school this week, Lord. I pray that your hand of protection will be on them and they will follow your way in all they do. Open Joshua's mind and help him understand math and get over his struggles. Keep Caleb sweet and kind. Take care of my little Molly. Watch over Mom and Dad and bless their ministry and be with Bryan's parents. Be with Matt and Aiden. Work out your perfect will in their situation, and I pray for Shannon. I'm not sure what to pray for her, Lord, but you know. In Jesus's name, amen.

Or Be Reconciled

The kids were worn out from their busy Sunday—two church services and a picnic. It took little coaxing to convince them to go to bed a half hour early that night. Jillian was pleased to have some quiet time. She felt she had not been spending as much time alone with the Lord as she had before they moved, and she wanted to change that. She knew her inner strength came from those quiet moments alone with her Heavenly Father. Tonight, her prayer had been brief; the yearning of her heart was to spend time in God's word. Reading in Matthew, she had just completed chapter eighteen, about teachings on forgiveness, a subject near to her heart and one she had struggled with. When she saw that the heading for chapter nineteen was "Divorce," she almost closed her Bible. However, that little voice inside said, *Go ahead, read it.*

> The Pharisee also came unto him, tempting him, and saying unto him, "Is it lawful for a man to put away his wife for every cause?" And he answered and said unto them, "Have you not read, that he which made them at the beginning made them male and female and said, 'For this cause a man shall leave father and mother and shall cleave to his wife; and they twain shall be one flesh? Wherefore they are no more twain, but one flesh. What therefore God hath joined together, let no man put asunder."

That was plain enough. One man and one woman equal one lifelong covenant. That was the message the speakers at church had presented. But the Pharisees were not content:

> Why did Moses then command to give a writing of divorcement, and to put her away? He saith unto them, "Moses because of the hardness of your hearts suffered you to put away your wives: but from the beginning it was not so. And I say unto you, Whosoever shall put away his wife, except it be for fornication, and shall marry another, committeth adultery: and whoso marrieth her which is put away doth commit adultery.

There it was, the so-called exception clause: *except for marital unfaithfulness*. It would have been so much easier to understand God's design if the Pharisees had left it well enough alone. Prodding Jesus to excuse Moses's actions led to an entirely different situation that was missing in Jesus's original answer. But then that answer appeared to open the door to situations like Matt's, where one party had been unfaithful, to not only divorce but to remarry. She pondered the Scripture. She remembered hearing her dad read this passage aloud to her mother when they were going through the difficult time at their church. Her dad was agonizing over the decisions he had to make as pastor considering divorce and remarriage. He wanted God's heart and researched the subject tirelessly. He sought counsel from other pastors and church leaders.

Her father had told her, "There are many voices out there, but I only want to hear one—God's." He had in due course taken a stand, in agreement with her mother, that he would not personally perform any marriage ceremony when either the bride or groom had been in a previous marriage that had ended in divorce. Some of the church members supported him; others called his stand judgmental and left the church. Her dad suffered many sleepless nights, crying out to God with the question, "Am I making an unrighteous judgment?"

That controversial issue caused her dad to resign as pastor from their church after twenty productive years. A new door of ministry opened soon afterward, but it required them to move five hundred miles away to a new church and a new life. That was where she met Bryan. The night Bryan asked her dad for her hand in marriage, her mother had told her dad: "God honored you for taking a stand for the sanctity of marriage and has given your daughter a good husband."

Well, Jillian contemplated her life since that night, *yes, Bryan and I shared some good years and the children. I can't imagine life without them.* She silently scolded herself. *Jillian, you're supposed to be reading the Bible, not reminiscing.* She determined to focus her mind on the words she was reading. *Not everyone can accept this word, but only those to whom it has been given.* Jillian read several more chapters before drowsiness began to overtake her. She checked the alarm one more time. Six a.m. would be here soon. Turning over on her side, she hugged her pillow close to her body and snuggled down under the comforter. When she closed her eyes, she did not see an image of Bryan, but of Matthew Morgan. Sleep came quickly.

Matt had been standing at his kitchen window, drinking the last cup of coffee in his pot—leftover from breakfast and warmed in the microwave—and saw there was only one light left on at the house next door. He knew, since the floor plan in the house was a mirror image to his own, that the light was coming from the master bedroom, Jillian's room. He thought a moment about that phrase, *master bedroom.*

A sudden and strong sadness overtook him at that moment. Flashbacks of the master bedroom he and Shannon had once shared appeared on the pages of his mind. He didn't want to dwell on those scenes, but when he attempted to erase his imaginings, he was confronted with a manifestation of Shannon the day they had met. She had been the girl of his dreams. They were both in college, he a senior and she a freshman, yet there was a six-year age difference since Matt had worked three years after high school to save money for college. Mutual friends introduced them at an after-the-game party. She was gorgeous with silky blonde hair, flirty blue eyes, and a perfect body. Although he had been in several serious relationships previously, he never looked at another girl after their first date.

They married nine months after they met, just a month after his graduation. Aiden was born five months later. Matt had no trouble finding a teaching and coaching position at an elementary school. Shannon chose not to return to college although Matt had encouraged her to do so. Instead, when Aiden was two years old, she found a job as an assistant at a prestigious law firm—probably because of her great looks—and put Aiden in day care. Matt wanted her to stay home with Aiden a while longer, but his teaching position did not allow them to live the lifestyle Shannon wanted. By the end of her first year at the firm, Shannon's salary was almost as much as Matt's. Matt felt threatened; he had wanted to be her provider. Still, he never considered she would find someone else.

Along with his memories of Shannon, Matt was fleetingly aware of the love he had once felt for her. He remembered how devastated he was when she told him she was leaving him for her boss. However, the cruelest cut was when she announced she wanted full custody of Aiden even though she had been a less-than-attentive mother to him.

Now she wanted to give Aiden back to him. He wondered if he was capable of being a successful full-time single father. Could he and Aiden regain the normalcy and happiness they had once experienced when their family was intact? As Matt stared at the house next door, the light in the master bedroom went out. *Jillian must be going to bed*, he thought. Abruptly, his reflections turned from the past to today. A few minutes later as he fell back into his bed for a good night's sleep, he dared to imagine, for the first time since his divorce, that his future held something as good or better than his past.

Chapter 14

Love Thy Neighbor

Dear Lord, please help this young woman deliver her baby safely.

Jillian had never hesitated to pray for her patients, and this young woman seemed especially in need of a touch from God. She breathed the prayer almost audibly as she prepared to initiate intravenous fluids.

"What's your name?"

"Stacy Whitley."

Jillian compared the spoken name with the one on the bracelet. "Are you right or left handed?" she asked the mother-to-be just as another contraction came hard.

"Help me, help me!" her patient gasped as she fought against the piercing pain.

"Just breathe through it, you can do it," Jillian reassured, then allowed Stacy to squeeze her hand tightly as Jillian directed her breathing.

As the contraction ended, Jillian repeated, "Right or left?"

"Why?" Stacy gasped breathlessly.

"I want to leave your dominant arm free so it will be easier for you to hold your baby."

"Oh, I'm right-handed." The reasoning seemed to comfort Stacey, and Jillian seized the moment to start the IV.

"This will help keep you hydrated and be available for any medications your doctor orders. Okay, I'm going to do a quick pelvic exam and see how far along you are." Jillian felt eight centimeters and knew there was no stopping this delivery now, even though the patient stated she wasn't due for five weeks. She breathed another prayer for God's grace and protection. "Is anyone here with you?" She used to ask mothers-to-be if her husband was with her. Often she was met with a negative reply, so now she was more generic.

"The baby's daddy isn't in my life anymore," was the stoic reply. "But my boyfriend said he would come if I needed him."

"I'm sending you up to delivery, so if you'd like me to call someone for you, I'd be glad to."

As soon as Jillian helped the transport assistants wheel Stacy to the elevator, she called the telephone number Stacy had given her. After ten rings and no answering machine, Jillian gave up. *The baby will be here before her support person*, she thought and then wondered how much of a support person the boyfriend would be anyway. She passed on the phone number to the department secretary with instructions to keep trying.

The rest of the day was uneventful—Mondays often were. Jillian was thankful that not only had she landed the day shift, but that she also worked only Monday through Friday. Working weekends would have wrecked havoc on her family life.

Before the end of the shift, Jillian called labor and delivery so she could complete her charting on Stacy. "She delivered a four-pound, fourteen-ounce baby girl at 12:30 p.m." Karen from OB informed her. "Mother doing fine, baby will be in neonatal intensive care a week or so, but she scored an eight on the Apgar and can suck from the bottle. Mom said no way to breastfeeding."

"Was anyone with her?" Jillian asked hopefully.

"Just the nurses and Doc. But she has a visitor with her now. At least, I guess you could call him that."

From the tone of her voice, Jillian could almost see the smirk on Karen's face. She decided not to pry. "Thanks, Karen. Take good care of her."

"You care too much for the patients that pass through the ED," Karen scolded, only partly in jest.

"Someone needs to," Jillian shot back good-naturedly. "Everyone needs someone to care about them."

"Talk to you later, Florence Nightingale."

Jillian considered being referred to by that name a badge of honor. Since she was a young girl, Jillian had dreamed of becoming a nurse because it was a caring profession. These days, it sometimes seemed *caring* was inappropriate, too much of an invasion into another's privacy.

As she punched on the time clock, she realized she would have to hurry to pick up the kids on time. The school allowed them to stay in the play yard until four in the afternoon without registering for or paying for after-school care. Joshua seemed to enjoy having the time to socialize, and Caleb often used the hour to start his homework. Molly usually sat at the teacher's table, waiting patiently for her mom to appear. Jillian appreciated the small-town feel of the school her kids attended as well as the many accommodations they made for working parents. So many pieces of the puzzle had fallen in place for them here. She once again felt reassured that it had been the right move.

Turning into the parking lot, she was surprised to see that Matt was directing traffic. He waved her toward him, and she pulled over, pushing the button to roll down her window.

"Mr. Martin called out today, so I'm standing in for him. Did you have a good day?" He had walked over and leaned his arms on the open window.

"Not bad. How about you?"

"It was okay." His face was so close she could see his four o'clock shadow developing. "But I missed you…kept thinking about yesterday and how much I enjoyed spending time with you and the kids."

Jillian felt her cheeks blush. "We enjoyed your company as well," she responded, then quickly diverting her gaze, searched for her kids in the sea of children playing in the schoolyard. "Oh, there's Molly. I better go round 'em up. See you later."

"Have a good evening, Jillian." The sound of Matt's voice made her heart skip a beat, and she didn't dare look back at him.

"Mom, what was Mr. Morgan talking to you about? Did he invite us over tonight?" Caleb had caught up with Molly and was breathless with excitement as he helped his sister climb into the car.

"No, honey, he was just saying hello. You know school nights are much too busy for socializing."

"Oh, phooey."

"Well, I'm here, and I'll be with you tonight," Jillian teased as she gave Caleb's shoulder a pat and reached back to give Molly a hug. "Where's Joshua?" She had given the kids strict instructions to watch for her at three forty-five sharp, and she was on time. Caleb and Molly were compliant. More often than not, she had to wait on Joshua.

"He's over there with Heather Browning," Caleb volunteered, followed by a candid "Yuck!"

Jillian looked in the direction Caleb was pointing and was surprised to see Joshua leaning against the fence, talking to a very lovely young lady. "So what's yucky about Heather?"

"She's a girl!" Caleb rolled his eyes as if she should have understood that from the start.

"I'm a girl," Molly volunteered and for good measure added, "and so is Mommy."

"That's different"

"Well, I'm glad to hear that. But it's still not nice to call someone yucky just because she's a girl," Jillian gently chided.

Caleb, always desiring to please, was quick to offer an apology. "I'm sorry...I just meant it was yucky to see my brother talking to a girl, not that all girls are yucky."

Jillian sensed the awkwardness he felt and didn't want to pursue this subject any further just now. "It's okay, honey. I know you didn't. It wouldn't be very polite to blow the horn. Would you mind running over and telling your brother we're here?"

Caleb saw his opportunity to make amends and grabbed it. "Sure, Mom," he called as he opened the door and jumped out. She watched as Caleb ran toward his older brother and was reminded once again how dissimilar the two of them were. She wondered if it was because Joshua reminded her so much of Bryan while Caleb was his own little man.

Joshua saw Caleb approaching and didn't waste any time saying good-bye to Heather. Without being told, he raced toward the car with Caleb trying to catch up.

"Hi, Mom. Sorry. I didn't see you," Joshua offered as he took his seat beside her.

Jillian decided not to inquire about Heather at this time. She tried to remember how eleven-year-old boys acted when she was in school, but she couldn't.

Joshua didn't give her a chance anyway. "Mr. Morgan came over and sat with me at lunch today. He said he had a good time with us last night."

Jillian was pleasantly surprised at this revelation. "How did that make you feel?"

"I liked it 'cause the other guys heard him, and they think Mr. Morgan is like really cool. They couldn't believe he had taken us on a picnic."

"Yeah, everybody likes Mr. Morgan. I heard that Ms. Caleche's in love with him," Caleb spoke innocently, with no idea how this statement would affect his mother.

For a moment, her heart sank, and she suddenly remembered what it was like to be an eleven-year-old girl and discover the cute girl in the front row also had a crush on the boy you liked. "Who's Ms. Caleche?" she ventured.

"She's a fifth-grade teacher," Caleb responded.

"And the cheerleading coach and dance teacher," Joshua added to her chagrin.

"She's really pretty, Mommy," Molly contributed. "Like my Belle Barbie."

Jillian considered that she couldn't compete with Belle, then immediately scolded herself, first for even thinking about competing with another woman for Matt's affection, and secondly for thinking that he would judge a woman only by her looks. However, an image of Shannon made its way into her brain, and she reconsidered. Her words gave not a hint of the emotional roller coaster she was riding. "I think we are very blessed to have such a nice neighbor as Mr. Morgan. I can understand why he is so popular."

She had hoped to end the topic with her declaration, but Molly didn't fall for her tactic.

"Do you love him too?" Molly's sweet little voice innocently delivered the loaded question.

Before she could answer, Joshua piped up in a mockingly sing-song rhythm, "Mom's in love with Mr. Morgan."

Jillian was embarrassed! She shot a hard glance at Joshua that wiped the smirk right off of his face. She paused for only a few seconds before calmly answering Molly. "The Bible says we are to love our neighbors, doesn't it?"

"Yes, Mommy."

"And we try to do what the Bible says, don't we?"

"Uh-huh."

"And Mr. Morgan is our neighbor, so I think it's right to say we should all love Mr. Morgan with the love of the Lord." Jillian knew it was a cop-out, but it was her best option. Out of the corner of her eye, she saw Joshua roll his eyes, but she ignored him. "I was thinking about tacos for supper. How does that sound?"

She was grateful for the chorus of "yes!" she received in response, not because she was hungry for tacos, but because the kids were now more interested in eating than in talking about who was in love with Mr. Morgan.

Chapter 15

What If?

Father, I thank you for loving me and taking care of me. I praise you for leading us to this place and giving us a new home with good friends. Lord, I place Joshua and Caleb and Molly in your hands and ask that you surround them with your love and protection. Help them to grow up loving you with all their hearts. Give Matt and Aiden a safe trip home and help Aiden adjust…and, Lord, speak to Shannon's heart." Amen.

Jillian's spirit quickened at the thought of Shannon; she had no idea what she wanted God to say to her, but she couldn't seem to get through any of her prayer times without having her come to mind.

As she stood up from the wicker rocker, thoughts of Matt were forefront in her mind. Unexpectedly, he dropped by last evening to let her know he would be leaving early this morning to drive to Charlotte to pick up Aiden. It was the first time she had seen him since the brief encounter in the parking lot on Monday, and it made her uncomfortable to realize how much she had missed him.

"I hope this works out. I don't know how Aiden is going to adjust." Matt had admitted he was worried that Aiden would miss his mom since he had only spent weekends away from her in the past.

Jillian understood his anxiety. She tried to imagine how Caleb would react if he was living away from her. "Matt, I'll be praying for both of you. You'll make this work." Jillian was cautious and didn't want to give false assurance. She considered there would be some difficult times ahead for both of them.

Matt had placed his hand gently on her arm. His kind brown eyes pierced hers as he spoke. "Jillian, I really appreciate you and your prayers. You're a good neighbor."

Their eyes lingered for just a moment. She almost wished he had used a word other than *neighbor* to describe her. It sounded rather indifferent. Then she remembered she had referred to him in the same way to the kids, yet her feelings were stronger than "neighborly love." She had wanted to say something to convey that...or did she?

"Thanks, Matt. I feel blessed to have you as a neighbor as well."

Last night and again this morning, Jillian regretted her choice of words. She so disliked her habit of replaying in her mind conversations that she wished had ended differently. Second-guessing her responses, she was always asking, "What if?"

"Well, today I don't have time for what ifs!" she declared out loud as if to convince herself. "There's too much calling me in the real world."

She picked up her teacup and Bible from the small wicker table on the porch before opening the front door. With Matt gone, she decided to catch up on everyday chores. First on her list was grocery shopping with the kids. "Okay, sleepy heads, time to get up!" she called as she walked down the hallway.

An hour later, the kids were dressed and fed, and they headed for a nearby strip mall where their new favorite grocery store was located. The prices were the best Jillian had seen in Lakeview, and she loved the fresh produce section. The employees were friendly and helpful, and the market had the small-town personality that Jillian preferred.

Not as detailed as she once was in making out a grocery list, she kept a basic list in her purse and added to it only when items were on sale. She wanted to provide for her family with her current salary. Unless absolutely necessary, she didn't want to touch the remainder of Bryan's insurance proceeds.

"Mom, can we get some ice cream please?" Joshua pled as he looked over the assortment of buy one get one free containers. "How about the cookie dough flavor? Joshua asked hopefully.

"That's a good choice," Jillian agreed.

"What other flavor should we get since its buy one get one free?" Joshua questioned.

"Actually, this store will allow you to just buy one and get it for half price, and I think that's what we should do today."

"Aw, Mom," Joshua complained.

Jillian decided to stick to her guns. "It's one or none. You decide."

Joshua looked annoyed but placed one carton of cookie dough ice cream into their cart as Jillian started toward the checkout.

Caleb and Molly were beguiled by a nearby display of Halloween candy. As Jillian pushed the cart past the neatly stocked shelves, she smiled and shook her head. When the cashier rang up the total, Jillian was pleased that she had come in under budget.

Or Be Reconciled

After putting the groceries away, Jillian assigned chores to the kids and headed toward her bathroom to give it a thorough cleaning before tackling the kids' bathroom. With that chore completed, she vacuumed the high-traffic areas and threw any out-of-place items into a basket for the kids to put up. When she glanced out the family room window at the empty driveway next door, she realized she was feeling a little lonely today. *It'll be nice to have Matt and Aiden back tomorrow*, she pondered.

A strange sensation came over her. She tried to collect her thoughts, but they were running in many directions. She reminded herself that she could never pursue a relationship with Matt because he was divorced. A voice seemed to call out: *But he was an innocent victim. His wife was unfaithful to him. He's alone through no fault of his own. He needs someone to love him, and Aiden needs a mother.*

But Aiden has a mother, she told herself. At that moment, she was overcome with feelings of compassion for Shannon and felt compelled to pray for her. She quietly escaped to her bedroom, knelt at her bedside, and began to intercede for Shannon's salvation. Before she closed her prayer, she also prayed for Matt and Aiden. *They were a family at one time*, she considered but without much conviction. Before she had time to ask herself "What if?," her quiet time was rudely interrupted.

Knock! Knock! Knock! Came three impatient poundings on her door. "Hey, Mom, are you going to fix lunch or not?" Joshua yelled from the other side.

Jillian stood up and opened the door before answering. "And if I didn't, would you starve to death?" she teased with a trace of annoyance.

"Maybe," Joshua shot back in true adolescent fashion.

She sighed. Sometimes she didn't know what to do with this boy growing into a man. "Well, let's not take that chance," Jillian's tone softened as she surveyed Joshua's expression and sensed a little hurt in his deep blue eyes, his father's eyes. Sometimes she forgot that of all the children, he was the one who suffered most when his father died. Bryan had adored Joshua and spent more time with him than the others. He would often tell Jillian, "You take care of the baby stage, and I'll take over when they can run and catch a football." Joshua and Bryan had been practicing for Joshua's first recreation league football game the day before he died.

Jillian put her arm around Joshua's shoulder and thought she felt just a little resistance. Caleb and Molly were still in their rooms, and Jillian decided, rather spur of the moment, to ask Joshua a question she usually avoided. She placed her other hand on his chin and lifted his face toward hers.

"Joshua, do you miss your dad?"

He briefly avoided looking into her eyes. When his gaze once again met hers, she could see he was struggling to hold back his tears.

"Not as much as I did at first…except sometimes when I miss him a lot."

As Jillian pulled Joshua close to her, she silently prayed he would not shun her affection as he often did. When she felt his strong young arms go around her waist, her heart leapt with a mother's joy. "I miss your dad too, Joshua," Jillian confided to her eldest son.

Their tender moment was short-lived as the doorbell rang and Caleb came bursting out of his room to answer it. "I bet Aiden and Mr. Morgan are back!" he shouted as he raced down the hall.

"Sorry to disappoint you, but they're not coming until tomorrow!" Jillian called after him even as she had a glint of hope that Caleb might be right.

Caleb pulled the door open wide and Jillian, who was just behind him, caught a glimpse of their visitor. As soon as Caleb realized it was not who he was anticipating, he shyly backed away, leaving Jillian to welcome their guest.

"Mrs. Cecil, how nice of you to come by," she greeted their elderly neighbor as she took her arm and assisted her inside.

"Just wanted to stop by with these flowers for you," Mrs. Cecil declared as she thrust a bouquet of brightly colored zinnias into Jillian's outstretched hands. "They're almost the last of the season. Seems like flowers just don't last like they used to," she added.

"They're beautiful, Mrs. Cecil. Thank you so much. Here, sit down while I put them in a vase," Jillian invited as she headed to her china cabinet to retrieve an appropriate container.

"Don't mind if I do," was her pleasant reply as she leisurely positioned herself in Jillian's favorite wingback chair. "Now, honey, don't forget to cut the ends on the diagonal under running water and put them into the vase quickly."

"Will that help them last longer?" Jillian asked graciously, remembering those were the same instructions she had always received from her Grammy.

"Works for me!" Mrs. Cecil chirped. "And I've been growing and picking flowers for a pretty long time now."

After aptly arranging the long-stemmed blooms in a tall crystal vase, Jillian placed the arrangement in the center of the dining table where Mrs. Cecil could view them. "I was just getting ready to prepare some lunch for me and the kids. Would you join us?"

Mrs. Cecil seemed to be considering the invitation, then stood up slowly and answered, "I appreciate your asking, but I best be going back home. One reason I came over, besides the flowers, was that I was wondering if you know where my fine young man Matt is. I needed him to change a lightbulb for me."

"Oh, he went to Charlotte to pick up Aiden. He'll be back tomorrow. Is there something I can help you with?"

"It's that light outside my garage…up pretty high. Matt has a ladder he uses to reach it easily. Guess I'll just have to wait until he gets back. It's not an emergency, you know."

"Well, if I see him before you do, I'll let him know," Jillian offered.

"I'm sure you'll see him before I do." Mrs. Cecil's eyes twinkled as she made her assertion, highlighting the numerous wrinkles lining her ivory face.

Jillian just smiled. "Thanks again for the lovely flowers."

Mrs. Cecil felt she had given Jillian an open door to squelch the rumors making their way around the cul-de-sac. When Jillian didn't take the bait, Mrs. Cecil considered the rumors must be true. "The whole neighborhood knows," Mrs. Cecil divulged with a childlike giggle just before she turned to walk down the steps.

Jillian almost countered, *Knows what?* Instead, she bit her tongue and smiled a clenched-mouth smile. She already knew exactly what Mrs. Cecil was referring to and inwardly enjoyed knowing that the neighbors were talking about her and Matt. She didn't want to say anything she might regret.

Chapter 16

Dream a Little Dream

Now I lay me down to sleep.

This evening Jillian began her bedtime devotions with the familiar childhood prayer. She felt vulnerable…and very alone. She continued through her routine requests and asked God to give Matt and Aiden a safe trip home tomorrow. Before she ended with "amen" she once again placed Shannon's name on the throne of grace, without adding a specific need.

The piercing sound of the doorbell startled Jillian awake. She had been sleeping soundly, but wasn't sure how long. She grabbed her robe and hurried to see who would be at her door at this hour. Before turning on the inside light, she switched on the porch light, pushed aside the edge of the filmy curtains and peered outside. Matt was waiting patiently for her with a bouquet of bright-colored zinnias in one hand.

Jillian flew to the door, her flowing robe fluttering behind her, her bare feet cool on the smooth hardwood floor. She flung open the door and met Matt's excited smile with her own. Before she could accept the bouquet, he threw his strong but tender arms around her, lifting her gently off the floor and twirling her as if she were weightless. He planted a soft kiss on the nape of her neck, then her chin and her cheek, and as his lips searched for hers, Jillian's heart leapt with elation!

"Jillian, I missed you so very much," he crooned just before his lips finally met hers.

Jillian melted into Matt's embrace and wished she never had to let go. She held on for dear life even when she felt the insistent tugging on her robe.

"Not now, Aiden, can't you see your dad and I are busy?" Jillian gently reprimanded.

"Dad, I miss Mommy. When is she coming back?" Aiden started to cry.

"Aiden, listen to Jillian! She said, 'Not now!' Leave us alone!" Matt's tone was harsh.

The magic began to fade, and Jillian felt herself falling from Matt's embrace…over and over and over she tumbled from dreamland to consciousness, awakening with a start. Breathless, she sat up in bed. The adrenalin rush was tangible. She longed to recapture the feeling of being held in Matt's embrace before it escaped her entirely. Gently, she reclined into the covers, lying still, placing the tips of her fingers on her neck and moving them slowly along the path Matt had used to find her lips. She so desired to hold on to that instant when his lips touched hers. Alas, it had vanished! She tried to forget Aiden's interrupting words, but they echoed in her mind: "Dad, I miss Mommy. When is she coming back?"

Jillian stole a glance at the clock on her bedside table. It was only three o'clock. *If I go back to sleep right away, chances are good I will dream again before morning*, she consoled herself. Closing her eyes tightly, she dared not move a muscle.

When the alarm stirred Jillian from a dreamless sleep at seven, she momentarily felt disoriented. There was something she wanted to remember…but what was it? She summoned her subconscious to reveal that for which her heart was longing. Less vividly than in the middle of the night, she saw Matt standing on her porch with a bouquet of zinnias, and she remembered.

Jillian and the children were almost late for church. Joshua had noticed that his mother was preoccupied during breakfast and preparations for church, and he thought she might be thinking about his dad. Joshua was surprised and pleased when his mother had asked him about missing his father yesterday. Sometimes, Joshua thought she had practically forgotten him. Those thoughts had increased since they had moved and had been doing things with Mr. Morgan. Joshua liked having Mr. Morgan for their neighbor. It made him feel special because his classmates were envious of the attention Mr. Morgan showed him at school. But it also bothered him because Joshua felt Mr. Morgan was trying to take his dad's place, and he knew no one could do that.

Jillian pulled into the crowded parking lot and hurried the kids out of the car and to their classes, then quietly slipped into the ladies' class as Mrs. Wilson introduced the day's lesson.

"Let the words of my mouth and the meditation of my heart be acceptable in thy sight." Jillian had memorized the verse her teacher was reciting when she was in children's church years ago.

She had often spoken it as a prayer. Though she tried to keep her mind on Mrs. Wilson's teaching, she couldn't seem to get past the phrase "meditation of my heart." *Does that include dreams or trying to conjure up the images and emotions experienced during dreams?* Jillian contemplated. *Dreaming is unconscious...you can't control your dreams,* Jillian argued with herself. *Reliving them over and over in your mind once you're awake...is that different?*

"Do you agree, Jillian?" Mrs. Wilson's direct question tersely interrupted her meditation; she did not have a clue what her teacher was asking.

Jillian sat motionless, pondering if it would be best to just agree or admit she wasn't listening. She thought she heard snickers behind her.

"Dear Jillian, were you deep in your own meditations?" Mrs. Wilson asked with just a hint of sarcasm.

Jillian felt her cheeks burn with embarrassment. "Yes, Mrs. Wilson, I'm afraid I was. Would you repeat the question?"

"Let me ask someone who was paying attention. Glenda, what do you think?"

Glenda Rogers was Mr. Roger's wife. She was as congenial as Caleb's teacher and glanced at Jillian as if to receive her permission to answer. Jillian responded with a vulnerable smile, and Glenda spoke up. "Certainly, if we continue having private thoughts of a sinful nature, that's not pleasing to God. We must guard our thoughts as well as our words and actions."

Jillian's humiliation was softened when Glenda added, "Jillian, it's okay. When I was young like you, my mind raced all the time with all the goings-on and family responsibilities, and I only had two children and you have three. Of course, now that I'm older, it's hard to get my mind to race at all."

There was friendly laughter throughout the room, and Jillian gave Glenda a pleasant nod that she hoped would convey the appreciation she felt for her expression of empathy.

Listening to every word Mrs. Wilson spoke during the remainder of the class was draining, but Jillian was determined not to fall into the inattentive trap again. She tried not to think about how rude she thought her teacher had been. When a wayward thought confronted her as to why she continued coming to this class, she quickly rejected it. When the class dismissed, several of the ladies sought Jillian out to offer cordial greetings, and though none of them mentioned what had happened, she felt it was their way of apologizing for Mrs. Wilson's insensitivity.

The children were allowed to stay in the sanctuary today. She missed having Matt here; they behaved well in his presence. She gave in to Caleb's request to draw on the back of the sermon outline, and when Molly leaned on her and drifted off to sleep, she decided it would be okay, just this once. Joshua appeared to listen attentively to the sermon, making her wonder if he was actually in deep thought about something else.

Just before Pastor Milkalski gave the benediction, Jillian realized she had been so intent on evoking her dream, she had forgotten to put lunch in the Crock-Pot this morning. To cover up her blunder, and because she wasn't really in the mood to cook anyway, she surprised the kids by taking them out to lunch at The Park. Coworkers at the hospital recommended it highly for its varied menu, including healthy selections, and the quaint ambience of this local family-owned restaurant.

Joshua begrudgingly ordered the turkey burger and baked sweet potato fries, complaining that he wanted a "real" cheeseburger and fries; Caleb and Molly ordered the kids' grilled cheese on whole wheat with veggie and fruit garnishes; Jillian opted for the low-fat tuna salad wrap. Their beverage of choice was water with lemon. While they waited for their food, Caleb asked the question she too had been wondering about, "When will Aiden be here? Will we have time to play?"

Anticipating seeing Matt's car in the driveway when they returned home after lunch, Jillian responded, "Maybe they'll be home by the time we get there. Won't it be nice to have a friend your age next door?"

"Yeah, nice for him. How about me?" Joshua whined.

"You can play with us anytime, Josh," Caleb proposed.

"Why would I want to play with little kids?"

"Because we have fun!"

Jillian thought she may have to referee this exchange, but the waitress brought their order and everyone's attention turned to the food that was placed in front of them. "Not bad," Joshua conceded as he wolfed down his "unreal" burger and fries.

"This is good, Mommy!" was Molly's complimentary review.

"I want to bring Aiden here sometime," Caleb gave his approval.

The tuna salad wrap was tasty, but Jillian wasn't feeling very hungry. She asked the waitress to put half of the wrap in a take-out box; it would be her lunch tomorrow.

Much to Caleb and Jillian's disappointment, their neighbor's driveway was empty when they arrived home. "Caleb, check and see if they parked in the garage," Jillian instructed in a calm voice, trying not to convey the disappointment she felt.

If he jumped high enough, Caleb could just see in through the row of high windows on the garage door. "No, they're not here yet," Caleb sighed, not at all attempting to hide his disappointment.

"I'm sure they will be back soon," Jillian reassured as she reached out for Caleb's hand.

Taking it in his own, he swung their hands back and forth as they went inside. "Well, I'm going to watch the DVD with Joshua and Molly."

Jillian wished she could bounce back as quickly. With the children watching the movie in the family room and no dishes to wash or kitchen to clean, Jillian decided to use her free time to send an e-mail to her parents. At least once a week, her mom and dad traveled by jeep to the nearest village—almost fifty kilometers away—that had Internet access so they could keep in touch. She always tried to have a letter waiting for them. She gave detailed accounts of the children's lives but was more vague about her own. She had not yet mentioned Matt by name but reassured them that she had "very nice neighbors." She had wanted to say something about Mrs. Wilson and her strange personality but decided against it. With her parents so far away, she tried to be positive and didn't want to give them any unnecessary cause for concern about the well-being of her or the children.

The thirty years that her parents spent in pastoral ministry had taken an immense toll, both emotionally and physically. When they resigned their last pastorate, Jillian was hoping they would take life easy, but she should have known better.

They had already made several mission trips to India, so she wasn't too surprised when they announced they were going to relocate to India to establish an orphanage. They moved to Kalinga in Odisha, India, only one year before Bryan was killed. When he died, it took her two days of intense effort before she was able to get word to them. Immediately they offered to return to the States and help her with the children. She declined their offer even though at the time she had no idea what she was going to do. "God knew the future when he called you to India. He will take care of us."

She knew they didn't fully understand when she insisted they not attempt to come home for the funeral. It was already scheduled for the next day, and she honestly felt it would be harder on everyone, especially the children, to wait. She reminded them they had shown abundant love to Bryan during his life when it really mattered. "He's not here. He's in heaven. I'll be okay," she had assured them then, and even now, two years later, she felt obligated to fill her correspondence with declarations that she and the children were doing fine. She ended up with two pages—longer than usual—and checked the spelling before choosing Send.

Joshua, Caleb and Molly were still watching the *Pilgrim's Progress* DVD that the children's pastor had loaned them. When she checked on them, her sons were immersed in the struggle between Christian and Apollyon. Jillian discerned this scene might be a little too intense for Molly, who was either cowering from the characters on the screen or drifting off to sleep.

"Anyone for a nap?" she offered. Joshua and Caleb stayed glued to the struggle on the screen, but Molly reached her diminutive arms up toward her mommy, and Jillian gathered her into a comforting embrace.

"Mommy's baby girl is getting to be a big girl," Jillian spoke softly as she carried Molly to her room and snuggled beside her on top of the comforter. Jillian pulled the patchwork quilt her Grammy had given her and Bryan as a wedding present around their shoulders. Molly's eyes were already closed as Jillian gazed at her precious daughter's perfect features. "He gives his beloved sleep," she whispered softly into Molly's blonde curls. Only a few moments had passed until two of God's beloved children were sleeping peacefully.

Chapter 17

Dreams Can Come True

Lord, please watch over Matt and Aiden and bring them home safely.

Jillian stood at the front door of her new bungalow. She had opened the solid wood interior door, leaving only the full glass storm door between her and the unobstructed view of Matt's driveway. It was ten in the evening, and the children had been in bed over an hour. She should be, but she credited her afternoon nap toward her needed eight hours so she could stay up just a little longer. She knew it was silly to worry that something had happened. Matt had not even mentioned when they were returning, but Jillian had assumed they would return as soon as possible. Up to now, her concerns had been about their safety. She knew the traffic on the interstate between here and Charlotte could be a nightmare on Sunday; strangely, this thought comforted her. She envisioned them stuck in a traffic jam on the interstate, Aiden sleeping soundly, and Matt becoming impatient. The vision brought a smile to her face. Of course, she was sure that was what had occurred.

As usual, her thoughts would not leave well enough alone. As she headed to the kitchen to retrieve her third cup of decaf tea, another possibility crossed her mind. *What if they had stayed? What if Shannon decided she wanted Matt back, that she couldn't lose both Matt and Aiden? Is that why I had felt compelled to pray for Shannon yesterday? Has God changed her heart?*

Jillian asked herself how she would deal with those circumstances. Immediately she was reminded that Matt had no interest in reconciling with Shannon. She reconsidered the traffic jam scenario and chose to believe that was the reason Matt and Aiden were not home yet. She sipped her tea until the cup was empty, then closed and locked the front door. Fatigue, not necessarily physical, was about to overcome her. She prayed sleep would come quickly.

Jillian was awakened by a muffled noise. She lay still and listened to hear it again. It was almost midnight. Someone was knocking on the front door, she thought, but why weren't they using the doorbell? She grabbed her robe and threw it on as she ran down the hall and across the family room. After turning on the front porch light, she cautiously peeked out the window. She shrieked with delight when she saw Matt.

Wasting no time in flinging open the entry door, she ran smack into Matt, who had already opened the glass storm door. Whether their embrace was an accident or deliberate, it seemed like the most natural thing in the world to both of them. Neither wanted to end it as quickly as they felt compelled to do so.

"I'm glad you heard me knocking. I didn't want to ring the bell and wake up the kids," Matt whispered breathlessly.

"So you didn't mind waking me up?" Jillian teased and quickly added, "I'm glad you did. I was worried about you, Matthew Morgan."

That was music to Matt's ear. "You were?" he questioned, hoping Jillian would reiterate her concern.

"Yes, I was. Is everything okay?"

"Now it is." He reached toward her and pushed a stray wisp of hair away from her face. He almost added, *Because now I'm here with you*, but wasn't sure if Jillian would welcome those words just yet. "Shannon insisted we go to the airport with them so Aiden could tell her good-bye there, and the flight was delayed until almost eight tonight."

"You made good time then. It's just after midnight, isn't it?"

"Yes, we drove straight through with just one quick stop for food. The traffic wasn't as bad as it could have been."

"I imagined you in a traffic jam—among other situations," Jill admitted.

Matt's interest was piqued. He wondered how Jillian saw him in her imagination. "Care to tell me about the other situations?"

"Oh, I almost forgot. Mrs. Cecil needs you to change a lightbulb for her," Jillian offered matter-of-factly.

"Are you trying to change the subject?"

"No…really, no," she fibbed with a straight face. "I just told her if I saw you first I'd let you know."

"Well actually, I've already seen her."

"Where?" Jillian was surprised.

"You didn't know she is the neighborhood night owl, did you? She saw me drive up and came over with a basket of her famous blueberry muffins for Aiden's breakfast. In fact, she's been sitting on her porch watching ever since I knocked on the door."

"You're kidding!" Jillian whispered, only slightly irritated at her nosey neighbor.

"No, I'm serious."

Jillian didn't dare look toward Mrs. Cecil's porch. She knew their cul-de-sac provided great views of surrounding neighbors' porches.

"Oh my," Jillian sighed.

"Are you trying to hide something from your neighbors, Mrs. Hamilton?" There was laughter in his voice.

"No, Mr. Morgan. I have nothing to hide."

Again, their eyes met and lingered, and Jillian began to recall the dream she had last night and knew she had to end this encounter.

"It's getting chilly out here. I better get back to bed. Six o'clock will be here soon."

"I wanted to let you know I'm taking tomorrow off so Aiden and I can get settled. He'll start school Tuesday. Speaking of Aiden, he's asleep in the car. I better get him to bed as well."

"I wondered where Aiden was. I was almost expecting him to tug on my robe."

Matt was puzzled by Jillian's comment, but the twinkle in her eyes satisfied his curiosity for now. He would remember that line and ask what she meant by it at the appropriate time.

Looking in the direction of Mrs. Cecil's porch, he whispered, "I would kiss you, but the spy has her binoculars focused this way."

"We could give her something to talk about," Jillian teased back, and her smile assured Matt she really wouldn't mind doing just that.

Ignoring their elderly neighbor joyfully scrutinizing their every move, Matt quickly leaned forward and pecked Jillian, ever so lightly, on her waiting lips.

Before she had time to respond, he turned and sprinted toward his car to retrieve his sleeping son.

Chapter 18

I Feel Giddy

"Father, thank you for another day to live for you." Her thoughts were racing a mile a minute with memories of her midnight encounter with Matt crowding out those of a more mundane nature. She was having a hard time concentrating on her prayer list. "Be with me and the children in all we do today. Thank you for bringing Matt and Aiden home safely, and take care of them today. Help Aiden adjust to his new home and surroundings, and bless Matt. Take care of Mom and Dad, Mom and Dad Hamilton, Pastor Milkalski and Marie, our friends at church. I love you, Lord!"

Jillian was almost giddy as she lay facedown across her bed, silently offering her morning prayer. She jumped up, feeling more alive and energetic than she had in a while even though she had missed out on her usual full eight hours of sleep. *Oh, but it was worth it!* She considered unhesitatingly as she hugged herself, trying to recreate the feeling she had experienced last night with Matt's strong arms around hers. *Mmm…even better than in my dream!*

As she drove the kids to school, her exuberance rubbed off on them, and their conversation and laughter were more reminiscent of a Friday afternoon than a Monday morning. Jillian considered how much her own demeanor affected her children and determined to work at making this heightened level of happiness the norm. *With Matt and Aiden next door, that shouldn't be hard*, she assured herself.

The morning flew by with a constant stream of sick patients, but there were no life-threatening emergencies. Mondays tended to be the calmest day of the week after what her coworkers reported were always hectic weekends. She had taken her full thirty-minute lunch break but decided to skip the cafeteria in favor of the hospital's Soda and Gift Shop. She ordered a fruit smoothie to go with her leftover tuna wrap, now slightly soggy. While she was waiting for the drink to be blended, she perused the racks of greeting cards with no special event in mind. In the contemporary all-occasion section, a white card with a single cobalt blue heart in the center caught her attention. She thought a blue heart unusual and picked up the card to see what was inside.

I'd rather be blue over you than be happy with somebody else, the verse read. Vaguely, she recalled hearing those words in a song once upon a time and started humming what she thought may have been the tune. *That's rather a strange way to look at a relationship*, Jillian concluded and replaced the card as the woman behind the counter called out, "Who ordered the triple tropical smoothie?"

Jillian sat on one of the swivel stools, slowly sipping the frosty drink and picking at her food while she contemplated the meaning of the curious verse. She asked herself under what circumstances someone would feel that way. *So from this point of view, it's better to have a sad relationship with a true love than a happy relationship with someone for whom you have less intense feelings?* Jillian pondered silently. For a moment, she considered purchasing the card, but when she looked at the price, *yikes!* She instead pulled a napkin out of the holder and a pen out of her pocket. She scribbled the words on the napkin and read them silently several times as if to correctly interpret this phrase would somehow provide insight into her own feelings. The whole exercise caused a spirit of melancholy to fall on her and she regretted having given any attention to the card in the first place. Nothing about it really applied to her or to anyone she would send the card to anyway.

As she used the long plastic spoon to retrieve the last bite of mango from the bottom of the tall glass, she slid off the stool and leisurely strolled down the long hall to the emergency department.

The afternoon was uneventful and therefore seemed to last forever when compared to the fast-paced morning when she had been busy attending to patients in distress. Most of the other staff were now gathered in the supervisor's office and were making unofficial bets on an upcoming football game. Several times she picked up various medical books that were kept in the department for quick reference, but none of the subjects on the pages she flipped to piqued her interest.

Finally she sat down in one of the vacant interview cubicles and began making a menu for the week's dinners: sloppy joes tonight, oven-fried chicken strips tomorrow. Matt, and secondarily Aiden, jumped into her thoughts, and she considered inviting them over for dinner tomorrow night. She rounded out the week's menus with old standbys. Her mind was not so much on the food as on the people for whom she wanted to prepare meals. Matt was at the top of that list. She knew the children would be satisfied with their usual simple meals, but for Matt, she wanted to do something special. Now that he was in the picture, meal planning and preparation once again became a task that she anticipated.

"I want to be a nurse and a wife and a mother." This had been her standard reply all through her childhood when she was asked, "What do you want to be when you grow up?" The desires of her heart had been granted; she had relished each of those roles in turn. At this moment, the realization of how much she had missed the wife part became very evident. Acknowledging without the least hesitation that being a mother without being a wife made the role much more difficult, she longed to have a man in her life again…and not just to cook for. She desired to be held and kissed and loved and—her dreamy thoughts had taken her far away from the emergency department when the intercom jarred her to attention.

"All staff on alert. Six-car pileup on Interstate 85; serious injuries reported."

Immediately Jillian left her little corner of dreamland and rushed, with the other emergency staff, toward the trauma receiving area. The wide double doors burst open as several of the staff hurried back in from an afternoon smoke break. She could already hear the shrill blare of sirens in the distance.

Chapter 19

We Are Family

> Thank you for our teachers and friends and for our mommy and grandmas and grandpas...

Joshua's loud sigh interrupted Molly's lingering blessing. Jillian shot him a "watch it" glare, and he looked down, with eyes wide open, as Molly continued

"And Mista' Morgan and Aiden, and help us all be good, and thank you for the food Mommy makes us. I love you, Jesus. Amen."

A chorus of amens followed, with Joshua's being the loudest.

"Molly, you just need to thank God for the food. I'm hungry," Joshua chided his little sister.

Jillian started to scold Joshua, then decided to let it go. Matt came through with an appropriate response.

"Molly, I thought your blessing was very nice. I'm glad you're thankful for Aiden and me. We sure are glad to be your neighbors."

"You can say that again," Aiden seconded as he reached for one of Jillian's oven-fried chicken strips. "You cook better than Mom."

Jillian felt her face flush, but Matt's smile of approval put her at ease. Yesterday she had followed through with her idea to invite Matt and Aiden over for dinner tonight, and Matt readily accepted. At two-thirty, her supervisor advised that her replacement was going to be an hour late and asked if she would work over. Jillian's first inclination was to decline; she was looking forward to getting home and preparing dinner for Matt. However, she also wanted to be seen as a team player and agreed to stay. When she telephoned Matt to ask him to pick up her kids from school, he was more than happy to oblige, even suggesting that he could take everyone out to eat when she got home. She appreciated his thoughtful offer but insisted that everything was ready to pop into the oven, which it was.

Angela, the second-shift nurse, was actually only forty-five minutes late, so Jillian rushed home, taking advantage of the extra fifteen minutes to shower and change. She preheated the oven for the chicken before calling Matt to let him know she was home.

"You need me to come over and help out?" he had asked.

"That would be great," she readily accepted his offer, "at least you can keep me company."

When Matt and their children walked in the front door a few minutes later, she had been overcome with feelings of contentment. As they worked together in the kitchen, sharing the more-pleasant anecdotes of their work days, she tried not to chide herself for allowing her feelings for Matt to develop. Still, something in her subconscious nagged at her when she acknowledged that with every passing day, she found something new to like about him. *Then why don't you tell your parents about him?* She had heard the voice say. She chose to ignore the illusive question.

It didn't take long for the six of them to devour the crispy chicken, the comforting macaroni and cheese, and the steamed-just-right broccoli florets. As Jillian rose from the table to start clearing the dishes, Matt offered, "Let me do the dishes for you, and you can relax awhile."

Jillian almost refused. Even when she and Bryan were married, he hardly ever helped around the house. She could get used to being treated this way!

"I'll take you up on that tonight, Matt," Jillian accepted his offer. "But it's not so I can relax. I have to help with homework."

"All done!" Matt replied matter-of-factly, but she saw a flash of achievement in his eyes.

"All done? You mean…"

"I mean we all sat down as soon as we got home, and everyone's homework is complete…and correct," Matt declared as the kids backed him up. "Remember, I am a teacher."

Jillian sometimes forgot. He didn't remind her of any teacher she had ever had…except maybe Mr. Moser for eighth grade history. Now he was also charming.

"Wow, I could get used to this," Jillian cooed as she stood just behind Matt's chair. Feeling sincere appreciation, combined with something else she wouldn't admit, she placed her left hand on Matt's shoulder in a lingering pat. She began to casually massage his shoulder just as she would for a coworker who had helped her with a difficult task, but her hand tingled from the touch, and Matt turned his face toward hers and searched her eyes with his own. Her hand froze in place, and then he placed his right hand over hers and held on gently, but tightly.

"So could I," he spoke almost in a whisper, but still the kids, hers and his, seemed to sense the romantic overture that was transpiring in front of them and burst into a gaggle of giggles.

Jillian ignored her first instinct to be embarrassed and instead, placed her free hand on Matt's. Together they joined the happy laughter. Anyone stealing a glimpse of the man, woman, and children in that room in that moment would have surmised that this was just one big, happy, intact family.

Jillian chose helping Matt with the dishes over relaxing by herself—actually, a very easy choice to make. *Working with a good friend…ahem, a special friend*—she reconsidered her description—*can be much more enjoyable than relaxing alone.*

After placing most of the dishes in the dishwasher, Matt washed the pots and pans while she dried. He almost overflowed the sink with bubbles, and once as she reached for a pan lid, he picked up a handful and blew the soapsuds playfully in her face. She reciprocated, and for a few moments, they were carefree, fun-loving kids until they stopped laughing long enough to seek each other's eyes. Effortlessly and in one accord, they found each other's hands. Neither spoke a word, but both of their minds raced with unspoken thoughts they wanted so much to say. Matt didn't want to move. Jillian silently prayed the feeling in her heart could last forever. He gently withdrew his right hand from her left and silently brushed a bubble off the tip of her nose. Then his warm lips brushed ever so gently against her welcoming ones and lingered just long enough for Aiden, who had run into the room, to see. His loud footsteps startled the two, and with faces still touching, they turned toward the sound.

Aiden's eyes were wide and wild with wonder. "Wow, I can't believe it. My dad is kissing your mom!" he shouted to her kids in the family room. She was sure Mrs. Cecil had also heard.

A little too sternly, Matt rebuked him, "That's enough, Aiden."

"Well, you were," he confirmed as Molly, Joshua, and Caleb ran in to see for themselves.

"They're not kissing, they're just touching," Caleb reasoned.

Oh, children sure can inhibit a romantic interlude…especially when they are his and mine, Jillian mused to herself. She wondered

Or Be Reconciled

what Matt was thinking. What he was feeling. Had the kiss sent him over the moon as it had her? Did it remind him of kissing Shannon? Was he comparing the two of them?

Shannon was the furthest thing from Matt's mind. "I think it's time for Aiden and me to call it a night."

Was that reluctance Jillian sensed in his voice?

"But I sure hate to…" he added, a fulfilled smile breaking across his face "Because it's been…" He searched for the right words. "The best night in a long, long time."

Silently, Jillian shared Matt's summation of the night. She couldn't remember when she had felt so contented.

The kids protested that it wasn't that late, but it seemed right to Jillian to concur with Matt. "Thanks, Matt, for everything." The sincerity in her voice gave way to pure mischief, "And I do mean *everything*," she almost broke out into laughter as she spoke those words.

Knowingly, they shared one last lingering gaze, almost forgetting their children were watching. Matt and Aiden said their goodnights and headed to their own home next door. They walked silently and slowly, but Matt's thoughts had turned to the subject of conserving energy—sort of. *Why should two households live separately when they could become one big happy family?* He asked himself. Then he grabbed Aiden like an oversized football and raced with him through the open garage door.

The following weeks flew by as the Hamiltons and Morgans shared more and more time together. At least a couple of nights each week they all ate together at one of their homes. When Matt had to coach a soccer game, Jillian and the kids went along, with Jillian watching over Aiden as if he were one of her own. Most Friday nights provided an opportunity for family activities at which the two families easily blended into one. Some Saturdays, they even did their grocery shopping together, and every Sunday found them worshipping together at New Life Center.

Jillian was scheduled to work Thanksgiving Day. Matt volunteered to plan activities for the children until Jillian arrived home at three-thirty in the afternoon. She had prepared most of the traditional meal Wednesday night, so Matt just had to keep watch on the turkey in the oven. It took her less than an hour to heat all the side dishes. With Matt's help, dinner was ready at four-thirty.

"I'm starved!" Joshua complained from the floor of the family room where he was sprawled, watching a football game.

"Sorry, I only gave them a snack at lunch so they would be hungry tonight," Matt took responsibility for Joshua's famished state.

"Good, that's all they needed. Look at this feast! Kids, our dinner is ready!" Jillian announced as she slipped her arm around Matt's waist. "Thanks for taking care of the kids today."

"My pleasure, my dear," he reciprocated and drew her close.

The first Saturday in December still felt like fall. The skies were overcast, and the temperature was in the high sixties. They woke up early, packed a picnic lunch, piled into Matt's van and headed to the mountains for a day trip. They chose two Christmas trees at a tree farm in Boone. By noon, the sun had broken through the clouds, and they shared their lunch together on a grassy knoll at a roadside park before returning home to their cul-de-sac.

It didn't take long to decorate the Morgans' tree. Matt insisted that colorful twinkling lights and a star topper was all that was needed. Decorating the Hamiltons' tree required a little more time. Jillian unpacked over two hundred individual ornaments—from a huge jeweled ball she had received from her Grammy when she was in high school to a tiny Christmas angel Bryan had given her on their first Christmas Eve as man and wife. Going through the boxes reminded her she had not added any new ones to her collection since their last Christmas together.

When the last ornament was hung on the Hamiltons' tree, Jillian stirred together cocoa, sugar, milk, and vanilla and poured the mixture into her hot chocolate maker. Matt retrieved the popcorn from the microwave. The kids plopped miniature marshmallows into their mugs as Jillian dispensed the frothy chocolate delight.

Jillian and Matt shared a cozy spot on the sofa, watching as their children, sprawled on the floor, built a futuristic city with Legos. Matt's arm fell longingly across Jillian's shoulder, and she tenderly but eagerly responded by laying her head against his chest. The mellow voices of James Taylor and Natalie Cole were crooning "Baby, It's Cold Outside" on the CD player. Jillian snuggled closer.

"You know, decorating two trees in one evening can wear a man out," Matt murmured with his lips against her left cheekbone.

"Decorating one tree would wear most men out," Jillian flattered.

"It does make more sense to me to just have one tree," Matt was slowly getting to his point.

"So who goes without the Christmas tree?" Jillian questioned, having not yet grasped where Matt was going.

"No one goes without the tree. We combine the households."

Jillian didn't speak but smiled up at him, allowing her head and shoulder to lean even deeper into his strong embrace.

This was not Matt's first overture, suggesting that the two families become one. Several nonlingering kisses and even more well-timed hugs had been shared by the two since their first real kiss at the kitchen sink, which of course, had been preceded by the midnight peck at the front door for the benefit of Mrs. Cecil. As their relationship developed, they had both felt the need to be discreet about displays of affection in front of the children. Still, Jillian and Matt longed for the other's touch. His hand on her arm, her hand against his cheek, a warm embrace—each of these met a longing that was growing stronger day by day.

Their conversations were usually practical discussions about their lives and children. There were the occasional overtures. Neither had yet uttered the words "I love you" out loud, but each had rehearsed that phrase over and over in their hearts, waiting for the right time to say those three little words. Jillian had come so close just the other night, but she wanted to wait until she heard them first from Matt. Tonight, sitting with him on the sofa, she knew it was only a matter of time.

Molly had fallen asleep on the floor at nine o'clock. Matt had tenderly picked her up and carried her to bed, gently tucking her in. As Jillian witnessed this touching scene, she considered once again what an amazing father Matt could be to her children. At ten o'clock, she and the boys had reluctantly told Matt and Aiden good night as they left for their own home.

Jillian was putting the mugs in the dishwasher when she noticed the stack of mail she had left on the kitchen counter earlier, most of which appeared to be Christmas cards. She decided to just take a peek at the return addresses. When she saw the gold foil label with the *H* in calligraphy, she recognized her mother-in-law's elegant style and immediately opened it.

> Surprise, dear! We're planning a trip north during the holidays and are hoping to visit you and our grandkids from December 26 until New Year's Day. Let me know if this does not work for you.

Any other time, Jillian would have been—if not exactly thrilled—at least pleased that her in-laws planned to visit, and she knew the children would love to see them. However, she wondered how her in-laws' stay would affect the plans she and Matt had already made. Thanksgiving had been so special for all of them. Now they were looking forward to celebrating Christmas together. *Well, at least they won't arrive until the day after Christmas,* she consoled herself, relieved that Christmas Day would still be an intimate family affair. She felt guilty for even contemplating that the visitors wouldn't be welcome. Surely, Matt would understand that she couldn't say no to her former in-laws.

Waiting until after church the next day, she broke the news of Grandma and Grandpa Hamilton's upcoming visit while Matt and the kids were hungrily devouring her oven-fried chicken and mashed potatoes. "Guess who's coming to visit us for Christmas?"

Matt looked at her questioningly but didn't respond.

Aiden answered matter-of-factly, "Santa Claus."

"We don't believe in Santa," Joshua retorted rather rudely. "So who's coming?"

"Grandma and Grandpa Hamilton. I got a letter from them yesterday. They'll actually arrive the day after Christmas."

The kids responded with much less excitement than she had anticipated. Matt seemed a little uneasy, muttering, "You got the letter yesterday?"

However, it was Aiden's response that really surprised her. "Dad, can I write Grandma and Grandpa Stewart and ask if they'll visit us for Christmas too?"

Matt was equally shocked by his son's request. Maggie Stewart, Shannon's mother, didn't have much to do with Aiden, even when he and Shannon were still married. And Shannon's father, who was divorced from her mother, had only seen Aiden on a dozen or so occasions since his birth eight years ago.

"I don't see a problem with that," Matt responded casually, successfully concealing the apprehension he was feeling at the thought of either one of them accepting Aiden's invitation.

"Yes! Let's go home now so I can write them!" Aiden was eager to pursue this prospect and pushed his chair away from the table.

"Slow down a minute, buddy," Matt cautioned. "We haven't had dessert yet." He eyed the apple pie Jillian had placed in the center of the table.

"I'm full, really, I don't want any pie. Let's go."

Jillian felt uncomfortable at Aiden's enthusiasm about writing Shannon's parents, especially since it was coupled with his desire to leave her house so soon. *Was that a pang of jealousy she was feeling?* Aiden had adjusted so well to living here with his dad; he hardly ever mentioned his mother.

She was grateful that Matt, as usual, took control of a sensitive situation. "You can't mail the letters until tomorrow. So settle down and watch the rest of us devour the apple pie. You'll have plenty of time to write your letters this afternoon."

"Ah, Dad." Aiden pouted to no avail.

Matt was already reaching for the knife to slice the pie. Molly, Caleb, and Josh had sat silently during the exchange, not seeming to grasp the significance, or insignificance, of what had just transpired. Still, the happy familial mood seemed somewhat dampened. Jillian wondered if Matt was reading as much into what had just happened as she was. He didn't appear to be. He was contentedly downing a large slice of pie.

Her much smaller slice sat in front of her. Her appetite had taken flight in the same way that her image of Matt and Aiden and her and the children as one big happy family had momentarily faded.

Matt sensed her uneasiness but misunderstood the cause. As they left to go home, Matt shooed Aiden on ahead, then whispered to Jillian, "Don't worry. Shannon's parents have no interest in visiting us for Christmas."

"Oh no, Matt. That would be great if they visited Aiden. I'm sure he would love to see them."

They both seemed a little confused at this point. "But you seemed to be concerned…"

"Not about Aiden's grandparents visiting. It's hard to explain. I guess…just that…he has grandparents…your wife's parents…"

"My ex-wife's parents," Matt corrected.

There was a moment of awkward silence between them.

"Still, Aiden's your son, and Shannon's his mother..." Jillian couldn't finish. She didn't know what she wanted to say.

"And that's a big problem with you, isn't it?"

Jillian disliked the tone of Matt's voice, a tone she couldn't recall hearing before. She wanted so much to make this conversation go away, to bring back the way it was before Aiden had asked about his grandparents visiting for Christmas. She wanted to throw her arms around Matt and tell him the past didn't matter.

Matt was waiting for a response. He wanted Jillian to say something that would dissipate the sick feeling in his stomach. He wanted her to say it was the future, not the past that was significant. He wanted her to reach out for him and make everything right again.

"It's not a problem, Matt," she spoke so tenderly that his heart melted and the irritation he had briefly felt evaporated as the morning fog. "It's just a little complicated, but we'll work through this."

Her hopeful words were enough for him just now. He opened his arms, and she welcomed his embrace. With her lovely face against his strong chest, she knew in her heart, that with God's help, everything would work out well.

Chapter 20

Love Is in the Air

Lord Jesus, thank you for this wonderful time of year to celebrate your coming to our messed up world to deliver us. As we celebrate, help us to keep our eyes on you and make you the center of all we do. Give me strength to do all the things on my list or at least the wisdom to know which ones really need to be done.

During the middle of her prayer, Jillian considered her list and began mentally numbering the tasks in order of importance. Momentarily, she dismissed the interruption and continued her requests, with a special note to God concerning her in-laws upcoming visit. Once again, a name entered her mind, more so

Or Be Reconciled

than her heart, and she was unable to ignore the prompting. "Be with Aiden's mother, wherever she is, and help her to love Aiden as she should."

At that moment she realized she had not been including Shannon in her prayers as often as she once had. Occasionally her name—or sometimes even a vision of her reclining on Matt's sofa in that seductive pose—would flash through her mind while she was praying. She chose to ignore it, considering it a distraction. She knew she had been avoiding praying for Shannon as if doing so might somehow change her own relationship with Matt.

How do people handle these situations? She asked herself as she made her bed. Recollections of two families that lived in her neighborhood in Richmond came to mind. They had divorced and married each other's ex-spouses. She thought that was strange enough, but then she heard that they went on vacations together "for the sake of the children." *How bizarre would that be?* That thought put a scowl on her face as she imagined the mêlée that would result if she had to share a vacation with her former husband's new wife. *Weird, weird, weird.* She groaned out loud. *I don't think I could deal with that!*

Soon thoughts of how she could complete everything on her Christmas to-do list crowded out the jumbled thoughts of broken and blended families. December was flying by as it always did. Christmas would be here in just over a week. She hurried to get ready, get the kids to school—their last day before Christmas break—and get herself to work on time. Carefully planning her work schedule, she had saved all her vacation days for Christmas week. Pleasantly surprised when her request to take off the week between Christmas and New Year's had been approved, she was as excited as her children as they planned their celebration.

Since she was a little girl, Christmas and New Year's Eve services were two of her favorite occasions. She loved the candlelight service with Christmas tree lights twinkling and Christmas carols being sung by a congregation of joyful people who seemed to put aside their differences for one special night. Not quite as special as Christmas Eve, New Year's Eve also had a special place in her heart: it meant a time of new beginnings, of putting away the old, and walking bravely into a brand-new year, a clean slate full of promise.

It was another uneventful Monday in the emergency department. Most of the patients were children with hacking coughs and high fevers who couldn't get in to see their own doctors. A few elderly people came in with chest pains that in most cases turned out to be indigestion. The day seemed to drag on and on, and Jillian felt great relief when her replacement arrived at shift change. "Not much to report. No one's in triage. It's been a slow day."

"I hope it's even a slower night," the second shift nurse responded.

The weather forecast had called for a dusting of snow, and though the clouds were low and thick, Jillian didn't see a single snowflake on her way to pick up the kids. They were more than excited as they scrambled into the car, loaded down with goodies from their teachers and friends and stories of their last day of school before Christmas: programs in the all-purpose room featuring Santa and his elves, a live Frosty the Snowman handing out snowballs—popcorn balls wrapped in cellophane—and singing "Jingle Bells" and "Rudolph."

"When I was growing up we had a live nativity and sang 'In the Little Village of Bethlehem,'" Jillian lamented. "How times have changed."

Tonight the Hamiltons were on their own. Matt and Aiden were going Christmas shopping, probably to buy Aiden's gift for Shannon. At least that's what Jillian imagined but didn't dare say. She threw together a quick pot of chili and served it with shredded cheese and Fritos. Fresh veggies with Ranch dip served as the side dish. The kids said they were still hungry after cleaning their plates, so Jillian let them eat their snowballs for dessert. Molly was the only one who seemed a little sad that she wouldn't be going to school for two weeks. When Jillian reminded her that Mr. Morgan would be their babysitter, her countenance immediately changed.

"I love Mista' Morgan, Mommy!" her sweet five-year-old exclaimed.

"He loves you too Molly," Jillian assured. *And he would be a wonderful father to you*, Jillian contemplated dreamily.

The week went by in a whirl of work, shopping, and anticipation. Matt graciously suggested that Jillian do any remaining shopping on her way home from work each day. Her Christmas list was dwindling, and it looked as if she might actually pull off everything she had planned to do before the Hamiltons arrived the day after Christmas. Matt invited them over for supper the Friday before Christmas and surprised them by inviting them to go ice-skating the next day.

"Matt, I've never ice-skated in my life!" Jillian disclosed to his amazement.

"You're kidding? Never, even once?"

"Not once."

"Why?"

"I was always too busy playing basketball in a nice, heated gym in the winter."

"Well, I haven't seen you shoot any hoops lately. Are you ready to give a new sport a try?"

Against her better judgment but unable to say no with all the kids yelling yes, Jillian consented, but not without apprehension. "Okay, but Matt, if I break something, you'll have to promise to do all the housework until I recover."

"It would be my pleasure, ma'am!" he responded way too quickly, not even considering the possibility that she may actually break a bone or two.

Matt and Jillian cleaned up the kitchen together while the kids played in Aiden's room.

"Our kids play together really well, don't you think?" Matt prodded as he placed his strong arms around her waist.

"Yes, they do," she replied.

"Remember that crazy movie *Yours, Mine, and Ours*?"

"Actually, I saw the old original one with—wasn't it Lucille Ball?—as well as the remake. A little too much for me."

"Well they had a dozen kids—"

"At least…it was a houseful!"

"Do you think we could move our two houses together?" Matt's eyes were full of laughter. "We'd need the room if we decided to add an 'ours.'"

He tightened his hold on her, and Jillian felt just a little awkward. "Don't you think we should have a wedding first?" she asked, not as a proposal, but as a reminder that I dos should come before baby making.

"Are you asking me to marry you?" Matt gasped, feigning astonishment.

"Absolutely not," she replied in mock dismay. "Just a declaration of my values."

"So if I asked you to marry me and you said yes and we did, then you would consider adding an 'ours' to the equation."

"That's not what I said," Jillian blurted while feverishly trying to think of a response that would convey her feelings. *Honestly,* she considered, *I have never given a thought to having a baby with Matt, if we were to ever get married of course, although I had thought of him as becoming the father of my children…maybe that's what I should say.*

"I think you'd make an amazing father to my children. I already see what a great dad you are to Aiden, and Joshua's behavior has improved significantly since you've been in the picture."

"So you have thought along those lines…us being a family… right?"

"A girl has a right to dream, doesn't she?"

"Am I in your dreams, Jillian?" his tone turned serious.

"Sometimes."

"Then let's make them come true!"

Was he proposing? What did he mean? Why don't I have the sense to ask him to explain himself? Her mind raced.

His lips melted against Jillian's, and his arms, tender in their strength, held her close for what seemed like a long, long time. She felt euphoric, peaceful, helpless, strong.

"I have a surprise for you, but I'm saving it for New Year's Eve."

"Then why are you telling me now? To make me crazy?"

"No, I just couldn't wait."

"Then why not just give it to me now?"

"I can't. It's rather involved, and New Year's Eve is the perfect time."

"Do you want me to guess?"

"Not out loud. Maybe in your dreams. But there is something I can tell you tonight." He paused much too long before he continued, "I love you Jillian. I love you so much."

She had wanted to hear those words and waited to hear those words and practiced how she would respond, and now she couldn't think, couldn't speak. He kissed her again, even more eagerly than before, and once more whispered into her ear those three words with a desire and longing that both warmed and chilled her heart.

"I love you, Jillian."

"I love you too, Matt."

There. Those three little words had been spoken. There was no turning back.

Chapter 21

Be Careful Not to Fall

Good morning, Jesus!" Thank you for this beautiful, beautiful day and my beautiful, beautiful life, for Molly, Caleb, and Josh, my parents, my in-laws, my neighbors, especially the one next door that loves me—"He loves me! He loves me!

Jillian repeated the cherished words out loud before she continued her prayer. "Help me to be able to stand up on the ice!" She giggled as she imagined falling to the rink floor as Matt reached out to catch her in his strong arms. "Father, forgive me for being silly this morning. My heart has not felt this carefree in some time; but I don't want to be foolish."

Is it foolish to be so in love? She silently mused. *What's wrong with me? Why can't I just enjoy what's happening instead of scrutinizing every thought?*

"Mom, I can't find my gloves!" Joshua's plea broke into her self-analysis. So far, the central North Carolina winter had been mild, and the kids had not unpacked all their winter gear. Today, on the ice in the indoor rink, it would be different.

"I already have them in my bag," she called back.

Aiden rang the doorbell at eight-thirty sharp. Matt was a stickler for promptness. She had just barely cleared the breakfast dishes from the table and decided to leave them in the sink. "Do you have everything you need, guys?" she hurriedly asked the kids as she grabbed her bag filled to overflowing with gloves, caps, and extra socks and jeans, just in case.

"Hello, Sunshine!" Matt greeted as she slid into the front seat of his van. "Are you ready to learn to skate?"

"I'm ready to give it my best effort, but please don't expect much."

"Everybody buckled up?" Matt glanced in the rearview mirror, then placed his right hand on Jillian's folded ones.

"Any good dreams last night?" he inquired with a not-so-shy grin.

"Honestly, once I got to sleep, I slept so soundly I don't recall dreaming. But I was thinking lovely thoughts as I drifted off," she added.

Neither wanted to say too much in front of the kids…yet. Their knowing smiles expressed what they were feeling inside, feelings neither had experienced in sometime, feelings each one had thought may be impossible to ever capture again.

Matt relinquished his hold on Jillian's hand just long enough to put a Christmas CD in the player. The haunting lyrics of "Mary, Did You Know" floated from the speakers.

"That's one of my favorites. Do you think Mary did know?" Jillian asked.

"Well, if an angel appeared to me and told me I was going to have a baby, I think I'd know something was up."

Jillian laughed at the image Matt had just evoked but wished he had taken her question more seriously. "I can't imagine what it must have been like for her, but God chose her, and she rose to the occasion."

Sensing that Matt wasn't in the mood for a serious theological discussion, she moved the conversation to preparations for Christmas and the activities they had planned together. "Thanks for helping out this past week with the kids. I don't know how I would have gotten everything on my list done without you. I'm even ready to face Mr. and Mrs. Hamilton."

"As always, it was a pleasure to be of assistance. I want to be indispensable in your life. That reminds me. Shannon's parents won't be visiting. Thank goodness." Matt spoke in almost a whisper. "But at least her mother responded to Aiden's letter and sent a Christmas card and a generous check with her regrets. Her father just left a message on the answering machine...a 'thanks, but no thanks' response."

"Um..." Jillian uttered softly, then turned to look behind her. The boys were playing games on their iPods in the back seat; they definitely were not paying attention to the conversation she and Matt were sharing. "That must have stung."

"Actually, he didn't seem to be bothered that much, especially when he saw the amount on the check. Maybe you can't buy love, but sometimes those dollars signs can keep the tears at bay." Matt glanced at her, waiting for a response.

"Money doesn't make up for time and attention."

"No, but if you aren't going to give them anyway, money's a tolerable substitute."

Jillian hoped he didn't really feel that way. She certainly didn't want to get in a discussion about love versus money, so again she changed the subject to avoid controversy.

"Doesn't Shannon's mother have a name?" Jillian wondered out loud. It always bothered her when Matt referred to Aiden's grandmother that way. Couldn't he call her by her name and circumvent her having to hear him say Shannon's name?

"I like to call her the Mother Witch!" Matt responded without missing a beat.

Surprised, Jillian cautioned him. "Matt, please don't say such things in front of the children."

"Well, you asked." He didn't realize Jillian had been offended by his answer. She quietly considered her response options, settling on saying nothing.

"Hey, did that really upset you? Oh, Jillian, if you only knew... I could tell you a few things that would make you understand."

"I don't think I care to know."

"Sometimes you're so prim and proper."

"I just would rather talk about pleasant things."

"Then we better not talk about Shannon's—sorry, I mean Margaret, also known as Moth...I mean Maggie." Matt thought he was being funny.

Jillian wondered if she sometimes did act too prim and proper.

The skating rink was just opening when they arrived. Matt expected the rink to be crowded later on and wanted to get there early. A few other families were already there, and kids were lining up to be fitted for skates. Matt and Aiden brought their own; Jillian said she didn't mind waiting with her kids to get their skates, but Matt insisted on helping.

"Especially yours. I want to make sure they fit just right so you can't use that as an excuse."

"Gee, thanks. Glad to know you'll be there for me."

"I want to always be there for you," he replied, a little too loudly, considering the kids were right beside them. Jillian looked at the kids, but they were engrossed in checking out the skates, lined up neatly in rows behind the counter. She turned back to Matt, who was waiting for a response.

"I want that too," she said, just above a whisper.

"Okay, who's next?" the middle-aged woman behind the counter asked brusquely.

"We are," Matt answered.

The woman's "I'd rather be somewhere else" demeanor quickly changed.

Jillian thought, *She must be trying to impress her handsome customer.*

"What a lovely family you have," she cooed.

Matt looked at Jillian, his face glowing. "Thank you very much, ma'am. They are a good-looking bunch, aren't they?"

Her kids had some experience with in-line skates, and they were up, for the most part, on the ice in no time. Josh sailed around the rink behind Aiden while Caleb and Molly stayed as close as possible to the rink wall.

Matt was a great skating coach, just as Jillian knew he would be. After all, he was a natural athlete. Even a great coach needs someone with at least a little ability if his teaching is going to succeed. When it came to skating, Jillian had none. After three awkward go-rounds with Matt practically carrying Jillian and more than a few near-falls, Jillian bowed out.

Though disappointed, Matt was tactful. "I just knew I'd be twirling you around on my shoulders before this day was over," Matt teased as he walked Jillian to the spectator area.

"I'm sorry I let you down," Jillian responded.

"The only way you could let me down is by not accepting the New Year's gift I have for you."

Jillian looked into Matt's eyes, wanting to say the right thing but still not knowing for sure what surprise awaited her on the last night of the year. He had hinted several times, and she could not help but believe he was going to propose, but she would not take anything for granted at this point.

"We'll just have to wait and see, won't we?" Now it was her turn to tease. She let go of Matt's arms and turned to walk toward the wooden benches, but her feet didn't cooperate.

"Oh!" she shrieked as they reached out for each other in a desperate attempt – she to keep from falling – he to keep her from falling. Together they went down in a strange sort of bear hug, collapsing side by side with a thud on the frigid ice.

Simultaneously they called out to each other, "Are you okay?"

Again, in sync, as if they were kindred spirits, they answered in the affirmative, "I'm fine," and broke out into embarrassed, but happy laughter.

Chapter 22

Merry Christmas!

Jesus, happy birthday! Thank you for allowing our family to celebrate your birth in so many wonderful ways with such dear people this year. I praise you for your constant care that protects us and blesses us and meets our needs. Bless today as we honor you. Be with Mom and Dad as they celebrate with the orphans. Be with Mom and Dad Hamilton as they travel; keep them safe. Be with all those who are sick or sad or going without today. Let them feel your presence and realize that you are the best gift anyone can receive. I do love you so, Jesus.

Jillian had always loved Christmas mornings. Except for one, or maybe two Christmases, they had always met her expectations.

Presents had never been the most important aspect. Being with the people she loved and that loved her and being contented—that's what meant the most. The past week had been grand—the amusing ice-skating excursion, the completion of her to-do list with time to spare, the planning of fun activities for the kids each day, the moments spent alone with Matt, all topped off by the sacred service last night. Jillian sat on her bed, hugging her pillow while reveling in all that was happening in her life. A year ago, she would have not dared to believe the blessings she was now experiencing. Her heart was so full.

After a quick shower, she dressed in a comfy pair of jeans and a Christmassy sweater, pulled her hair back into a ponytail, brushed on some makeup, and kissed her lips with bright red gloss. For good measure, she sprayed her favorite perfume behind both ears, then decided to put on her Christmas earrings, small ruby-red crystal spheres that Bryan used to describe as, "Glowing like Rudolph's nose." She laughed as she remembered the time he suggested she use them as nose rings. Recalling that, she realized this was the first time she had worn them since Bryan died. *Quick! Change the thought pattern!* She told herself and then scurried to the kitchen to boil some water for the Christmas tea. She put in her favorite Christmas CD and turned it up loud enough to wake the kids. She couldn't believe they were sleeping this late on Christmas morning. It was already seven o'clock. They were up late last night though. Because it was Christmas Eve, the skating rink had closed early. Jillian was thankful; otherwise they may have missed the church service. Matt and Aiden invited them over for snacks and games afterward. She and Matt had sat on the sofa, watching the kids play and reinforcing each other's determination that there would be no gifts opened until morning, even though the kids pleaded.

They had lingered until Molly fell asleep on the floor in front of the fireplace. Matt carried her home with Jillian and the boys at his side. He insisted on tucking Molly in bed and the sight

Or Be Reconciled

of him kneeling on the floor beside the bed to kiss her daughter good night sent goose bumps all over Jillian.

"Mommy, it's Christmas!" Molly squealed as she ran down the hall in her bare feet. She leapt into Jillian's outstretched arms, and they shared a lingering Christmas hug. Jillian burrowed her face into Molly's soft blond locks and inhaled deeply. "Of all the Christmas smells I love, you are my favorite, Molly."

Molly giggled, then reciprocated by snuggling her nose into the soft skin of Jillian's neck. "Mmm…you smell like the flowers."

"Christmas flowers?" There was joy in Jillian's voice.

"No, like the flowers Mrs. Cecil gave us from her garden when we first moved here."

"Mrs. Cecil!" Jillian exclaimed. "Oh my, I forgot to wrap her presents, and she'll be joining us for breakfast soon."

"Why is she coming?" Molly asked innocently. "I thought it was just going to be our family."

"Don't you mean our family and Aiden and his dad?"

"They are our family," Molly asserted.

"Yes, well, sort of…and Mrs. Cecil is joining us because otherwise she would be alone. She doesn't have any family nearby."

"Then I'm glad she's coming, but I like it better when it's just our family."

Jillian understood Molly's point of view. Their family, including Matt and Aiden, had shared so many great times over the past few months. Life always seemed complete, somehow, when the six of them were together.

"Help me wrap Mrs. Cecil's presents, and then we'll wake your brothers," Jillian spoke softly, deciding she could use a few extra minutes before the boys got up.

"Okay, Mommy," Molly whispered as they tiptoed to Jillian's bedroom. Hastily, the gift-wrap was retrieved from her closet, and the presents she had carefully chosen for the children to give Mrs. Cecil were wrapped in shiny paper and adorned with brightly colored bows.

"I think she'll like the gardening gloves and apron best," Molly guessed.

"I think she'll love all her gifts," Jillian responded.

"Merry Christmas! Merry Christmas!" The boys ran into her room just as Jillian had put away the tape and scissors.

"When are we opening presents?"

"I'm hungry!"

"Are we going to eat or open presents first?"

"Boys, be patient! Aiden and Matt are coming over…and so is Mrs. Cecil."

"Mrs. Cecil?" Josh balked. "She's an old lady, and sometimes she smells funny."

"Josh, don't make me ashamed of you on Christmas. Someday I'll be an old lady, and sometimes *you* smell funny." Jillian had adopted Matt's way of correcting Joshua with a hint of humor; it seemed to be working.

"I don't really mind," he declared, and Jillian thought she detected a spark of compassion in his tone. "I know she doesn't have family like we do."

"That's kind of you. I bought presents for each of you to give her. Joshua, here's the one from you." She added as she held up a wrapped box, "It's a towel set."

"What's a towel set?"

"It's some towels for her bathroom."

"Yuck, I hope nobody gets me a towel set."

Jillian laughed at his comment, remembering Matt's advice to not take everything Joshua says so seriously. "He's just a kid," he had often reminded her.

"What did I get Mrs. Cecil?" Caleb asked.

"A very lovely apron. She loves to wear aprons when she cooks."

Molly added, "And I'm giving her garden gloves, three pair, and she's going to like to wear them when she plants flowers."

"From all of us, I got a gift card for Stella's Cafeteria because I know that's her favorite place to eat. Let's all help Mrs. Cecil have a lovely Christmas, okay?"

Her reminder that Matt and Aiden would be arriving soon met with a course of "yeses." "So hurry and get dressed," she instructed as she headed to the kitchen to prepare breakfast.

"Thank you so much for inviting me to share your Christmas with you," Mrs. Cecil gushed as Matt pulled out the dining chair for her. "I hope you have looked as forward to this as I have."

Jillian had hardly used their dining room at the front of the house, just off the frequently used family room. This occasion called for it, especially since the table in the eat-in kitchen could only comfortably seat six people. Jillian had set the table with her grandmother's lace tablecloth and her white china. An arrangement of red and white mixed flowers and candles served as the centerpiece. The overcast skies allowed just enough light to see and just enough darkness for the candles to shine brightly from their holders.

Jillian poured her Christmas tea, a concoction she had learned to make from her mother: tea steeped with cloves and cinnamon, then mixed with sugar and lemon, orange, and pineapple juices.

Matt had brought over his Belgian waffle maker that was turning out golden waffles to accompany the big platters of crisp bacon and scrambled cheesy eggs Jillian had prepared. There were three flavors of syrup: maple, butter pecan, and blueberry. Strains of "I Heard the Bells on Christmas Day" played in the background.

"Shall we pray?" Matt asked as he reached out for Aiden's hand on his right and Mrs. Cecil's on his left. Caleb and Joshua sat on the side with Aiden; Molly was next to Mrs. Cecil, and

Jillian sat at the end opposite from Matt. When all hands were joined, Matt spoke in a soft yet masculine voice, "Our Father in heaven, we thank you and honor you on this special day that we celebrate the gift of your Son, Jesus. Help us to be grateful for all our blessings and to love you as we should. Thank you for this food, and bless the hands that prepared it."

A chorus of amens rang out. The ample platters were passed around the table, and good food and fellowship were enjoyed by all.

Mrs. Cecil insisted on helping Jillian clear the table. Matt took the kids into the family room to wait patiently for the opening of the gifts.

"Let's just put them in the sink. I'll fill the dishwasher later," Jillian suggested to no avail.

"Oh, dear, if you leave them now, there will just be that much more to do later."

Jillian gave in to Mrs. Cecil's counsel, and together they had everything in order in a few minutes. Mrs. Cecil took Jillian's hand as they moseyed to the family room.

"Mrs. Cecil, you'll be comfortable in this chair," Jillian offered the upholstered wing chair to the elderly woman. Holding onto her bony, ill-aligned fingers reminded Jillian how frail Mrs. Cecil was becoming.

With her ever-present grin, she accepted, "Yes, and it looks like one I'll be able to get up out of after a while."

At Jillian's request, Matt read the Christmas story from Luke, and then, rather formally, each presented their gifts to the others. Aiden no longer believed that Santa brought the gifts, which was helpful as Jillian had reared her kids to celebrate Christmas as Jesus's birthday, not a time to receive gifts from Santa Claus. Jillian and Matt had agreed that each child would receive only three gifts from their wish list, but with everyone buying gifts for everyone else, there were still plenty of presents to open.

Each person opened a gift in turn, oohing and aahing over what the others received. Jillian was pleased that her children expressed gratefulness for each gift, even the packages of white socks Mrs. Cecil had lovingly wrapped for each of them. Matt and Aiden gave her a gift card to the only grocery store in town that provided delivery service. Their neighbor showed genuine appreciation for her gifts, insisting that each child come and receive a thank-you kiss. Molly, Caleb, and Aiden offered their cheeks appropriately; Joshua, however, held back until Matt nudged him forward.

In addition to the white china teapot Mrs. Cecil gave her, Jillian received a paisley-printed blue silk scarf from Molly, a mom's devotional book from Caleb, and a basket filled with bath products from Joshua. She had suspected that Matt had secretly taken them shopping one evening when she had to work late, and the well-chosen gifts had confirmed her suspicions.

With a little prodding from Matt, Aiden handed her a small shiny blue gift bag. "This is from me and dad." Inside, enveloped in glittered tissue paper, was a small box bearing the name of a popular jewelry store. She opened it slowly, imagining for a second that it might be—but no, couldn't be—an engagement ring from father and son. She was relieved to see that it was a nurse's watch and, as she lifted it from the box, recalled that she had casually mentioned several times that she needed a new one. "This is great, just the one I wanted too!" she exclaimed. "Now every time I look at it at work, I'll think of you, guys."

"Okay, everyone, I think my present is best of all, and I really do appreciate your honoring my request," Matt interjected. He proudly held up a certificate from the orphanage Jillian's parents directed in India, which read, "A gift has been given in honor of Matt Morgan to House of Hope on the occasion of the celebration of Jesus's birth."

"It was very kind of you to make that request, Matt," Jillian responded.

"It's a perfect gift especially for a man that already has almost everything he needs." Matt looked directly into her eyes as he spoke, hoping to convey to her the only thing he wanted that he didn't have.

If they had been alone, it would have been a romantic moment.

"Well, I didn't know about the orphanage, so I bought you some socks too," Mrs. Cecil intoned as she pushed the last unopened gift into Matt's hands.

"How did you know, Mrs. Cecil? Socks are the one thing…"

Mrs. Cecil, still intellectually perky for her age, stopped him short. "Matt, my dear, don't try to convince me for one second that socks are the one thing you need that you don't have. I know better than that." Her eyes twinkled as she cast a perceptive smile in Jillian's direction.

"You are very clever," Matt responded before bending over to give Mrs. Cecil a quick peck on the cheek.

"Oh my," she gushed as her pale, wrinkled cheeks turned rosy.

"Can we sing some songs together?" Molly requested. "Please, like 'Away in A Manger.'"

"I want to play with my new game," Joshua protested but was quickly overruled by his mom.

"There's plenty of time to play before we go to the dinner at church. Let's sing some songs and celebrate Jesus's birthday."

Joshua knew better than to object to his mother's instructions and even enjoyed, just a little, singing along with the others. Jillian responded by making it as painless as possible. After the fifth song, she announced, "Okay, everyone, time to enjoy your Christmas presents."

Without further encouragement, Caleb and Joshua grabbed their presents and headed off to their rooms. "Mommy, can I play in here with you?" Molly whispered, clutching her new baby doll to her chest.

"We would love to have your company!"

Caleb realized Aiden hadn't followed him. Returning to the family room, he called out to him, "Aiden, are you coming in to play with us?"

"I don't think so. I've got presents at home to open."

Matt looked at Aiden, then Jillian. She knew the look on his face was saying he would prefer to stay with her.

"Dad, can we go home? I haven't opened up my gifts from Mom yet. You said I could open them when we were finished here." Then he commented directly to Jillian, "My mom bought all my gifts in Europe."

Jillian shook her head gently, indicating, "That's okay," while thinking, *He didn't mention that Shannon had sent Aiden gifts. So much for three gifts per child.* "That sounds very exciting, Aiden. You'll have to let us know what your mother sent you."

Mrs. Cecil held on tightly to the arms of the chair to push herself up. "It's time for this old woman to take her Christmas nap. I really have enjoyed sharing Christmas with your dear family, Jillian. And by that I mean Matt and Aiden too."

"It's been a pleasure, Mrs. Cecil. Do you need help getting home?" Jillian offered.

"Aiden and I will help her since we're going home for a while. What time do you want to leave for church, Jillian?"

The church was providing a late-afternoon Christmas dinner where church members served and ate alongside their special guests. Those who would otherwise be alone, the elderly, even some homeless people attended.

It was already noon. "I think we should leave at four so we can get there before the guests start arriving."

"Sounds good to me. See you then."

Jillian stood at the door as Matt and Aiden walked with Mrs. Cecil toward her house. She had hoped Matt would stay all day, but as she saw them hand in hand, walking away, she understood that Aiden probably wanted some one-on-one with his dad.

Chapter 23

A Time To Grieve

Lord, thank you for yesterday. It was such a beautiful way to celebrate your birthday. Bless all those who attended the dinner last night, especially those who don't know you. Help them to remember Pastor Milkalski's message of the greatest gift, your salvation. Thank you for extending that gift to my children and me and to Matt and Aiden. Lord, I feel so blessed. There have been many tears in the past, but you have brought me through those times. Bryan's parents will be here this afternoon; help us to have a good time together. I want them to get to know their grandkids better. I'm not sure how to deal with Matt and Aiden while they are here. Help me know what to say and do. I want your will in our lives. Take care of Mom and Dad and all the orphans and workers. I love you, Jesus. You are so good to me.

The kids were still asleep, which gave Jillian the quiet time she needed to get the house in order for her guests. She would be moving into Molly's room for the week so her in-laws could stay in her room with the master bath. *I'm going to miss that*, she thought to herself. *But it's just for a week.* She stripped her bed and made it with new four hundred–thread count white cotton sheets she had bought on sale last summer and never used. She tossed her warm and fuzzy cream-colored microfiber ones into the washing machine, then cleaned her bathroom from top to bottom, vacuumed, moved her toiletries to the kids' bath and the clothing items she would need the next few days to Molly's closet.

She surveyed the rest of the house quickly to find and correct any housekeeping indiscretions. The Christmas tree made the family room appear much smaller, but it also made it beautiful. She plopped down on the sofa to admire the tree when she heard a strange noise, pecking at the front window. "Good grief, I hope they haven't arrived early," she sighed and then peaked around the curtains to find Matt standing on her porch. Hurrying to open the front door, she laughed at her neighbor's antics.

"Sorry to bother you," he smiled mischievously as he stepped into the foyer. "I thought you'd be up, but I didn't want to wake the kids. I forgot to give you something last night."

He placed his hands on her shoulders and leaned forward until his lips touched hers in a warm, almost lingering kiss.

"Mmm," she approved when he eventually stepped back.

"I had planned to do that last night, but I could never get you alone."

"It was worth waiting for," Jillian responded.

"Thanks for the best Christmas I've ever had."

"Oh really?"

"Definitely. First, because it was centered around Christ, not Santa Claus. Shan…"

He had started to say something about Shannon and her affinity for an all-things-Santa Christmas but changed his mind. "Even Aiden didn't mind not having *A Hundred and One Santa Clauses.*"

"I thought it was Dalmatians," she teased.

"Santa Clauses, Dalmatians…what's the difference?" Matt responded, indifferent to both Santa Clause and Dalmatians at this moment.

"You know what? You're fun to be around," Jillian cuddled into Matt's embrace, thinking how happy he made her.

"You know what? You're more fun to be around!"

"Me? I'm just a prim and proper preacher's kid."

"Yeah, I've heard about those preacher's kids."

He made her feel young, almost carefree. "I love you, Matt Morgan."

"I love you, the future Mrs. Matt…" he stopped, not because he did not mean what he was about to say, but because the timing was not right just yet.

Jillian sensed his hesitation and broke the silence. "And the second reason this was your best Christmas?"

"You, of course, my Jillian. You and Aiden and Joshua and Caleb and Molly."

"Don't forget Mrs. Cecil."

"Actually, I had forgotten Mrs. Cecil."

For a moment, they stared into each other's eyes conveying feelings that needed no words. Jillian broke the trance. "You know, my in-laws are arriving about three this afternoon."

"And when do I get to meet them?"

"I'm not sure. I'm trying to figure that out."

"Do you want Aiden and me to hide out while they are here?"

"Of course not. I'm just not sure how to approach it."

"We'll knock on the door, you say, 'Come in,' and then you say, 'I'd like you to meet my neighbors Aiden and Matt who are like family to us.'"

"That's a little sudden, don't you think? However, I would like to have you over for dinner tomorrow tonight. I want to give the kids some time to renew their relationship with their grandparent first."

"Are they close?"

"Well, as close as you can be when you only see someone once a year. I wish it could be more, but they'd never leave Florida now that Jim is retired. They dreamed of that all their lives."

"Well, you can't blame them for living their dream...and listen, Jillian, I understand. I promise I'll be on my best behavior tomorrow night. I won't grab you and kiss you the moment I walk in."

"Be serious. I was married to their son."

"I'm sorry, hon. Didn't mean to be irreverent. I'll look to you for cues."

"I'd rather you pray and take cues from God. I'm not sure what cues I'd give."

The boys woke up just after Matt left, and in turn, their enthusiastic voices awakened Molly. They were excited at the prospect of seeing Grandma and Grandpa Hamilton this afternoon. After breakfast, Jillian announced a quick run to the grocery store. "I don't want to have to go after they get here."

"Grandma and Grandpa don't eat that much." Josh sighed. He disliked grocery shopping.

"No, but they do eat something and our fridge and pantry are bare."

"Why do people eat so much at Christmas?" Caleb asked.

"Tradition, I guess. It's a way of celebrating."

"Are there any holidays when we don't eat?"

"Not yet, but it might not be a bad idea...like the day after Christmas. We could call it Free from Food Day."

"No, I'm starved!" Josh declared. "Can I stay home by myself while you take the others shopping?"

"Not this time. Maybe in a year."

"But, Mom, I'm growing up. I'm not a kid."

"Exactly, and I need your help to carry the groceries, especially since you're starving."

Jillian hurried the kids as much as possible. Although her in-laws had said they would probably arrive about three, she knew, unlike most people, they were always early.

By noon they had returned from the market; she had let the kids pick out deli sandwiches for lunch. While they ate, she put away the groceries and put together her best lasagna recipe to serve for dinner. She would toss a salad while the lasagna was baking and put in the breadsticks when she removed the foil for the last fifteen minutes of bake time. She had only bought her father-in-law's favorite ice cream, butter pecan, for desert, knowing her mother-in-law never allowed herself to indulge in sweets. She liked having everything organized; she no longer felt the same need to impress her in-laws that she did when she and Bryan were married, but she still wanted them to think well of her.

As expected, they arrived early. At two-fifteen, she opened the front door in response to the ringing of the doorbell. Her mother-in-law's first words were "Oh, I hope we didn't arrive too early and you're not ready for us."

"We're always ready for you. We've waited a long time," Jillian forced more excitement into her voice than she actually felt, but she was glad to see them.

The boys responded immediately; Molly took her own time but warmed up to her grandpa first. He was the quieter type, like Molly. Just as she had climbed onto his lap and was engaged in conversation, Grandma Hamilton jumped up. "Jim, for heaven's sakes, go get the presents from the car."

Dutifully, Grandpa Hamilton lowered Molly to the floor, stood up straight, and like a good soldier, sauntered out to the car, returning a few minutes later with three large gift bags and a smaller but more ornate one for Jillian. The ever-doting grandparents had brought a second round of Christmas with them, more presents than the kids had opened yesterday morning. Inwardly Jillian groaned, but she didn't let it show outwardly. The kids were delighted.

Maybe you can make up for a lack of presence with presents, she considered tartly. When she removed a generous gift card from her sequined gift bag, she regretted her wayward thoughts. "Thank you so much, Mom and Dad Hamilton." Jillian's acknowledgement was sincere.

"I never know what to get you," Elizabeth explained.

Jillian inferred that her mother-in-law might have well added, "Because you're so hard to please." Rather than take offense, she smiled sweetly and responded, "You can never go wrong with a gift card!"

For the boys, there were several new video games as well as what seemed like a complete winter wardrobe.

At least there is some practicality involved, Jillian consoled herself. She just wished they wouldn't go overboard. The doll they gave Molly was much more elaborate than the simple baby doll Jillian had given her. There was a change of clothes for every day of the week and a small wardrobe in which to store it all. Three of the doll outfits were replicated in Molly's size.

Elizabeth saw Jillian's surprised expression and responded, "Oh, a good friend of mine is a talented seamstress, and I had her sew the dresses to match. Aren't they adorable?"

Jillian had to agree; she just wished it didn't make her gifts to Molly seem so ordinary.

Elizabeth had let Jillian know the only gift she and Jim wanted were recent photos of the grandchildren. Although she had not specifically asked, Jillian included an eight-by-ten framed photo of her and the children, along with individual five-by-seven photos of each child.

"Oh, what gorgeous grandchildren I have!" Elizabeth purred as she held the framed portraits to her heart. "And these frames are lovely, Jillian. You didn't have to buy the frames, I could have done that."

Jillian wondered if that meant Elizabeth would have rather chosen them herself and almost asked that question. Before she could get the words out, Dad Hamilton spoke up.

"Best-looking grandkids in the world, yes, they are," Jim agreed with Elizabeth. "Joshua sure reminds me of Bryan when he was that age."

Jillian knew he didn't mean to put a damper on their mood, but the mention of his deceased son seemed to have that effect, especially on Elizabeth, who so uncharacteristically sat speechless as she stared at Joshua's picture.

"You really think I look like my dad, Grandpa?" Joshua probed.

"I sure do, son," he replied as he reached his arm around Joshua and pulled him close. Joshua thought himself too old to sit on his Grandpa's lap, but he did place his arm around his shoulder.

An awkward silence descended on their celebration. Jillian wondered if she should start a conversation about Bryan. Maybe her in-laws needed to talk about their deceased son.

"Oh, Jim, you're going to make us all cry," Elizabeth sniffled as she dabbed at her eyes with a tissue.

Jillian walked over to her mother-in-law, who was now standing by their Christmas tree, sobbing. As she tenderly embraced her, Molly and Caleb promptly joined their mother.

"Why are we crying?" Molly questioned. She hardly remembered her daddy and, as far as Jillian could tell, had never grieved for him as the boys had.

"Because Daddy's not here with us anymore," Caleb sobbed.

Jillian gazed over her mother-in-law's shoulder and saw Joshua burying his face in his Grandpa's bulky sweater. His sobs

Or Be Reconciled

were audible. Grandpa Hamilton pulled a handkerchief out of his pocket and handed it to Joshua.

Jillian's tears wouldn't come. It hurt to see the boys crying and Molly's perplexity. She had to be honest with herself. It had been sometime since she had grieved over her husband's death, especially since Matt had entered her life. She knew it was different for the children, yet Matt had filled a void in their lives as well. An idea flashed in her mind. *Should she?* Gently, she released Elizabeth from their lingering embrace. Molly and Caleb continued to hug their grandmother. Jillian took a deep breath and then cleared her throat.

"I think we should take some time to remember Bryan today. This is only our third Christmas without him," her voice wavered slightly. "Of course we miss him and feel sad that he isn't here." With that acknowledgment, the previously unrelenting tears cascaded down her cheeks in a river of relief.

Joshua left his grandpa's embrace and hurried to his mother's waiting one. Caleb and Molly let go of their grandmother and rushed to her side. She held her sobbing children close.

Only a few moments had gone by, but to Jillian, it seemed like an eternity. Silently, she prayed, *Lord, now what?*

"Jillian, I didn't mean to..." Grandpa Hamilton thought he was responsible for everyone's tears.

Before Elizabeth could reprimand him, Jillian spoke with reassurance, "Oh no...no, Dad Hamilton. You did nothing wrong. Today is a good time to remember Bryan...even if it makes us sad for a while. In fact, I want to bring out some of our photo albums, and we can look at them together."

Jillian retrieved the albums from the bookcase in her room where she had placed them the weekend after they moved to their new home in Lakeview. As she removed the photo albums holding memories of the last two years before Bryan's death from their perch on the top shelf, she used her damp tissue to wipe off the dust that had collected.

For the next hour, they scrutinized the photos, each reminiscing about good times, the children asking questions, and the grandparents commenting on how the children had grown up so quickly.

"I wish you had more photos of Bryan and the children," Elizabeth opined as she surveyed the last page of the second book.

Jillian recalled that she had not taken as many pictures those last two years as she had earlier in their marriage. Maybe if she had known. "I have more current photos on my computer if you would like to see them," Jillian offered before she remembered that many of her recent photos included Matt and Aiden.

Thankfully, Elizabeth wasn't interested. "That's okay, dear. But don't you have the previous ones, when Joshua and Caleb were babies?"

"I do. Would you like to see them?"

"Oh yes, I want to see all the ones with Bryan in them."

"I'll get them for you."

There were six previous albums, more than enough to keep Mrs. Hamilton occupied for the rest of the evening. Jillian excused herself to prepare dinner, fending off her mother-in-law's offers to help. "Please, spend time looking at the photos with the children. I have everything under control."

At seven o'clock, they set down to a "perfect little dinner," according to Jim. True to form, Elizabeth refused dessert, which gave her a chance to talk while the others ate their ice cream.

"So tell me, what's going on in your lives?" she looked around the table at each grandchild and then focused on Jillian.

Jillian waited, hoping one of the children would reply, and someone did.

"Mom's got a boyfriend!" Josh offered as if this bit of information was a news alert.

Jillian knew her face had turned as red as the marinara sauce in the bottom of the lasagna dish. Grandpa sat quietly, but not Grandma.

Or Be Reconciled

"Jillian, why haven't you told us?"

Jillian wanted to respond carefully to this sort of, but not exactly accurate news. Sure they were talking about marriage, but no one had referred to Matt as her boyfriend.

"Well, I think..." she paused and cleared her throat, then awkwardly continued, "I think Josh is talking about our neighbor, a coach at his school, Matthew Morgan. He has a son Caleb's age, and we have all become good friends since we moved here. We do a lot of things together."

"Well, Jillian, is it serious? He has a son? Is he a widower?"

Jillian did not want to come face-to-face with this question. She paused too long.

"No, his wife took off to Europe with her boss. That's what Aiden told me. But he still loves her." Joshua's stunning declaration floored his mother.

"He still loves his wife? Is that what you said, Joshua?"

"I don't know. I meant Aiden still loves his mom. That's what I said." Joshua stammered his reply.

"Jillian, do you think this relationship is wise?" Elizabeth asked in a tone that Jillian knew implied she certainly did not think so.

Trying her best to stay calm, she guarded her response. "Elizabeth, really, it's just a good friendship. We go to the same church, his son and the boys play together, we're neighbors...and yes, his wife did leave him." From her point of view, that sounded so much better than "he is divorced."

Jillian stared at Joshua as she finished, with a glare he knew all too well. Without a word, she had told him, "Don't you dare say another word about this," and he got the message.

"Well, honey, I just want you to be careful now. I know how your Dad and Mom feel about such things."

Jillian did not have to be reminded; she finally admitted to herself that was why she had not told her parents about Matt. She absolutely could not get into a discussion about this with Elizabeth either.

Jim, bless his heart, came to the rescue. "This was a delicious meal, Jillian. You're still the great cook Bryan always said you were. I'm so glad Elizabeth and I can spend a few days with you and the children."

Jillian felt dizzy. *Lord, help me respond appropriately*, she whispered her frantic prayer. "We're glad too, Dad Hamilton. We have really looked forward to your visit. Now I want you and Elizabeth to relax with the kids while I clean up. You traveled a long way today, and I know you're tired."

"Actually we spent the last few nights in a wonderful resort in Myrtle Beach, so we only had a three hour drive today," Elizabeth revealed.

"Oh, that sounds lovely. You'll have to tell us all about it later." Jillian grabbed a handful of plates and headed to the kitchen before her mother-in-law could respond. Even with the faucet turned wide open, she could still here the sound of chairs being pushed away from the dining table and cheerful chatter from the children as they led the way to the family room to visit with their grandparents.

She took her time cleaning and putting things away. Thankfully, there were no leftovers to deal with. She was almost afraid to join the others. Where would the conversation go?

Grandpa Hamilton was snoozing in the lounge chair, and Grandma Hamilton was yawning on the sofa when she entered. The boys were playing video games, oblivious to their visitors. Molly had brought her Christmas baby doll—the one Jillian had given her—from her room and was rocking her to sleep while sitting in front of the fireplace.

"Mom and Dad Hamilton, your room is ready for the night," she announced grandly as she waved her hand toward the master suite. Neither of them offered objections as they stood, and she realized they were probably more tired than they wanted to admit.

"Say good night to Grandma and Grandpa." She wished she didn't have to coach the kids to show their grandparents affection. Molly came running with her baby doll in tow. Caleb was second in line for hugs. Joshua continued his game.

"Joshua…" she prodded, thinking how differently he was acting than the tearful young man grieving the loss of his father earlier that day.

"Oh, all right," he moaned as he hit a few more buttons before turning the game switch to off. "Goodnight, Grandma. Goodnight, Grandpa. Thanks for the gifts." He crossed the room slowly and stood rather motionless as he received a hug from each.

Jillian led her guests down the hall to the master bedroom. As Elizabeth realized Jillian had prepared her room for them, she cooed, not too convincingly, "Oh, you didn't have to give up your room, dear."

"No problem." For good measure and to stop the inevitable debate before it started, "And Molly's excited about having a sleepover with her mom."

That was a good-enough excuse for Elizabeth. "Okay, if you're sure now."

Jillian knew Elizabeth had probably secretly expected the master suite. She laughed to herself as she imagined Jim and Elizabeth sharing Molly's twin bed or the boys' bunk beds.

"I'm sure. Let me know if you need anything, and please sleep as late as you want."

Grandpa Hamilton was already sitting on the bed, taking off his shoes.

"Oh, we'll be up by seven. Can't sleep later than that," Elizabeth asserted.

"Speak for yourself. I might sleep till eight," Jim chortled.

Jillian sent Molly to the bathroom to get ready for bed and then stopped by the boys' room. She was curious about just how much the boys and Aiden had talked about his mother. *Should she ask?*

"Josh, please be careful what you say to Grandma and Grandpa about Mr. Morgan."

"Don't you want them to know he's your boyfriend?"

"He's not my boyfriend."

"Then why do you kiss?"

"Son, I believe you saw us kiss one time, and that was just a…a…well, we are good friends."

Joshua screwed up his face as if to say, "Yeah, right," but thought it best to let his expression do the talking.

"You said Aiden had talked about his mother. What does he say?"

"He's always talking about her—how much he misses her and how he wants her to come back home."

"Really? I've never heard him…" she paused as she remembered on several occasion she had heard Aiden talk about his Mom. Maybe she just didn't want to hear him. "Uh, so he talks about her a lot?"

"Almost every time we play together when his dad isn't around. He doesn't think his dad wants him to talk about her. He said it makes his dad sad."

Mad is more like it, Jillian thought. *Or maybe…*she wondered.

"Mommy, I'm ready," Molly called out from her room.

"I'll be right there, Molly. Good night, sons. I love you. God bless."

"Mom, Aiden talks to me about his mom too," Caleb offered in a whisper. "Last week, he said all he wanted for Christmas was for his mom to come home."

Jillian had bent down to kiss him, not expecting this bombshell. "That's sad, isn't it? But she did send him presents."

"Yeah, but I think he'd rather have his mom than presents. I'd rather have you than presents," Caleb disclosed.

"You are my present." She wrapped her arms around Caleb, feeling ashamed that she had been annoyed this morning when she learned Aiden had received Christmas gifts from Shannon. "The bathroom is all yours, guys. Brush you teeth well. I love you. Goodnight."

Jillian wished her own bed wasn't occupied so she could throw herself on it and cry herself to sleep.

"Mommy, here's the books I want you to read," Molly welcomed Jillian into her room. "This is going to be so much fun!"

Jillian's mind was preoccupied. She had to force herself to put on a happy face and a pleasant tone to read the dozen or so books Molly had chosen for their special time together. Jillian felt relieved when Molly fell asleep just before the end of book number five. "And they lived happily ever after," were Jillian's last spoken words as she pulled the cover up over her sleeping daughter's shoulders and pressed a kiss to her rosy cheek. She turned out the light and headed to the bathroom to get ready for bed. Physically and mentally exhausted, she prayed she would sleep soundly without dreaming. After all the emotions she had experienced today, she could only imagine which unwelcome characters might show up in her dreams.

Chapter 24

Oops!

The ringing phone awakened Jillian from a deep sleep. Forgetting she was in Molly's bed, she reached for her phone, knocking over the lamp on Molly's nightstand. The resulting crash caused her to sit straight up in Molly's bed. "Good grief," she muttered. "Whoever's calling is going to wake up Elizabeth and Jim!"

She jumped out of bed, tripping over Molly's toys as she fumbled with her robe. Just as she reached Molly's barely opened door, Elizabeth appeared.

"There's a gentleman on the phone for you, dear. I asked who was calling, and he said his name is Matt."

Warily, she reached for the phone in Elizabeth's hand. "Thanks, Elizabeth."

"Good morning."

"I didn't know if I should bother you…"

"No, that's fine. I needed to get up anyway." Elizabeth appeared to have no intention of leaving while Jillian was on the phone with this man.

"Hi, Matt, what's up?" Jillian attempted her best neighborly inflection.

"Hey, did I wake you up?" Matt was one of those people who woke up every morning raring to go. She thought he was almost yelling into the phone.

"Oh, yeah, that's okay. Christmas vacation, you know."

"I'm sorry, I should have known you might want to sleep in, but actually I needed to know what time you want Aiden and me to come over for dinner tonight."

She was groggy, not yet fully awake. "That's really nice of you, but my in-laws are visiting from Florida this week."

"Huh? I know that. Was that your mother-in-law who answered?" Matt was beginning to realize he had made a bad decision to call so early.

Seemingly satisfied that nothing unsavory was transpiring over the phone, Elizabeth turned and went back to Jillian's room.

"Sorry, Matt. She was standing here listening. She's gone now."

"I shouldn't have called this early, should I?"

"Yesterday was a hard day for us. They are still grieving their son's death."

"Of course they are." Matt understood.

She didn't want to tell him there were other reasons it had been a difficult day for her. As the boys' comments about Aiden missing Shannon moved to the forefront of her mind, she made a decision she hoped she wouldn't regret. "Matt, I was thinking that maybe it's best you don't come over just yet. Joshua blurted out something last night about my having a boyfriend, and I think Mom …uh, Mrs. Hamilton seemed upset."

"Josh called me your boyfriend? Good for Joshua!" He wanted to make her laugh but when she didn't respond right away, he realized she wasn't in the mood.

Jillian considered his reply flippant, not what she had expected.

There was an awkward moment of silence.

"Oh, sure, sure, no problem." Matt tried to sound indifferent, but she heard the disappointment in his voice—or thought she had.

"Actually, that will work out great for us because Aiden wanted to go back to the ice-skating rink today. That's why I called to see what time we needed to be back for dinner. Now we'll grab some unhealthy junk food at the snack bar and stay at the rink until it closes. Aiden will love that."

Matt's reply seemed much too glib. Jillian didn't blame him, considering she had just rescinded her dinner invitation.

"Oh, okay," was the only response Jillian could muster, and though she was the one who had made the decision to cancel their dinner together, there was definite disappointment in her voice.

"Have a good day. We'll see you later in the week."

Jillian didn't like the sound of that. They couldn't say good-bye without confirming some plans. "We're still on for New Year's Eve at the church, aren't we?" She hoped her tone wasn't too pleading.

"Hey, that's up to you. Whatever you feel comfortable with," Matt replied coolly.

"Oh yes, I want to spend New Year's Eve with you and Aiden. The kids would be so disappointed if we didn't. I'm sure it will be fine."

"Okay, let me know if you change your mind."

"I won't, Matt." She wanted to make sure he knew she wanted to be with him. "Have a great day."

"You too." The phone clicked off.

Oh, that's what I get for running my mouth before saying my prayers. What have I done? I was upset about Shannon and took it out on Matt.

> Lord, help me not to be so stupid. I didn't want to hurt Matt, and he actually didn't seem to be upset…maybe that's why I'm upset, because he wasn't. What's wrong with me, God? I feel so foolish. Help me to seek you with all my heart, Lord. I want your will, not mine. I don't know what to do anymore.

Jillian took a deep breath.

> Take care of my kids today, Lord. Bless our time together with Bryan's parents. Be with Mom and Dad and give them strength for the work you've called them to do. Let Matt and Aiden have a great day together. Oh, what is that heavy feeling in my chest? Lord, wherever Aiden's mom is, watch over her and help her.

Those words did not come easily; it was a sacrificial prayer offering. But as soon as she prayed for Shannon, the burden lifted.

Chapter 25

All in the Family

Father in heaven, as we begin a new year tomorrow, help each one of us to look to you for guidance. May we seek you through your Word and prayer so that we can know what you want us to do. I especially pray for my grandchildren that they will grow strong and healthy and follow you, Lord. Be with Jillian in all she does—being a mother, a nurse, a daughter, a daughter-in-law. Encourage and strengthen her. As we head home, give Elizabeth and me a safe trip and help us to put you first in the New Year, and thank you that we've had this wonderful week together with our family. Amen.

Jillian was touched by her father-in-law's words. She had not often heard him pray and was pleased that he had not hesitated when she asked him to say the blessing over their brunch. Before she let go of his hand, she gave it a gentle squeeze.

"Well, I say let's eat this beautiful breakfast Jillian has prepared!" Elizabeth reached for the platter of fluffy, almost-made-from-scratch biscuits.

"Would you like one, dear?" she asked her husband.

"Yes, thank you," Jim replied and then winked at his grandchildren as he grabbed three. "Make sure there's enough to go around," his wife scolded.

"Oh, there are plenty of biscuits...more in the kitchen," Jillian assured as she passed the sausage and egg casserole she had learned to prepare from her mother.

Good recipe for company because you prepare it the night before, her mother had told her. Jillian was thankful she had something to do last night. It had been a long week without Matt and Aiden around. After beginning to feel they were both just holding out on each other, she had given in and called him yesterday morning. Matt didn't pick up until the sixth ring, and she knew it would go to the answering machine on the seventh. She breathed a sigh of relief when she heard his voice, even as she imagined him holding the phone in his hand and waiting until the last minute to answer.

"Hey, Jillian, how are you?"

"Just wanted to check on you and Aiden."

"We're doing great. Have had some really good times together this week...ice skating Tuesday, we went to the *Cars* movie Wednesday night, and last night I took him to a hockey game in Raleigh."

"Sounds like it has been a special week for you two."

"You're right. It's been great. How are you and the kids?"

"Tired. Elizabeth and Jim"—that was what she had being calling them all week, purposefully dropping the *Mom* and *Dad* titles—"have kept us busy shopping and going out to eat. I haven't cooked since Tuesday night."

"I haven't done much cooking myself this week. We had chili burritos at the rink, and since then we've been grabbing a bite wherever. I did cook oatmeal for breakfast this morning."

Jillian managed a laugh. "Good for you. I wouldn't want you to lose all your skills."

No response.

When she could no longer bear the silence, Jillian asked tentatively, "You will be at the service tomorrow night?"

"Sure," he responded quickly. "But I wasn't planning on sitting with you and your in-laws…sort of awkward, don't you think?"

"Oh, they won't be there. They've decided to leave early in the morning and go to Asheville for a few days. Elizabeth wants to see the Christmas decorations at Biltmore House."

"More than visit with her grandkids? Sounds like Shannon's mom."

"Actually, I was relieved when they told me. We'll have the night to ourselves." Jillian hoped Matt would hear the anticipation in her voice.

"Ourselves, our kids, and the congregation," Matt quipped. "I wish I could be alone with you on New Year's Eve." Jillian heard the longing in his voice.

"Mmm…sounds nice to me."

"So what time do we need to leave for church tomorrow night?"

"I told Marie I would come early to help set up for the games and snacks before the service. Would it be too much to ask you to watch my kids from eight to nine and bring them to the church then? The actual service starts at eleven."

Matt was not at all put off by her request; in fact, he was pleased that they would be functioning as a family again. "Sounds good to me. Do I need to bring anything? Maybe some leftover oatmeal?"

Jillian laughed. "The church is providing the food, so maybe you can have the oatmeal for lunch."

"Mom! Mom! There're no more biscuits."

Before Jillian had a chance to scold Joshua for what she perceived as yelling at her, she noticed the stares she was receiving from the others seated around the table.

"Jillian, dear, are you okay? You seem so far away." Elizabeth was more curious than concerned.

"I'm sorry," Jillian apologized, realizing she had been mentally absent from the table for sometime. "Just thinking about all I need to do to get ready for tonight. Joshua, I said there were more biscuits in the kitchen. Here, take this and fill it up," she directed as she pushed the wicker breadbasket toward him.

"I hope we haven't made it difficult for you by leaving a day early," Elizabeth responded.

"Oh no, not at all," Jillian replied, hoping she had not conveyed the relief she actually felt about the early departure.

As her family consumed another round of biscuits, Jillian continued to replay the remainder of yesterday's phone conversation with Matt.

"Remember, I have a surprise for you!"

Jillian had thought about that surprise often during the past week. She was almost sure it was an engagement ring. "How could I forget? You've been tantalizing me for weeks."

"Do you still want it?"

"I love surprises. Sure, I still want it."

"And I want to give it to you....really bad!" Jillian recollected that Matt had sounded like an excited teenager when he talked about the forthcoming surprise.

There were a lot of hugs and kisses and a few tears as the Hamiltons said their good-byes just before noon. Jillian removed the luxurious linens from her bed and replaced them with her warm, cozy sheets. She couldn't resist the urge. Falling backward, she stretched out onto her queen-size bed. It felt lavish after being squeezed in with Molly all week. She closed her eyes for just a few minutes and imagined Matt slipping a shining diamond ring on her finger tonight. Then she envisioned her mom and dad as she told them her good news. She knew she should have already told them about Matt. *But how could she? What would they say?*

Chapter 26

Ringing in the New Year

> Let our lights shine for you in this New Year, Lord Jesus. We want our lives to reflect you, the Light of the world. Keep us from hiding our lights or letting them grow dim. May we shine them in all the dark places that we encounter this year. May they never go out, we pray in Jesus's name. Amen.

Pastor Milkalski led the congregation in prayer to open the New Year's Eve service. Cindy and David, the children's ministers, hurriedly lit the candles the children's choir members were holding.

"One, two, three," Cindy raised her hands and directed the robed group of children in singing "This Little Light of Mine."

Molly's grin was from ear to ear. Joshua appeared solemn, maybe a little embarrassed. Caleb and Aiden were trying to sing and blow out each other's candles at the same time. Matt and Jillian sat "church-close" together, barely touching, and for the first time in church, he positioned his strong left arm around her on the back of the pew.

"Our kids," he whispered into her ear, "are the best-looking ones." He grasped her shoulder with his left hand, sending goose bumps scattering up her arm. When the song ended, he moved his arm to join in the applause. As soon as the kids had scooted in around them, he replaced it…a little closer and tighter. She looked at him, and they shared a lingering gaze.

I love him, Jillian contemplated.

I want to spend the rest of my life with this woman, Matt declared in his heart.

Pastor Milkalski's message for the New Year was one of hope and trust in Jesus. Noting that the days ahead may be difficult ones, he encouraged the congregants to put God first in their lives and teach their children to do the same.

It was a few minutes before midnight. The string trio was playing a stirring arrangement of "What Wondrous Love Is This?" Mr. Ockenhouse, the head usher, had turned off the overhead lights, leaving only the candles burning. The other suit-clad ushers joined him at the front of the sanctuary where the communion table had been prepared.

Jillian closed her eyes, basking in the serene ambiance.

Matt manipulated the small box he had hidden in the pocket of his slacks. As he surveyed Jillian's face in the glow of candlelight, the anticipation was almost overwhelming.

Just as Pastor Milkalski asked the congregation to stand, Matt's cell phone blared like a foghorn in the still of the night. Fumbling to turn it off, he grabbed it out of its case, poked at the keypad, then cringed in disbelief as it slipped from his hands and went flying underneath the pews. There was muffled laughter throughout the sanctuary. Unfortunately it was not loud enough to prevent the whole church from hearing the plaintive voice on the speakerphone:

"Matt, Matt, this is Shannon. Baby, answer the phone! Matt, Matt, don't ignore me! Where are you? Matt, I'm standing on your front porch. Answer me Matt!"

There was a look of disbelief on Matt's face. Jillian's left hand reflexively came up to her face, and with her right one, she held the back of the pew in front of her for dear life. Matt lunged to the floor to retrieve the phone.

Hearing his mother's voice, Aiden called out enthusiastically, "Mom! It's Mom! Dad, she did come! Let's go see Mom."

A loud gasp, probably Mrs. Wilson's, and muffled snickers sounded throughout the church. After an eternity, Matt found the phone and, without responding to Shannon's pleas, hit the off key. He stood to his feet looking more broken than Jillian had ever seen him.

"Pastor," he offered humbly in a voice barely audible, "and friends," he continued as he turned his head toward the congregants seated behind him but with eyes focused on Jillian, "I am so, so sorry for this disruption…please forgive me."

Pastor Milkalski was hardly ever ruffled by distractions, and even this conspicuous one was no different. "We forgive you, Matt. Go. We excuse you."

Matt looked at Pastor Milkalski in disbelief. He had no intention of giving in to Shannon, especially not tonight. By this time, Aiden was beside him, jumping up and down in excitement. "I knew Mom would come see me for Christmas!" he proclaimed.

Matt wanted to shout, *She's a week late!* He wanted to throw his cell phone through the stained glass window and pretend this never happened. He didn't want to acknowledge her, and he definitely didn't want to go to her. But he had no choice. His pastor's words felt like a command.

"I am so sorry," he repeated, almost in a whisper, his face focused on the floor in front of him. The sanctuary felt like a dark, damp cave closing in on him. His shoulders slumped, his palms sweated. The words "humbled, broken man" might as well have been written across his chest.

He longed to meet Jillian's eyes, to see a glimmer of hope in them, but he did not have the strength to look in her direction.

"Come on, Dad, Mom's waiting!" Aiden pleaded as he pulled on his dad's arm. Matt didn't remember being tugged down the aisle by his son, even when a blast of frigid air hit him across the face when one of the ushers pushed open the exit door.

Dear Lord, dear Lord, Jillian cried out silently from the depths of her soul. *Be with Matthew just now…whatever is happening. Father, give him strength and help him Lord to do the right thing. Oh God, he looked so broken…devastated.* Her mind was racing. *What was happening? Why was Shannon at his house? She's supposed to be celebrating New Year's Eve in Rome with her lover*, Jillian told herself. She tried to stay focused on praying for Matt but could not escape the nauseating thoughts that were cascading over her. *What was it she called him? Honey? Dear? No! It was baby. She had addressed Matt—my Matt—as baby. Jesus—*it was a desperate plea from her heart—*Jesus, help Matt. Help me.*

"Amen," Pastor Milkalski ended his communion blessing of which Jillian had not heard a word. "You may be seated."

The worship band was playing a hauntingly soulful rendition of "Silent Night." As Emma Grace, the gifted young harpist, skillfully glided her fingers over the strings, Jillian felt that a strong man was plucking her heartstrings into a tangled mess. She knew that in a few seconds, an usher would present a silver tray laden with bread and wine. The word *mortified* continued to flash across the screen of her mind. She opened her eyes wide to stop it. To her right, Molly lay sleeping on the padded pew, sprawled out in the place where Matt had been sitting only a few minutes earlier. To her left, Caleb and Joshua sat very still, looking in her direction until she looked in theirs; both boys quickly looked toward the floor before she made eye contact.

The usher tapped Joshua softly on his shoulder and offered the silver tray. Awkwardly, Joshua took a tiny piece of bread and one of the small cups and handed the tray to Caleb. Jillian reached over to help Caleb, then served herself and reached across Molly to hand the tray to the usher waiting at the other end of the pew.

She thought she saw a look of pity on his face. *No, no it's just my imagination*, she told herself. She tried so very hard to focus on Christ, on his costly sacrifice, on his shedding of blood to save her, her children, and every other person in the world. *Even Shannon*, the thought came out of nowhere, and she tried to banish it from her mind, but she couldn't. *For God so loved Shannon... Shannon...Shannon...that he gave his one and only Son that if Shannon...Shannon ...Shannon...believes in him...Shannon... Shannon...Shannon will not perish but will have eternal life.* It took everything in her to shut down her thought process. She focused intently on the pastor and the words he was speaking.

"That whoever believes on him will not perish but have eternal life."

Whoever includes Shannon reverberated in her mind. She tried, oh so hard she tried, not to think anything, just to keep a blank mind. *No thoughts, no thoughts*, she said repeatedly to herself.

Then, as if Jesus himself was standing beside her whispering into her ear, she heard those words gently but clearly spoken, "*Whoever* includes Shannon."

"Let us take the bread together," Pastor Milkalski invited the congregation to participate in the sharing of Christ's body. Jillian slipped the morsel into her dreadfully dry mouth and tried to swallow it but could not.

"Let us take the wine, the symbol of the blood that was shed for our sins." She washed the bread down with the grape juice. All over the church, she heard the clink of communion cups in the holders on the backs of the pews.

"Jesus, Jesus," she whispered plaintively. Jillian's mind was spinning, but she could barely form words with her lips. *What should I pray?* She asked silently. More than ever before, she understood the Scripture about the Holy Spirit interceding with groans that words cannot express. Prayer had never been more arduous. Her groanings were inaudible but earnest.

Both Joshua and Caleb had fallen asleep—or pretended to—on the way home; neither had said a word. She had even been able to slip Molly into her booster seat without rousing her from her peaceful rest. Now she sat in her driveway, the gearshift set on park but the engine still running to keep the kids warm. Matt's car appeared to be parked haphazardly in his driveway. His usual parking space was occupied by Shannon's flashy red convertible.

Almost an hour had passed since Shannon's telephone call to Matt had interrupted the New Year's Eve service and rocked Jillian's own little world. As soon as the service ended, Jillian gathered her children and headed for the side exit, hoping to avoid the crowd now joyously welcoming the New Year. Pastor Milkalski called after her, and hesitantly, she turned toward him. Marie was beside him and gave her a gentle hug, taking care not to disturb the peacefully sleeping Molly. "Jillian, call me if you need me."

"I'm praying for you," Pastor Milkalski reassured.

Mr. Ockenhouse, ever the compassionate encourager, put his hand on her shoulder. "I'll be praying for you and Matt," he promised. Knowing he planned to include Matt in his prayers for her gave Jillian a glimmer of hope.

Several other parishioners wished her and her family a happy New Year in what she perceived as subdued tones. Just when she thought she was safely out the door without too much confrontation, she heard the one voice she had dreaded the most.

"Well, well, my dear," were the only words she allowed Mrs. Wilson to utter before she pushed the door closed and rushed her kids out into the cold night air. Now, a few minutes later, Jillian felt she had probably been too abrupt, even angry, but at the time, and maybe even now, she didn't care.

Suddenly, like a drone attack, a random, crazy idea coursed through her consciousness, just long enough to make her feel both queasy and frightened: *Just pull the car into the garage, Jillian. Use the remote to close the door. Leave the car running.*

Immediately she hit the remote to open the garage door, pulled the car into place, opened her door wide, hitting the lawn mower in the process, and frantically reacting to that voice, turned off the ignition and yanked out the keys. Out loud she replied, "No way, no way am I going to do such a foolish thing."

"Who are you talking to, Mommy?" The question came from Caleb, yawning in the back seat.

"Oh, honey, did I wake you up? Sorry, but it had to be done. I can't carry all three of you sleepyheads inside." She hoped Caleb understood her words to mean she needed to wake them up. She did not want to explain to her eight-year-old that she was rebuking the devil himself.

Joshua slowly opened his eyes. "Are we home?"

"Yes, we're home," she sighed woefully and wondered if the boys heard the pain in her voice. She had been dreaming of becoming a whole family again this year, a mom and dad and four kids…maybe even five. *Now what?*

The boys seemed much too tired to pick up on anything but the obvious. She didn't even remind them to brush their teeth as they headed straight to their room. Tenderly, she changed Molly into her soft pink gown Grandma and Grandpa Hamilton had given her for Christmas and placed the baby doll with the matching gown beside her.

Molly stirred. "No, Mommy, I want the one you gave me," she declared as she pulled the plain, diaper-clad baby to her chest. Gently, Jillian pushed Molly's golden halo of hair from her face and lovingly pecked her precious little girl on her forehead. Tugging the comforter around her shoulders, Jillian pined, "Oh, if only I had loving hands to tuck me in." She hungered for a strong masculine touch.

Knowing better than to do so but also aware that she wouldn't get a wink of sleep until she did, she made her way to the front of the house. Without turning on any lights, she was guided by the glow from the street lamp in front of Mrs. Cecil's house. She took a deep breath, then carefully pulled the curtain back just enough so she could see Matt's driveway.

Shannon's convertible still sat proudly beside Matt's van. Jillian stood staring at the cars for a moment before a disgusting realization made her reel quickly away. From her view, Matt's house was completely dark. There were no lights on anywhere in his house. Of course, she reminded herself, she could not see if his bedroom light was on; it was on the other side, in the back. She wasn't sure that thought was very comforting. She hurled herself on the sofa, collapsing into tears. Each time she felt sleep trying to overcome her, her mind would start replaying the evening's happenings. She pulled her favorite throw around her shoulders, swaddling herself in its warmth. Mercifully, God granted his beloved child sleep.

Chapter 27

Full Disclosure

God, you are going to have to give me the words to say. I am so confused, so depleted. Help me explain this to Jillian, Lord, and help her understand.

Matt stood outside Jillian's bedroom window, shivering in the early morning cold. The sun wouldn't be up for another four hours, and the wind was blustery. At least the cold helped him stay awake while he waited for her to respond to his calling her name; not only had he not slept, he had also been involved in a verbal knock-down drag-out with Shannon. He was afraid knocking on the window would frighten Jillian; after what he put her through last night at church, he didn't want to cause her any more turmoil.

Jillian had startled awake and looked at the clock in the dining room. It was two o'clock in the morning. Her bladder was aching. She pulled herself up from the sofa and stumbled down the hall to the bathroom. She started to go to the kids' bathroom in the hallway but then thought she heard someone calling her name. As she listened, she was sure she heard someone calling from outside her bedroom widow.

Just as Matt was about to turn and leave, he saw a faint light streaming through the bedroom curtain. "Jillian, Jillian!" he called louder, assuming his previous calls had awakened her.

The light disappeared.

Jillian had just flipped the switch on her bedroom wall when she again heard someone call her name. Immediately she turned off the light. Warily, she made her way in the darkness to her bedroom window. Standing to the side, she pushed the curtain open only slightly.

"What in the world!" she exclaimed, stunned from seeing a man outside her window. It took only a second for her to recognize Matt's strong, lean form.

Still in the emerald green sweater she was wearing at the service last night, Jillian appeared to Matt as if she were sleepwalking. Her hair was disheveled around her expressionless face.

"Jillian, oh honey, thank you for answering me. I need to talk to you."

Jillian could barely hear him through the window. "Okay, okay, I need to go to the bathroom, and then I'll meet you at the front door."

"Hurry, please. It's freezing out here."

Jillian was in a sleep-induced haze. Gradually she recalled what had transpired last night. She remembered Shannon's car still being in the driveway when she threw herself on the sofa. "At least she didn't spend the entire night," Jillian consoled herself.

Instead of heeding Matt's plea to hurry, she took her time in the bathroom. After splashing cold water on her face, she swished a capful of mouthwash and spat it in the sink. These she did for her own comfort; her eyelids were matted from tears mixed with mascara, and her mouth was dry. At the moment, she could care less how she presented herself to Matt.

Still feeling no call to urgency, she paused to turn on the two lamps in the family room and then the outside entry light before turning the deadbolt lock. Matt almost opened the door before she had a chance to move out of the way. A gust of frigid wind carried him into the entryway.

"Oh, cold!" she exclaimed, not at all attempting to hide her annoyance.

"I told you it was freezing out there."

"So?" Last night had all come back to her now: the humiliation, the hurt, the hopelessness.

"Jillian, please, baby." He had prayed she would give him a chance to explain before she jumped to conclusions. He reached out to embrace her, but at the sound of *that* word, she jerked and turned away.

"*Baby*? Don't call me baby! That's what she...your ex-wife called you in front of the whole church."

Matt kept his composure. "Do you...do you want me to leave?" he asked hesitantly, afraid her answer would be yes.

"Yes, I do, I want you to leave right now. Go away. Go back to your Shannon!" she spoke from her head, not her heart.

"Shannon's not here. She's gone to a hotel, and she's not mine."

"Well, she was here when we got home tonight," Jillian asserted, still in an uncharacteristically angry tone.

"I know...I saw you," Matt's words wee calm and gentle.

"Where? I didn't see you," she retorted, continuing their back to face confrontation.

"We were sitting in my van. I wouldn't let her go in the house."

"You wouldn't?" Jillian's icy demeanor was beginning to thaw around the edges.

"Are you kidding? Of course I'm not going to invite her in. Aiden and I sat in the van and talked to her. The last hour I spent on my cell phone trying to find her a hotel room for the night. Have you ever tried to find a hotel room on New Year's Eve?" He was attempting to insert a spark of humor into the conversation, but it didn't resonate with Jillian.

"No," she replied matter-of-factly.

"Well, it wasn't easy, but there was no way she was going to stay in my house."

A little more melting took place, just a little, but enough for Jillian to turn around and face him. *He looks like a lost puppy*, she considered. The corners of his lips turned up ever so slightly.

"It is so good to look into your gentle, beautiful eyes instead of Shannon's ferocious ones."

"This is no time for flattery, Mr. Drop-Your-Cell-Phone-in-the-Middle-of-Church." A full defrost was on the way. She imparted a slight grin. "After hitting the speakerphone key no less." The tone of her voice had changed dramatically. She still had no idea what was going on, but knowing that Matt had sent Shannon away made her willing to listen to the rest of the story.

"I was going for the off key…huge blunder." The gust of frigid air had dissipated; the atmosphere was warming.

"You didn't leave Aiden at home alone did you?"

"No. He wanted to spend the night with his mom. I finally found a room for them in Durham, a rather less-than-swanky place for Shannon's taste, but I guess she thought it was better than spending the night in her car."

"You wouldn't have!"

"Oh, wouldn't I? Jillian, I don't think you understand the degree to which I plan to not have anything to do with that woman ever again." His cold-hearted words warmed Jillian. "And I am so sorry about the spectacle at church. What happened after I left?"

"Communion…music…prayer…Mrs. Wilson scolding me—"

"Oh no. I didn't know she came out at night. Did she really scold you?"

"Not really. Just her usual not-so-kind comments. Pastor and Marie and a few others said they were praying for me. Mr. Ockenhouse said he was praying for us."

"That was thoughtful."

"Yes, it was."

"The kids?"

"Asleep…or pretending to be…hardly a word."

"I am so very sorry. Will you forgive me?"

"For what?"

"For the commotion, for embarrassing you, for hurting you."

"It wasn't your fault."

"I take full responsibility for turning on the speakerphone," he grinned as the combination of his humble words and timid smile tugged at her heartstrings.

"That's all?"

"Well, the darn phone should have been off. You've warned me about that before."

The angst she had felt only moments before continued to fade away. "Yes, I have, haven't I? Did you learn your lesson?"

"I'm pretty sure I'm throwing the phone in the garbage in the morning."

Matt and Jillian yawned almost simultaneously.

"It is morning," Jillian reminded him. Still, she felt a greater need to know, than to sleep, at this moment. She wanted Matt to tell her why Shannon had shown up at his house last night without her having to ask the question. *What was that urgent message broadcast to the entire congregation all about?*

Matt had become proficient at reading Jillian's thoughts. "I guess you're wondering why Shannon came."

She started to act uninterested, then realized how dishonest that would be. At this point, undeviating honesty would surely be the best policy. "Of course I am."

"Here, let's sit down." Matt placed his arm gently around her waist as he guided her toward the sofa. For an instant, he thought he felt her pull away. No, he must have misinterpreted her movement.

Jillian picked up the pillow that had been under her head during her fitful slumber and, holding it close to her chest, curled up at one end of the sofa. Matt retrieved her throw from the floor where she had dropped it when she got up to go to the bathroom. Silently, he tucked it around her, and then stretched out on the opposite end, kicking his shoes off in the process.

"Do you need some cover? I have another throw—"

"No, I'm fine, but it does feel rather chilly in here."

"I know. The programmable thermostat—it's set on 68, good for sleeping."

"Brrr."

"Let me get you a blanket," she offered as she started to get up.

"No, I'll get it. You look too comfortable," he insisted as he quickly stood to his feet.

"It's on the bench at the end of my bed."

As he walked down the hall, Matt observed the boys sleeping soundly in their bunks while Molly nestled under the comforter in her white four-poster bed. Approaching the master suite, he realized he had never been in Jillian's bedroom. The queen-size bed was still neatly made with a bright yellow bedspread. Colorful throw pillows were strewn along the headboard. It dawned on him that she had not been to bed; she just fell asleep on the sofa in her clothes from church.

With the faux fur throw over his arm, he attempted to walk silently back down the hall. One of the floorboards creaked as he walked past the boys' room; Joshua, on the top bunk, rolled over in his sleep, his left arm falling over the side rail. Matt paused; he didn't want to wake the kids. As quietly as he could, he pulled their doors almost closed before tiptoeing back to the family room. Jillian's eyes were closed. As soon as he eased himself onto the sofa, they opened wide.

"I wasn't sleeping, just thinking…"

"I noticed you haven't been to bed."

"I couldn't…too worried about what was happening next door. I wish I had seen you in the van. I noticed there were no lights on in the house."

"You didn't let your mind play tricks on you, did you?" He was genuinely concerned about what she might have imagined.

"Let's not talk about imaginings. Let's talk about what really happened tonight."

"That's why I came over. I want you to know everything that went on."

"Actually, you can skip all the gratuitous parts, just tell me why she showed up at your house on New Year's Eve, begging you to come to her." Jillian hoped her tone didn't sound as spiteful as the words made her feel. "Just cut to the quick." She knew that meant pain, but at this point, that would be better than not knowing.

His expression was serious. He stretched his arms up behind his neck, elbows bent; he bent his neck from side to side, then around in a circle. She sensed he was preparing for something he didn't want to do. This wouldn't be good news. Jillian just wanted this whole ugly episode to disappear.

"Shannon's boss bought her a one-way ticket back to America from Rome. She had been experiencing some health problems and was diagnosed with early stage breast cancer. He told her he was sending her back to get the best medical treatment possible, but when she called to tell him she had arrived safely in Charlotte, he told her he thought it was best they go their separate ways. When she asked about her job, he told her she could keep it so her insurance would be intact as long as she needed it."

Jillian gasped. Two words stood out to her. *Breast cancer.* She had asked for the hard facts, and Matt laid them out. It was too much to comprehend. She summed up the situation in her mind as she understood it. *Diagnosed with breast cancer. Dumped by boss. Wants Matt back.* Matt hadn't included the last part, but he didn't have to. She knew. She had known since she heard Shannon call him *baby* on the phone and asked him to come to her.

In the distance, there was the faint wail of a siren. Jillian was reminded she was scheduled to go back to work in two days. She would call out. She would just bury herself under her covers for a few days. No, she couldn't do that. She had to take care of the kids; they started back to school on Monday. She had to face this situation no matter what the outcome.

Arousing from her trance, she lifted her eyes to meet Matt's waiting ones. It was evident it had been almost twenty-four hours since he had shaved; the stubble was becoming.

Finally, she spoke. "Breast cancer…that's serious."

"She didn't seem all that concerned since it's in an early stage. Her mom had breast cancer years ago, and she recovered."

Jillian was thinking about the treatments she would have to undergo—or surgery. "No matter what stage, cancer is serious," she spoke from a medical perspective.

"She has good insurance; she'll get the best care."

"That's good." Jillian felt almost callous asking her next question, but she needed to know. "Did you leave anything out? Like why she showed up on your doorstep, unannounced on New Year's Eve?"

Matt bit his lower lip, then looked down, again rotating his neck from side to side. He stretched his head upright and met Jillian's eyes with his own. He couldn't speak the words.

"Well, did you?" She wasn't angry, just impatient. She wanted to know. "Does she want you to take her back?"

"When hell freezes over!" Matt declared much too loudly.

"Matt, shh," she cautioned, not because of his uncharacteristic response, but because she didn't want him to wake the kids. Normally she didn't approve of that expression, but it was comforting to hear him express his negative feelings about Shannon so strongly.

"What a mess she's got herself into." Jillian hadn't dealt with the "Shannon as a woman with breast cancer" aspect yet. Still, she felt not one iota of compassion for the woman. It was as if she was getting what she deserved.

Then Matt said the words that would cause Jillian's whole world to spin out of control.

"And she said she's found religion, that's she a Christian. Give me a break. She begged for forgiveness for leaving Aiden and me, saying she takes full blame, and she's sorry for all the hurt she caused both of us. She was crying like mad. Her mascara was smeared so badly she looked like a raccoon…a raccoon with bleached blonde hair."

Jillian wanted to yell, *Stop! Stop!* Now he was giving too many details and, she thought, becoming mean-spirited. That wasn't her Matt; he was kind and understanding. Then she considered the attitude of her own heart and breathed a prayer, *Lord, help me!* Almost immediately she felt a trickle of compassion in her spirit. For the first time since Matt's cell phone blared in the church last night, Jillian glimpsed this scenario from Shannon's point of view. The word *cancer* flashed in her mind. It was joined by the word *alone*.

Matt wondered what Jillian was thinking. He didn't want to argue with her about Shannon's supposed salvation, but he just couldn't bring himself to believe it. She had never, ever in her life gone to church except at Christmas and Easter. She still had fire in her eyes, but he had to admit he had never seen her so repentant, but then she was dealing with cancer and was probably frightened.

"That changes everything." Jillian's almost inaudible declaration stung both of them.

"I just can't believe she found God. She wasn't even sure she believed in him," Matt contended.

Jillian thought she heard a still, small, voice. She closed her eyes. She tried to shut out everything around her. Yes, she heard it again. *Remember all the times you felt led to pray for Shannon?* She knew God was speaking to her.

"Matt, we can't judge another's claim to salvation. If she says she's a Christian, we must take her word for it." *Maybe by giving Shannon the benefit of the doubt, God would make this whole ordeal go away.*

"Jillian, you only met Shannon once. You have no idea what she's really like."

Jesus came to save the lost no matter what they've done…whosoever… Jillian's mind reeled back to the words she had heard over and over in her spirit last night: *For God so loved the world, that he gave his one and only Son, that if Shannon believes in him, she will not perish but have everlasting life.* "Matt, anyone who seeks him will find him."

"I don't think Shannon was seeking Jesus."

"Maybe he was looking for her." Jillian couldn't believe the love and compassion she was feeling for Shannon now. She didn't want to; she knew it wasn't coming from her heart, but God's heart in her.

"Okay already, so she's a Christian. Great. Good for her. Now she won't go to hell. But she's not going to make my life a living hell again. Jillian, there's no way that I would ever take her back. She cheated on me. She flaunted her actions. She moved out taking my son, and then when it was convenient for her, she gave him back to me. She wanted the divorce. She broke Aiden's heart. She broke my heart."

It's a humbling sight to see a strong, grown man collapse to his knees, crying uncontrollably. His body rolled off the sofa until his knees hit the floor. His head followed, meeting the hard wood with a thump. He threw his arms out beside him, pounding his fists against the smooth surface. There was not enough strength in them to make much noise.

Jillian tossed her throw aside and knelt beside Matt. Their tears flowed. Their cries of despair, though consciously muffled so as not to wake the children, were fervent. Jillian wasn't sure how long they had prayed together. Had she fallen asleep?

When Matt took the initiative and began to pray out loud in a calm, strong voice, Jillian knew God was listening, and somehow he would answer the prayers of their hearts. "Jesus, I really need your help. I love you, Lord. You have been so good to Aiden and me through all this, bringing me to a closer relationship with you than I've ever had before. You carried me through dark nights when I didn't think I wanted to see another sunrise. Then you allowed Jillian and her kids to be a part of our lives, and I know you understand how I feel, and I'm asking you to help me to do what's right. I know I should be glad that Shannon says she has found you, but I'm stunned. This doesn't fit in with my plans. Thank you for Jillian. Help her as we go through this together."

Matt pushed himself up from the floor, and he and Jillian helped each other to stand. There was a quick, friendly hug, and then Jillian took Matt's hand and led him to the kitchen.

"I've got to have something to drink…would you like something?" she offered.

"Water's fine."

She filled two glasses with water from the refrigerator dispenser, and both drank thirstily.

"Yeah, I was parched," Matt acknowledged as he sat the empty glass on the counter.

They looked at each other questioningly. Both wondered what the other was thinking; both felt a peace in their spirits that had not been present earlier.

Eventually, Matt broke the silence. "The Bible does say that adultery is grounds for divorce, doesn't it?"

"Some people interpret it that way, but that doesn't mean it's a given."

"Oh, Jillian, I don't want to hear that. I don't want Shannon back in my life. I love you. You know what the surprise was that I had intended to give you tonight?"

"Oh, I did have a notion."

Matt reached in his pants' pocket and pulled out a small black box. He held it in his hands for a few seconds before opening it carefully and removing the ring. "I was going to ask you to be my wife."

Jillian gazed at the ring and saw the promise of joy it could have held for her if the night had turned out differently. "Oh, Matt, it's a beautiful ring." She didn't dare reach out to touch the sparkling diamond banded in platinum.

Matt continued. "I know the woman you are, and therefore, I'm putting this ring back in the box for now, not because my intention has changed, but because I know you think this is not a good time for me to propose. You want me to deal with this other situation first, am I right?"

Relief washed over Jillian. Dealing with a proposal on top of everything else would have been too much. Matt's understanding once again reminded her why she had fallen in love with this man. She smiled a grateful smile, kissed Matt softly on his cheek, and responded, "Yes, you are right."

Matt stuck the box back in his pocket, and the solemn expression lingered on his face. "Jillian, I want you to know that I really want to do what's right, but I believe God approves of divorce when one of the partners commits adultery. It's pretty clear in the Bible."

In the process of making a difficult decision, Jillian remained silent. *Should I?* Her heart was racing, just considering the possibility.

"You lost your husband to death. That's so different than having your mate cheat on you and tell you she doesn't want to be married to you anymore. It's a whole different ballgame. I don't expect you to understand how I feel. Sometimes I think losing a spouse to divorce is worse than having your spouse die." He noticed the distressed expression on her face. "I'm sorry, I don't have any right to speak to that."

His words had made her hard decision easier.

"Matt, I know it's almost four in the morning and we're both sleep deprived, but I want to tell you something I've never shared with you before."

"Uh-oh. This sounds serious."

"It is."

Before letting go of his strong hands, Jillian squeezed them lovingly. She had led him back to the sofa, and now they both sat upright on the sofa, next to each other, his arm gently draped around her shoulders. She felt awkward that she felt so much love for Matt during these confusing circumstances. It was almost as if the character of her love for him had changed.

"Well...I..." she started slowly, wanting her words to be precise without revealing unnecessary details. "I suppose, no matter what happened between us, that it was inevitable I tell you this someday."

Matt had no idea what secret Jillian was about to share with him; he wasn't sure he wanted to know.

Jillian continued, "I didn't really want to tell you, because... well, it hurts, and somehow I feel it's a betrayal of Bryan."

"Jillian, if you don't want to..."

"Oh no. I have to tell you, Matt. After I do, you'll understand." She inhaled deeply, propped her feet on the coffee table, and began. "The day Molly was born was an exciting one, of course. My due date was still two weeks away, and the boys had come generally on time, so I had planned to take it easy, maybe take the boys to the park. Bryan had worked the night shift and called at seven that morning to tell me he had to work late to take care of some training. He was one of the best and was always being asked to train new officers. I just rolled over to go back to sleep. About fifteen minutes later I woke up suddenly, feeling like I really needed to go to the bathroom. When I stood up, blood gushed everywhere. It was not my water breaking, mind you. It was blood, and as a nurse, I knew right away that my placenta was separating from the wall of my uterus. I tried not to panic, but I was there alone with the boys. I thought, *Only if Bryan had been able to come straight home.* I grabbed the phone and called the station. I didn't recognize the name of the officer who answered the phone. I'm sure I sounded distressed, and I could barely get the words out. I told him who I was and what was happening, and he immediately dispatched an ambulance, which, in hindsight, was the best thing to do, but I wanted to get a message to Bryan to meet us at the hospital. He just kept saying that Bryan was no longer on duty. I screamed into the phone that I knew he was off regular duty but was training a new officer. Finally I just screamed into the phone, 'I need my husband. Now get a message to Bryan Hamilton or else!' I guess I should be glad I didn't get arrested for threatening an officer." Jillian was beginning to feel woozy from lack of sleep.

Matt's somber expression did not change.

"Well, the next few moments, I called my friend Mona who lived two doors down. She had a key to our house, so she ran up just in time to let the paramedics in, and she took the boys home with her. The next thing I knew, literally, I was waking up in recovery. The doctor had performed an emergency C-section, and I had a precious six-pound, four-ounce baby girl. I lost a lot of blood. They had no choice but to do the surgery. But Molly was okay, and that was all that mattered."

"You never told me that."

"Well, I really never had the opportunity."

"Go on."

"So I felt really horrible. The anesthesia was still taking care of the pain, but I was so out of it and nauseated. It was a rather unpleasant experience, especially after having two normal deliveries with the boys. About noon, I was finally moved from recovery to my room on the floor. Bryan and the boys were waiting for me. Bryan kept saying how sorry he was that he hadn't got my message in time to be with me. I was just thankful that Molly and I were going to be okay. The outcome could have been very different."

Matt looked at her questioningly. He didn't understand what a C-section delivery had to do with him. Was she going to tell him she couldn't have more kids?

"I think I'm drawing this out too much. Let me summarize."

"It's okay. I'm wide awake."

"No, let me make it easy on both of us and make a long, sordid story a short, sordid one."

Matt closed his eyes; he was dreading going any further with this account.

"The officer was right. Bryan was off duty. The only training he was doing was not sanctioned by the department, but he was with a coworker. A young, pretty thing she was, and he was…well… they were involved sexually."

Matt's somber expression turned to one of loathing. "How could he do that to you? What a jerk! While you were pregnant?" Matt couldn't comprehend how Bryan could have cheated on Jillian. She was beautiful inside and out and such a great mother—and while she was pregnant. He shook his head back and forth indignantly.

Jillian didn't like the way this was proceeding. "I'm not telling you this to condemn my deceased husband. This is a story of redemption." Jillian spoke softly but sternly.

Matt felt ashamed—sort of. He certainly didn't want to hurt Jillian. He didn't know if it was his lack of sleep or the conversation, but he was feeling lightheaded.

"Do you want me to go on?"

"Might as well, but spare me the details, please."

"I'm trying." She paused to catch her breath. "I was released from the hospital two days later, and we went home with our little girl. We were so happy…or so I thought. Bryan had never explained what took him so long to get to the hospital the morning Molly was born. In hindsight, I realized he was vague about when he got my message and when he arrived at the hospital, but honestly, I never saw a reason to pursue it, until…" Jillian paused briefly, took another deep breath, and continued. "When Molly was two months old, I decided to take her and the boys down to the station one day to see Bryan. Jake, the officer who had answered the phone the morning Molly was born, the one I threatened, was at the front desk. When I introduced myself, he had this weird expression on his face, like he didn't know what to say, and I thought it was because I had been so rude to him that morning, and I started to apologize.

"He stopped me. 'Oh no, ma'am, you don't owe me an apology,' and then he added, 'I guess Officer Hamilton let you know he was off duty that morning and let me off the hook.' That made me feel strange. Bryan had never said anything about where he was when he got my message. To me, it was a strange comment, but I paid little attention to it. I didn't reply to Jake's remark, just smiled and told him we were there to see Bryan. He started to call back to his cubicle, and I told him it was okay, we were going to surprise him. That strange expression came back, and he just said, 'Okay.' So we went on back. Bryan looked more than surprised when he saw us. She…the one…was in his cubicle with him. Still, dumb me, didn't think anything about it. He was her training officer. Then, just sort of out of the blue, I told him what Jake had just said to me. I asked, 'Where were you that morning?' The color drained from his face, but it was her—I promised myself I would never say her name—it was her reaction that made the lightbulb turn on in my brain. It was almost as if she wanted me to find out. She said, 'Guess it's time for me to leave now,' and then she winked— she *winked*—at my husband and flounced out of the cubicle like she thought she was hot stuff." Jillian sighed. She was tired but wanted to finish her account and get it over with.

"Well, Bryan?' I asked him. The boys started climbing all over their dad, and he reached out for Molly. Officers in nearby cubicles saw us and came over to see Molly and the boys, and Bryan didn't respond. I felt a sick feeling in the pit of my stomach and knew in my heart this wasn't the place or time to get to the bottom of what was going on. All afternoon I replayed everything that had happened, repeatedly in my mind, and as soon as he walked in the door that evening, I confronted him. Bryan confessed almost immediately. I think he was tired of the sneaking around, the lying…and of her. At least he said he was. He took responsibility for his actions but blamed it on her 'seductiveness' and the close proximity involved in his training her. Calmly…I don't know how…but calmly, I asked him to leave. He begged me to forgive him…wanted to call our pastor and ask him to come over, but I wasn't ready for that. He did leave that night and stayed with one of his buddies. The next morning he went to his commanding officer and told him that to save his marriage he could no longer work with 'the woman.' He didn't tell the whole story though; his job would have been on the line, and that would have made things even worse for us—no income or insurance. The department gossip was that I was a jealous wife who didn't want her husband training pretty, young women. Funny, isn't it. I had always trusted him. So while he was asking for a new partner at work, a male partner, I was at my OB-GYN being tested for STDs. Thank God, all the tests came back negative. He had insisted he always used protection, but I didn't trust him, and just hearing that admission…that he had obviously planned their encounters…was sickening to me."

"And you still took him back?" Matt was hoping the answer was no even if that meant she had previously misled him. At least he wouldn't have to live up to her example.

"Oh, yes. It was the hardest thing I've ever done. We lived apart six months. I sought advice and counseling, which presented me with many options. My best friend suggested 'getting rid of the jerk and taking all his money,' not that he had any to spare. I never told my parents. They had spent two weeks with us after Molly was born and had gone back home to prepare for their move to India. I knew what they would say: 'marriage is till death do you part.' Bryan and I went to a marriage counselor that was covered by his insurance. He was much too secular for me, even suggesting "an affair can be healthy for a marriage." Right, like cancer. Oh, sorry, bad choice of words." Jillian did not intend the indirect reference to Shannon. "I read my Bible, read books, Googled *adultery*, which by the way, I don't recommend..." They shared a half-hearted smile before she continued. "Caleb and Joshua were fine. They were used to their Daddy working weird hours and probably saw him as much if not more than they had when we were together. He made a point of spending as much time with them as he could, but when he came over, I would leave the room. I don't know if this was a good decision or not, but we continued going to church together. I was too embarrassed to have the entire congregation know, but we were honest with a few close friends and our pastor. After giving up on the first counselor—we were not getting anywhere—Bryan begged me to go with him to our pastor for counseling. Reluctantly, I agreed. Our pastor's wife also attended the sessions, and I really appreciated that. In fact, it was something she told me that eventually convinced me to agree to try and restore our marriage. In one session, I was really struggling with what I should do. I told them that many sources, even Christian sources, stated that because of Bryan's adultery, I had scriptural grounds for divorce. I asked their opinion. His wife answered, and I'll never forget her words. 'Jillian, there are Scriptures that are used to support that belief. The Bible also states clearly that God hates divorce. Because Bryan committed adultery, you may come to the conclusion that you have scriptural grounds for divorce, but I can tell you without a doubt, that you have better scriptural grounds for forgiveness.'"

Matt threw his hands up to his face and massaged his forehead as if to expunge a bad headache. Jillian could hear the muffled groans he was attempting to suppress. She took a deep breath and continued, "When she spoke those words audibly, well, God immediately confirmed those same words in my heart. I knew from that moment that the only right thing to do was to forgive Bryan and let him come back home. But it didn't happen right away."

"Thank God," Matt interrupted.

Ignoring the remark, Jillian resumed, "We continued with counseling, together and individually. After six months apart, there were a few times when we were together when I began to feel just an inkling of what I had once felt for Bryan. There was certainly no romantic love—sometimes I still couldn't stand the sight of him. But as my Grammy used to say, 'It's not the love that holds the marriage together. It's the marriage that holds the love together.' So I prayed and prayed that God would give me the desire to restore our marriage, and our pastor referred us to a Christian marriage counselor. One day, after a counseling session—now we hadn't touched the entire time we had been separated because I would not allow it—but just out of nowhere, I had a desire to kiss him. Just a peck on the cheek was all I wanted, and I asked his permission. He seemed elated. I reached up and was going to give him just a touch with my lips but I lingered a few seconds...no hands...no other part of our bodies was touching...just my lips barely against his cheek. Then I felt something wet and warm on my face. He was crying. I pulled away. But after that, I didn't dread the thought of touching him so much.

"Are you too tired to continue?" she asked as Matt gazed into her eyes. "I think your eyes are fixed."

"I'm exhausted, but go on."

"So we did some of these touchy-feely exercises recommended in a book the counselor gave us, and about a month later, I told Bryan he could come home, but we would have to take it slow.

The first two months we were more like roommates than husband and wife. Gradually, the touching increased, and one night I thought I was ready to reconsummate our marriage."

"And?"

"And I threw-up."

"All right!" Matt obviously enjoyed that revelation.

"Well, it wasn't on purpose. It just made me physically sick. Gradually, I overcame those feelings. Learning to love him physically again was emotionally agonizing. But I can honestly say that the last two years we had together before Bryan died were good years. The first year after he moved back home was extremely challenging, more so than I had imagined. It wasn't easy to let go of the hurt and bitterness. Trust me, it did not happen overnight. There were setbacks when I almost gave up. Maybe it's true that time does heal, or at least lessens the pain. When Bryan died, I felt an incredible sense of loss. I will always be indebted to God for allowing us to reconcile our marriage. It would have been unbearable if we had been estranged when he died."

Matt sat motionless except for his twiddling thumbs. "Anything else?" he asked, knowing his mind could not comprehend another thought until he had some sleep.

"That's all…for now," she whispered.

Jillian put her arm around his waist and walked him to the door. Before opening the door, Matt turned to her, placing his lips softly against her forehead. "Later," he mumbled before heading home.

Exhausted, Jillian fell asleep as soon as her head hit the pillow.

Exhausted, Matt tossed and turned for the next hour before deciding to take a Tylenol PM. Fifteen minutes later he was, gratefully, dead to his chaotic world.

Chapter 28

Where Do We Go from Here?

Dear Jesus, help me get through this. Lead me. Speak to Matt's heart; help us both to do what is right.

Jillian whispered her urgent plea, then looked at the clock. Nine o'clock. She lay quietly but didn't hear a sound coming from the kids' rooms. She wanted to curl up under the covers and go back to sleep but knew her mind would be too busy to let her body rest. Instead, she threw the covers back and lithely jumped out of bed, not giving herself an opportunity for second thoughts. A long hot shower helped. She figured that altogether, before and after Matt's visit, she had slept about five hours and knew she could manage on that for a little while. She pulled on her fuzzy lounging pajamas. Tiptoeing down the hall, she hoped the kids would sleep just a while longer so she could have some quiet time. After putting a kettle of water on the stove to make a pot of tea, she opened her Bible, reading in Psalms. Good, encouraging words, but no direct answer to her situation.

Show me, God. Please show me what to do now, was the prayer of her lips and her heart.

"Good morning, Mommy!" Molly had slipped quietly into the kitchen. "I'm hungry."

"Me too! Go wake up your brothers, and I'll throw together some breakfast for us."

Jillian opened the refrigerator, surveying the contents. She pulled out a tube of cinnamon rolls. Jillian's mind flashed back to one of the last breakfasts she and the kids had shared with Bryan before he died. She had planned cinnamon rolls that morning, but Bryan asked her for eggs and bacon to go with them.

"I need a he-man breakfast!" he had teased.

She had complied. She could still see him cutting a cinnamon roll in half and stuffing it with eggs and bacon before gulping it down. The kids laughed at their dad's strange concoction, but when he made another one and gave them each a bite, they clamored for more. Smiling at the memory, Jillian reached in the fridge for the microwavable bacon and a carton of eggs.

"We haven't had these in a long time!" Joshua exclaimed as he took a big bite of his egg and bacon cinnamon roll. "It's good."

Caleb and Molly hungrily agreed.

Jillian had just completed the after-breakfast cleanup when the doorbell rang. She assumed it was Matt although she had really expected him to sleep in. Their New Year's Day church service would not be held until two this afternoon. Quickly drying her hands on a dishtowel, she responded and flung open the door.

"Good morning!"

Jillian was rendered speechless as she stared into Shannon's flashing blue eyes.

Or Be Reconciled

"Mrs. Hamilton, don't you have a key to our house?" Aiden asked as he stepped out from behind his mother.

"Oh, hi, Aiden," Jillian stammered.

"You do, don't you?" Aiden asked again.

Recovering from the shock, Jillian tried to reply nonchalantly. After all, there's nothing wrong with neighbors exchanging extra keys for 'emergencies,' she reasoned. "Oh yes, there's one here somewhere. Come on in while I find it."

"We rang the bell at least five times, but Matt didn't come to the door, and I know he's there because his car is in the driveway," Shannon explained with a hint of concern or irritation in her voice.

Jillian started to say that he had been up all night but thought better. "Sometimes he runs early in the morning," she offered instead, seriously doubting he was running this early after going to bed at five in the morning.

"Hey, Aiden!" Caleb had heard their voices and returned from his room where he and Joshua had gone to play after breakfast. "Mom, can Aiden come over and play?"

"Oh, that's sweet," Shannon oozed. "I'm sure he'd love that."

Whoa, wait a minute, Jillian thought. *Sure, you'd love to have the key to Matt's house and leave your kid here.*

Somehow, she kept her wits about her and addressed her reply to Aiden. "Gee, I'm sorry Aiden, but we have some things we need to do before we get ready for church." Then she turned to Caleb. "Besides, I'm sure Aiden wants to spend as much time with his mom as he can since he doesn't get to see her often." She smiled a saccharin smile at Shannon, who didn't seem to pick up on Jillian's sarcasm.

"You're right. I'm sorry. Don't know what I was thinking," Shannon responded kindly, and apparently sincerely, an attitude that surprised Jillian.

Jillian took the key from the kitchen drawer where she had stashed it. She had forgotten that Matt had put it on a key ring he bought for her: "When I'm sick, I want you for my nurse!" the engraved message announced. She almost removed it, then decided not to bother. Shannon didn't even look at the key ring as she stuck it in the pocket of her fake white fur jacket. Her golden tresses spilled out over the collar. Jillian could not help but notice Shannon's beauty. She wondered how cancer would change her looks.

"See you later, Aiden," Caleb said, disappointed.

Aiden barely waved.

Jillian had second thoughts about just handing over the key; she wouldn't have considered it had Aiden not been with his mom. "Don't you think you should call first?" Jillian questioned as they walked toward the door.

"We tried…no answer. It'll be okay. He won't mind." The heels of Shannon's knee-high leather boots clicked on the oak floor. "Thanks so much, Jillian." She smiled a bright white smile as she walked out the door.

Jillian had opened up her prayer journal and was praying through her list, trying to focus on the names and the needs instead of what was taking place next door, when the doorbell rang once again. Shannon hadn't been gone five minutes. She jumped up from her chair, almost knocking over her third cup of tea in the process. This time she peeked out the window before opening the door.

It was Matt!

He saw her and mouthed, "Hurry!"

Unlike the last time he visited, she rushed to the door. "Everything okay?" she probed as she let him in.

He wrapped her in a bear hug without responding.

"I didn't know what to do about the key." She felt she owed him an apology although he didn't seem to be annoyed.

Or Be Reconciled

"That's okay. I'm sure Shannon didn't give you a choice."

"Actually she was very nice about it."

"Yeah, right. Well, at least she let Aiden come in and wake me up. Can you believe she wanted me to go out to brunch with them?"

"I'm sure Aiden would have liked that."

"Don't go trying to make me feel guilty now."

"I wasn't. I'm glad you didn't go," she started to put her arm around his waist but instead, barely touched his cheek with the fingertips of her right hand.

He responded by taking her hand in his and pulling it up to his lips, gently nuzzling the back of her hand. "Yeah, me too. Man, I was finally sleeping soundly, but I am still dog-tired. May I borrow a bed for a few hours? I want to go to church with you and the kids, but I really need some more sleep." Matt was clutching his king-sized pillow under his arm.

"You can borrow my bed, Mista' Morgan." Molly had slipped into the room unnoticed.

"Well, thank you, Molly. Is that okay with your Mom?"

"If you don't mind princess sheets and a ruffled comforter," Jillian responded as Molly looked on, giggling.

"Sounds great to me! Could you wake me up about one so I'll have time to get ready for church?"

"Be glad to…but what about Shannon and Aiden?"

"She's cooking breakfast for him. Poor child," he added with a touch of cynicism. "I can still remember her flat, rubbery pancakes."

His comment made Jillian wonder if Matt had any pleasant memories of his life with Shannon, but she did not dwell on that possibility. "You better go crawl between those princess sheets before it's time for church."

She felt contented as he brushed his lips against her forehead, bent down to give Molly a hug, and ambled down the hall. He was hugging his pillow tightly to his chest, wishing it was Jillian.

Jillian asked the boys to play quietly in their room since Matt was "napping" in Molly's room, a scenario that both of the boys found interesting.

"I didn't know teachers took naps in the morning," Caleb wondered audibly.

Jillian almost confessed that she and the teacher had been up all night but caught herself in time to avoid a long drawn-out explanation. Just after she and Molly made themselves comfortable on Jillian's bed, Molly asked for her new baby doll and some books to read. Jillian was glad to oblige; she jumped up and quietly slipped out the door to the room across the hall. She pecked at the closed door until she heard Matt respond. He was already stretched out under the covers, his sneakers and sweatshirt thrown casually on the floor beside the bed. He sat up just slightly, and she caught a glimpse of his bare chest. With a flirtatious grin on his face that showed off his adorable dimple, he motioned her to come over.

She contemplated the idea fleetingly. "I just need to get Molly's baby doll and some books." Her voice was just above a whisper.

"How disappointing," he returned as he lay back and pulled the pink, frilly covers over his head.

Has he forgotten all about our conversation last night? Jillian mused as she quickly gathered the doll and books. In spite of that conversation, even she couldn't deny the feelings bordering on desire, which she felt as she allowed herself a quick parting glance of Matt's form lying underneath the comforter.

Six books later, Molly slipped off into dreamland on Jillian's bed, the baby doll cuddled in her arms. Jillian considered joining her but decided she would feel better if she got up and expended a little energy. She didn't want to do anything noisy and wake Matt; that left few options. She surveyed her bookcase, pining for some light, take-my-mind-off-my-reality reading. Instead, her eyes came to rest on a thick navy-blue notebook. She immediately realized what it was and tried to avoid it but couldn't. She retrieved the heavy binder from the shelf, made herself comfortable in the corner upholstered wing chair, put her feet up on the ottoman and let the pages fall open where they may. "What the Bible Says about Remarriage after Divorce" was the title of the magazine article that presented itself. Her eyes were drawn to the bold script in the center of the page.

> And unto the married I command, yet not I, but the Lord, Let not the wife depart from her husband. But and if she depart, let her remain unmarried *or be reconciled* to her husband; and let not the husband put away his wife.
>
> 1 Corinthians 7:10–11

She leaned back and closed her eyes, remembering so clearly the day she had first come across that article and read that verse. During her separation from Bryan, she had sought every trace of information she could find about divorce from a Christian perspective and had found much of it contradictory. Some authors presented "an exception clause" that allowed divorce and remarriage when the guilty party had committed adultery as Bryan clearly had. Others declared that divorce, but not remarriage, was permitted. Some claimed there was no innocent party in a broken marriage; this concept had made her feel extremely guilty as if she had not been good enough in bed for Bryan or he would have never had an affair. Through counseling and much soul searching, she was able to work past those feelings of condemnation. However, the idea that marriage was a partnership, and if it ended in divorce, neither party was completely innocent or guilty was a hard pill for her to swallow. Eventually, she had concluded that the Bible was vague on the subject and that the many commentaries were just people's opinions, leaving her in a quandary as to what she should do. She asked God to show her "the writing on the wall."

Then she came across this article in a Christian magazine while waiting in Molly's pediatrician's office. She asked the receptionist if she could make a copy of the article, but when she handed it to her, the woman read the title and handed it back to her, saying, "Here, just take the magazine with you."

When she got home with it, she sat down with her laptop and had looked up that verse in every version of the Bible available. In essence, they all said the same thing: God commands a woman separated from her husband to remain single or be reconciled to her husband, and the husband is not to divorce his wife. At that point, she had not even thought about getting married again; marriage was a painful experience she didn't want to repeat. But being single with three kids, the rest of her life didn't offer much comfort either. That verse had spoken to her heart; she remembered the word *reconcile* seemed to throb in her brain until it was engraved. That word, as well as the pastor's wife's admonition concerning forgiveness were the two guiding principles that convinced her she had to try to rebuild her marriage. Now, that verse spoke to her in a new way. Shannon was seeking reconciliation with Matt, her former husband. Would Jillian stand in the way?

When she went to Molly's room to wake up Matt at one o'clock, she thought she had her emotions under control. She knocked repeatedly on the door and, when she didn't get a reply, opened it slowly. Without entering, she called Matt's name until he rolled over. "Time to get ready for church," she announced and closed the door.

A few minutes later, he staggered out, looking like he could still use a few hours' sleep. He stood directly in front of her as she finished cleaning up from the kids' lunch and, stretching his arms high into the air, growled an endearing yawn. Dropping his arms to his side, he then reached out for her left hand with his right one and traced around her ring finger. Pulling her hand to his lips, he kissed the place where a diamond, if centered on a platinum band, would be.

"The best-laid plans of Matt and men go astray…"

"Taking a little literary license there, are you?"

"I need you to do me a big favor," he implored, still caressing her hand with his kisses.

"What's that?" she responded tentatively, not sure she could comply with his request.

He must have seen the apprehension in her face. "Don't be afraid. It's not anything improper."

"I should hope not."

"I need you to go over to my house with me while I get ready for church."

"Oh, do you think that's necessary?" Jillian thought she would feel silly complying with Matt's request, even though she was glad he asked.

"Yes."

She expected him to offer some rationalization but was pleased with his straightforward answer.

"Okay. I'll need to bring the kids. It'll take us a few minutes to get ready."

"I can wait."

Jillian went to Matt's house with some apprehension but was not prepared for the chaos that followed. Almost as soon as they walked in the door, Shannon announced that she also wanted to go church, noting that her newfound Christianity gave her the desire to worship God.

Matt's response was one of derisive laughter, which caused Shannon to throw herself on the sofa as she burst into crocodile tears while all the kids looked on, traumatized. Jillian not so subtly began directing her kids toward the door. She stopped in her tracks when, remarkably, Shannon pulled herself together.

"You're right, Matt," she proclaimed through gulping sobs.

"I didn't say anything!" he asserted.

"Your laughter said a lot, and you are right. I have given you no reason to believe that I have changed, and many reasons for you to believe I couldn't change. So you go on to church together. I'm going back to Charlotte tonight. I should have never come here. I was just hoping and praying—"

Jillian regretted not leaving when she had the chance. The kids didn't understand what was happening, and she understood all too well. Matt was doing all he could to avoid Shannon's contrite demeanor. Aiden broke the silence with wails that tore at Jillian's heart.

"No, Mommy, no!" he cried. "Don't go, please don't go, you just got here. I love you, Mommy, don't go!" Aiden pleaded as he threw himself onto his sobbing mother.

Neither Jillian nor Matt could think of a feasible plan of action. It was Shannon who made the decision. She gently stroked Aiden's hair as he lay across her, still gulping. "Matt, go on to church with Jillian and the other children. I will stay with Aiden."

Matt turned to Jillian. "Give me a minute to change clothes."

"We'll wait in the car," Jillian somehow managed to respond as she jostled the kids out the door. She intended not to look back, but when she heard Shannon whisper, "I'm so sorry, Jillian," she felt compelled to respond.

Shannon was still holding her sobbing little boy tightly in her arms. Jillian discerned a repentant spirit. Having been taught long ago that the only appropriate answer to a sincere "I'm sorry" is a sincere "I forgive you," Jillian spoke the words softly. As she pulled the door to Matt's house closed, confusion and sadness tore at her heart.

Matt joined them in the car in what must have been record-breaking time for even a man to change clothes. Neither said much on the ride to church; several times she caught a glimpse of Matt shaking his head and mumbling. None of the children said a word. They arrived at church just as the service began, allowing them to escape awkward welcomes although there were the awkward glances from a few of their fellow worshippers. Cindy and David were singing "Love Never Fails" when Jillian noticed a distraction behind her. She turned ever so slightly and caught a glimpse of Shannon and Aiden slipping into a pew across the aisle. She hoped Matt had not seen them and assumed he didn't because he was sitting calmly beside her. *What were the other people in the congregation thinking?* Surely some of them realized who Shannon was since she was with Aiden. *What if Mrs. Wilson is here?* That thought struck dread in her heart. Jillian could only imagine, considering her past inappropriate remarks, what she would say if she realized Shannon was Matt's former wife. She tried to listen to Pastor Milkalski's sermon, but her mind was going crazy with speculation. *Oh Lord, please don't let him say anything about marriage or divorce,* she pleaded silently.

A half hour later, when the pastor concluded his message, Jillian had no idea what he had said; she presumed he had not mentioned *marriage* or *divorce* because surely either of those words would have broken into her thoughts.

"Please stand for the closing hymn."

She wanted to look behind her as everyone in the congregation stood to their feet, but she didn't dare. *Praise Father, Son, and Holy Ghost. Amen.* As she placed her hymnal in the rack on the back of the pew, she turned ever so slightly and saw an empty space in the pew where Shannon and Aiden had been sitting. Had it been an irrational figment of her imagination?

She was beginning to think so when Joshua reached over and nudged her. "Did you see Aiden and that woman sitting across from us?" he asked in amazement.

"Shh," she instructed Joshua but with a grateful smile for his having answered her unspoken question. Maybe she wasn't losing her mind after all. *But what am I losing?* That question was at the forefront of her mind as Jillian Hamilton looked apprehensively into the new year that was just beginning.

Chapter 29

Alone

Jesus, forgive me for making such a mess of things, not just my marriage, but last night. I don't know a whole lot about how to live this Christian life, and I need help to change and make up for everything I've done wrong, if it's not too late. Take care of Aiden. I love him so much. I want to be a good mom to him. Thank you that he still loves me. I know I don't deserve it, but if you could give me some time to make things right. I won't even ask you to make this cancer go away, but if I could just have some time with Aiden. I know it's probably too late for Matt and me to ever be together again. Take care of him anyway.

Shannon and Aiden left the New Year's Day church service as the congregation sang the closing hymn so they could have dinner together before she returned to Charlotte. Aiden cried when she brought him back to Matt's, but her promise that she would be back to see him soon gave some consolation. He did not really comprehend cancer, but she told him she needed to keep some doctors' appointments because she was sick and wanted to get better for him.

It was hard for Matt, feeling awkward around his own son. He tried to see the situation from Aiden's point of view, but his own intense dislike of Shannon, along with his feelings for Jillian and the plans he had for their future together presented a rather serious obstacle.

As soon as she got to the Charlotte city limits, Shannon pulled off the interstate at a Ramada for the night. She would worry tomorrow about where she was going to live. Tonight she just wanted to get some sleep so she could report to her job in the morning.

As soon as she arrived at the law firm, Shannon found out from Moriah, the receptionist, that her former boss had more surprises in store for her. Since the night she had knelt in the small village church and asked God to reveal himself to her, Shannon had refused to sleep with him until he married her, and once she left him to fly back to America, she knew in her heart she had no desire to be his wife. She was actually relieved when he dumped her. Immediately, her thoughts had turned to Matt. She understood that her chance for winning him back was remote; still she tried and failed.

"I'm sorry honey, your position has been filled. I thought Mr. Miller would have told you," Moriah gently informed her.

"No, Moriah. He told me I would still have my job. I guess his other promises were lies too." Shannon was beginning to sink into despair.

"Well, I know he did deposit a check for severance pay into your account, and he's taking care of your insurance for a while, and here is an envelope from the Ritz Carlton. He made reservations for you for this next week."

"A week? Then what will I do?" Shannon did not want to break down in tears in front of Moriah or her other former coworkers, but at that moment, she thought there was no alternative.

"Have you talked to Matt, honey?"

Just the sound of his name gave Shannon a glimmer of hope, but her tone was still skeptical. "Oh yes…I went to see him and Aiden for New Year's Eve. It didn't turn out the way I had prayed it would."

"Shannon, you know I don't like gossip, but honey, there's some rumors going around the office."

"I bet there are."

"Well, do you mind if I ask?"

"No, please, I'd like to have the opportunity to clear up any false accusations."

"Well, they're not exactly accusations, but the word going round is that while you and Mr. Miller were in Italy, you were diagnosed with breast cancer, and then you found religion?" Moriah ended her statement as a question.

"Well, what do you know? Office gossip that gets the facts straight!" Shannon actually smiled, albeit cynically, at this bit of information. "Yes, Moriah, I noticed some symptoms with my breasts and went to a doctor in Rome. I was diagnosed with early stage breast cancer, which is the excuse Mr. Miller used to send me back…so I could get 'the best medical treatment…' and yes, I stopped by a quaint little church one day and low and behold, I found God there! I'm sorry Moriah, I didn't mean to sound flippant. I did ask God to come into my life."

"Well, that's just wonderful, honey! I mean the God part, not the cancer part, but I'm sure God will take care of that for you.

You know, when you put your trust in him, he can do miracles for you!"

Shannon appreciated Moriah's exuberance but considered it somewhat out of place considering all she was facing. Moriah read her expression appropriately and toned down her discourse.

"Oh, Shannon dear, don't let ol' Moriah's pontificating bother you. In time, you'll learn how powerfully God can work in your life when you let him."

"Oh, what you said didn't bother me, Moriah. It's just…I guess all this believing and faith stuff is still so new to me."

"You're just a baby Christian, but you'll grow up."

An incoming call momentarily distracted Moriah. As she pushed the button to put the caller on hold, she once again directed her comments to Shannon. "Yes, you'll grow up if you don't give up! Now I better handle this call. It's been so good to see you. I always did think so much of you and Matt and your little Aiden. We'll have to get together for lunch sometime soon and reminisce."

"I'd like that, Moriah. Now let me go so you can get back to work."

"Take care, darling. God be with you."

Shannon knew, no matter what Matt or anyone else thought, that she had found God. So instead of going out for a few cocktails, as she would have after receiving bad news before, she checked in the hotel suite that had been reserved for her. She was surprised to see all her personal belongings from Mr. Miller's house stored in one of the rooms. Apprehensively, she dialed her mother's telephone number. It was the first time they had talked in weeks, and Shannon gave her all the sordid details of her breakup, job loss, and her diagnosis. After ranting and raving and cursing the former boss, her mother insisted that Shannon move into her condo with her while she was undergoing medical treatment. Being a breast cancer survivor herself, her mother dealt with this news nonchalantly, as if she had an abscessed tooth that would have to be pulled. Her reaction didn't surprise Shannon.

Shannon was most concerned about explaining her newfound religion to her mother. She didn't expect her to understand. Shannon visualized her laughing, just as Matt had done. Still, when she got the opportunity, she planned to tell her about her experience with God.

Lying on the king-sized bed, she prayed, *It's strange, God. The past few days have been terrible, and I don't have a job, and I have cancer. Yet somehow, I feel...I feel something in my heart I've never felt before. Is that what peace feels like?*

Her prayer was simple, childlike. She had so much to learn. No one had ever taught her about living a Christian life. Early in their marriage, Matt had wanted to take her to church, but she balked at the idea. Matt's parents took him to church through his teen years. Once he was out on his own, his attendance was hit-and-miss. Shannon had only attended church on holidays and believed religion was a crutch, certainly not something she needed in her life. If only she had gone to church with Matt. Maybe she would not have been swept away by her desires for pleasure and riches. She knew she had made a mess of her life. Was it too late to make amends? Aiden wanted her back, but Matt had a much better option, and she could not blame him. *Why would he want to take me back after what I did to him?*

The cinema of her mind started rolling once again, almost imperceptibly at first; then vivid, sordid scenes from the past flashed through her mind as if she was riding in a swiftly moving railcar. There she was, sitting on her boss's desk in a short skirt with her legs crossed, flirting. There she was, staying late at the office to catch up on work. She started feeling dirty and guilty, and shame enveloped her like an ominous cloud. She turned over on her stomach, burying her face in the luxury linen encasing the oversized pillow. She tried to stop the memories of her past sins playing out before her, but she could not. The peace she had felt

Or Be Reconciled

only moments earlier had taken flight. *I don't know if life is even worth living anymore*, was her last thought as she drifted off into an exhaustion-induced sleep.

Father, I just really feel a need to pray for Shannon right now. Jillian had excused herself abruptly from the table she was sharing with four coworkers in the cafeteria. She had no appetite for food or the conversation laden with curse words and descriptions of their disgusting New Year's Eve celebrations. Two of her coworkers were divorced and unhappily remarried. Another was single but lived with her significant other. The last was thrice divorced and advertised herself as "available." Their lives outside of work seemed to revolve around partying and drinking.

She had been thinking, *Doesn't anyone lead a normal married life anymore?*, when her mind was suddenly invaded with thoughts of Shannon. She felt an urgency to pray for her.

"Oh Jill, did we offend you, honey?" Chelsea had asked sarcastically.

"I just remembered something I have to do before going back to work," she had replied with a forced smile while heading toward the exit.

She hadn't heard Darcy, the single coworker, retort, "She probably has to go read her Bible," as the others laughed mockingly.

Jillian had entered the chapel as quietly as possible. No need. It was empty, as usual. She had slipped into the back pew before calling out to God on Shannon's behalf. *I don't know why or what she needs, but I have a heaviness in my heart for her. Dealing with a diagnosis of cancer is bad enough, but not having someone close to help you go through that…and she must really miss Aiden. Lord, I really don't know how to pray for her, but I know you love her and want what's best for her. Help her to feel your presence and take care of her.*

Shannon had often come to her mind, and even though Jillian tried to be open to the Lord's leading and pray for her, it was difficult to find the words. Jillian didn't want to pray for anything specific; she didn't want her own desires to interfere. She just wanted God to take care of Shannon in his way.

The remaining hours of her shift went by quickly; she kept busy with minor emergencies—cuts requiring stitches and a sprained ankle. Going back to work after a few days' vacation was always challenging. Combined with the emotional roller coaster she had ridden during the holidays, she couldn't remember when she was so thankful to see her second shift replacement walk through the double doors of the ED. She couldn't wait to get home to her kids.

Shannon slept for several hours and awoke feeling rested and peaceful. She decided to wait until the next morning to go to her mother's condo. She would need to find someone to help her move her things; they wouldn't fit into her convertible. Remembering the New Testament that the kind, elderly usher had given her at Matt's church last night, she pulled it out of her purse. She had no idea where to start. Opening it at random, she began to read the book of 1 Corinthians.

Matt couldn't wait for Jillian to get home. His first day back at school after vacation was a tough one. The students were rowdier than usual, and he admitted to himself that he was not giving the attention to his lesson plans that he needed to. If he wasn't organized, how could he expect the children to make their best effort? Being a single dad was another challenge. Even though Shannon and he both worked when they were married, she did halfheartedly fulfill her role as *homemaker*. He chuckled as he said that word to himself, remembering how she hated it along with *housewife*. She always insisted she was a *married career woman* and a *mother*. The *mother* title she didn't seem to mind, especially when it was acknowledged with the usual comment, "Oh, you look too good to have had a baby!" as if every woman who had given birth immediately turned into a frump.

An image crept into his subconscious: Shannon, tanned and toned, reclining on a blue velvet chaise, a baby shower gift from her mother. Her long golden tresses fell softly around her bare shoulders; she was wearing a white gown with tiny straps and a lace bodice. In her arms she held a bundle of joy, a newborn baby boy with a wisp of blonde hair, wrapped in a snug white blanket. Matt tried to stop the image, but it lingered, just a second longer. The woman, the mother of his son, looked into his face, her blue eyes glistening as a tear of joy rolled over her left cheekbone and down her perfect face; he wiped it away with his right index finger. Violently, Matt shook his head, shutting down the scene he did not want to remember. "Yeah, some mother you were!" he spewed the words. They were uttered with such venom that Matt was immediately convicted of the hatred he held in his heart.

Chapter 30

Troubled

Lord, I'm a sorry excuse for a Christian man. I can't stand the sight of my ex-wife; but look what she did to me! I want to do what's right. I want my life to please you, but I am in such turmoil. I really believed you had sent Jillian into my life to make up for what——for what Shannon did to me. Jillian is such a wonderful woman and mother, and I know she would be a loving, faithful wife, what I need. Oh Lord, I don't know what I need. Coaching has become a chore. I can't concentrate, and I couldn't care less whether or not we win. Teaching is even worse. What do I have to teach these kids? My life is a mess. Where do I go from here?

Undoubtedly, Matt's pleas to God were earnest. He was not used to praying out loud. Jillian had often mentioned how she liked to pray by herself in her room, verbalizing her requests because it kept her focused. Recently, Matt had given it a try. At first it felt awkward, but he had begun to see how it made his prayer time more profitable than just thinking through his daily list, which was admittedly short and sweet: "Bless Aiden, bless Jillian and the kids, help me at work."

Last night, he yearned to spend the evening at Jillian's but ended up just seeing her for a few minutes when she got home from work. In fact, he caught her as she was getting out of her car.

"Hey, nosey neighbor, you know I don't like you to see me this way before I change and freshen up. Nursing is a physically demanding activity," Jillian had teasingly complained as he opened her car door.

"You look great to me!" Matt was totally sincere.

"Well, thank you, sir, but I feel grubby."

The kids spilled out of the car, eagerly surrounding Matt.

"I waved at you during fourth period today," came Joshua's plaintive greeting, "but you didn't wave back."

"I'm sorry, Joshua. If I had seen you I not only would have waved, but I would have gone over and slapped you on the back," Matt responded jovially as he reached for Josh's shoulders, turned him around, and gave him several playful whacks.

The smile on Joshua's face indicated the previous slight was forgiven. Caleb high-fived Matt, and Molly presented him with her usual leg hug.

"Okay, guys, go inside and start your homework. I'll be in in a few—"

"I don't have any homework!" Molly announced, pleased with herself.

"Then set the table for dinner. Go on, I'll be in soon," Jillian shooed them toward the front door.

"Ah, Mom, can't we stay out here with you?"

There was no verbal reply, just "the look" and the kids were on their way.

"Nice going, Mom," Matt complimented.

"They better do what they're told, especially after a long day at work."

"Rough day?"

"Not really…just that I…" she started to say "have this tremendous burden," then decided to keep her burden for Shannon to herself. "It's just everything that's going on."

"Yeah, I feel it too. I'd love to spend some time with you tonight." There was a sweet pleading in his voice.

"I'd like that too, but maybe we should just stay home tonight and rest up from the holidays."

Matt understood but was disappointed. "It's too bad holidays are such a drain."

"It's not the holidays as much as what happened during the holidays, you know, Shannon and all." There, she said it—her name—acknowledging that she too was thinking about the significance of Shannon's intrusion in their lives.

"Okay, if that's what you want."

Jillian thought he sounded so defeated. "You know, things have changed."

"Only if we let them."

"Do me a favor."

"Whatever you ask."

"You're brave."

"I trust you, and I love you."

Jillian didn't want to hear that. It made her request more difficult. "Matt, please pray and ask God to show you what he wants us to do."

Matt resigned himself. He had not yet fully realized how much Jesus loved him and that he wanted what was best for Matt and Jillian and Shannon.

"Yes, ma'am, if you insist."

"It's a request, not a demand. But isn't that what you want?"

"I want you, Jillian. I love you."

"Then pray for God's will, please."

Feeling dejected, Matt went home to Aiden and threw together supper, a frozen pizza and salad from a plastic bag. After they ate, he and Aiden played some video games before going to bed earlier than usual. Still feeling the effects from his New Year's Eve all-nighter with Jillian, he longed for sleep but only tossed and turned. At midnight, he fumbled through the medicine cabinet for a Tylenol PM. When the alarm went off at seven, he felt that he had hardly slept. Keeping the promise he had made to Jillian yesterday, he had begun to pray.

"Dad, who are you talking to?" Aiden peaked through the barely open door.

"Hey, good morning, son." He felt a little embarrassed. "I was praying. Guess you could say I was talking to God."

"Yeah, I do that sometimes too. Caleb told me his mom does it all the time. Do you think he answers quicker if we ask him out loud?"

Matt smiled at his son's childish faith. "Oh, I don't know about that, but I do believe he likes it when we talk to him."

"I hope so because I've been asking him to bring Mommy back home. She is going to be okay, isn't she, Daddy?"

Matt decided to avoid commenting on Aiden's prayer request and moved quickly to address his question.

"What did your mom tell you, son?" Matt wasn't sure how much detail Shannon had given Aiden.

"She said she was sick and was going to a special doctor that would make her better."

"That's what she told me too. So you need to pray for her."

"She is going to get better and come back home, isn't she? She's not going to die, is she?"

Matt paused to consider his reply. He realized that he had not given much thought to the possibility that Shannon might die. The doctor in Rome told her they had caught her cancer in an early stage. Her mother had breast cancer and recovered. He just assumed…

"Daddy, could she die?" Aiden was beginning to tear up.

"No, Aiden. She's sick and has to go to the doctor and get treatments, but she'll get better." He wanted to add, "That doesn't mean she'll come back. We're divorced, remember?" but decided that for now it was best to just reassure Aiden.

Aiden had put his arms around Matt and hugged him tightly. "I'm glad because I really miss Mommy."

Matt struggled through another day at school, finding it more difficult than ever before to keep his mind on the lessons he was suppose to be teaching and the sports teams he needed to coach. He seriously considered asking for a few days off, but they had just returned from Christmas vacation, and he didn't want to have to explain to his principal all that was going on in his life.

He would just try harder to concentrate at school, not allowing his mind to wander, and think and pray through his personal problems in the evening.

Jillian realized she was spending more time thinking about and praying for Shannon than Matt these days. She felt bad, turning down Matt two nights in a row when he had asked to see her, but she felt they needed to spend some time apart. Her feelings for him were still real and deep. Love. Yes, she loved Matt. He had been such a blessing to her since the second day her family had arrived in Lakeview. She believed that moving in next door to him was part of God's perfect plan for her life. She imagined how hard the last few months would have been without him. Now she was starting to wonder how hard the next few months would be because of him.

Chapter 31

Cancer

God, go with me today and help me. I love you.

Shannon rose early Tuesday morning and anxiously prepared for her first appointment at the cancer center. Her mother had insisted on going with her and picked her up at the hotel.

"Darling, you look wonderful! No one would ever know you have cancer," was her mother's unfortunate greeting, especially since it was loud and in earshot of several guests in the hotel lobby.

Shannon hugged her mother warmly, something neither of them were accustomed to doing. Shannon closed her eyes to avoid the stares of the guests whom she perceived must be looking at her with pity. Feeling her mother's resistance, she released her from the awkward embrace.

"Is that the way one is greeted in Europe?" Mrs. Stewart inquired, once again appearing to be asking her question to everyone in the lobby. It was her way of letting the others know her daughter had just returned from abroad.

In a more serene voice, Shannon replied, "It's the way a loving daughter greets her mother whom she has not seen in several months."

Mrs. Stewart laughed, almost mockingly. "Oh dear, that man did leave you in a sorry state, didn't he?"

How she wanted to say her actions had nothing to do with her former boss, that she was glad he was out of her life. She wanted to tell her mother about the new Man in her life, but she dared not mentioned her conversion experience…not yet.

The oncologist Mr. Miller had arranged for Shannon to see became unavailable at the last moment. Instead, the cancer center had assigned her to another doctor on staff. Shannon immediately liked this woman who was to provide her primary care during her treatment. In her mid-fifties, she was herself a cancer survivor and appeared very optimistic. Looking around her well-appointed office, Shannon saw some evidence that led her to believe her doctor was also a Christian.

"I love that framed Bible verse you have on the wall," Shannon gushed, momentarily forgetting her mother was sitting on the sofa behind her. Mrs. Stewart's ironic laughter drew a look of displeasure from Dr. Walker.

"Yes, that's one of my favorites. 'Delight yourself in the Lord, and he will give you the desires of your heart,'" she read from the plaque before turning back to her patient.

"What are the desires of your heart, Shannon?" The question was asked not intrusively, but with genuine interest.

"Well, I'd like to get better, but more than that I want to be reunited with my husband and son."

"Ex-husband, Shannon dear," Mrs. Stewart chortled from the sofa.

Dr. Walker glanced kindly, but not approvingly, at Maggie Stewart before addressing her response to Shannon. "Sounds as if you're facing more than one battle in your life just now. Let's get to know each other better and see how we can work together to help you win those battles. Mrs. Stewart, I'm so glad you came with your daughter this morning. It has been nice meeting you. Now if you'll please wait in the family lounge down the hall, I'll begin my examination of Shannon. We'll be doing several tests. It's going to take two or three hours."

"Several hours?" Maggie didn't want to sit in a waiting room all day.

"Feel free to leave and come back. Do you have a cell phone number where Shannon can reach you when we're almost through?" Dr. Miller was bothered that her patient's mother had complained about the wait. That was not a good sign that she would be a compassionate companion during a long and often arduous process.

"Shannon, I wish you had told me it was going to take all day."

"I'm sorry, Mother, I didn't know. This is all new to me." Shannon didn't turn around to see the expression of what she knew would be annoyance on her mother's face. She kept her eyes focused on the framed scripture as Dr. Walker rose from her chair, walked to the door, and opened it for Mrs. Stewart.

"I'll remind Shannon to call you," the doctor smiled charmingly as she swept her hand in the direction of the waiting area.

Reluctantly, Shannon's mother rose from the sofa, and for a second, Dr. Walker thought she might balk at being asked to leave. Instead, she smugly rolled her eyes and strode confidently from the room.

Three hours later, Shannon felt physically depleted but emotionally buoyed as Dr. Walker completed the thorough examination and what seemed like a thousand questions. Dr. Walker had mentioned the Scripture on the wall again, giving Shannon the opportunity to disclose to her that she had recently become a Christian. Responding with genuine joy, the doctor noted that she had become a Christian at a youth camp when she was a teenager and that soon afterward she felt God's call to the medical field.

"You must have delighted yourself in the Lord, then, because he gave you what you wanted." Shannon marveled at the possibilities.

"I've come to believe it all works together. When you delight in God, then his desires for you become your own desires for yourself. When you seek him with all your heart, you are not going to want something that he doesn't want. Does that make sense?"

"Yes, I guess so. I really don't know a lot about God or the Bible. We only went to church on holidays. It was only after I found out that I had cancer that I went to a church to pray. It was like I heard God's voice calling me. Is that crazy?"

"No, not at all. God does call out to us. He wants us to come to him. And often, he allows circumstances in our life to get us to the place where we do seek him." She pulled a business card out of her desk drawer and handed it to Shannon. "This is where I go to church. Why don't you visit us next Sunday? I think you'll like it there."

"Thanks," Shannon replied as she carefully placed the card in her purse. "I didn't know where to start looking for a church, but I do want to know more about being a Christian."

"We have a class that meets in the evenings for new Christians. Maybe you'd be interested in that."

"I have so much to learn. First I need to tell my mother I'm a Christian, and I know she's going to think it's just a crutch because I have cancer."

"Only you can show her that it's more than that."

"I'm going to try."

Dr. Walker stood and extended her hand. "It's been good talking to you. Stop at the reception desk, and Kendra will make you an appointment for next Monday. I should have all the results from your tests then, and we will discuss your treatment options."

"Okay," Shannon replied with a sigh. "Thank you so much for everything."

"See you Monday. I'll keep you in my prayers."

Awesome! Shannon exclaimed under her breath. *God gave me a doctor that's going to pray for me.*

Chapter 32

Letting Go

Thank you, Lord, for Saturdays! And thank you for helping me make it through this week. It wasn't an easy one, but you were there with me. I could feel your presence and your peace. Take care of my precious children and lead them in your way. Bless Mom and Dad and the Hamiltons. Be with Shannon and bring healing to her body. Watch over Aiden, and, Lord, please speak your will to Matt. Let him know the plans you have for him and help him to walk in them. I love you, Lord. Amen

Somehow, Jillian had avoided all but a few casual conversations with Matt this week. Every time he wanted to get together, she had produced a legitimate excuse, but she knew she could not continue to avoid him. It wasn't fair to Matt, and being distant was draining her emotionally. She just wasn't quite ready to deal with all that was happening. Once in a while, a wistful daydream raced through her mind: she and Matt and the kids, hand in hand, running and playing at the park—a happy family. Always, she would straightaway dismiss it, but it took a great deal of willpower. When the vision appeared yesterday while she was having lunch in the hospital soda shop, an idea popped into her head. She tried it. She closed her eyes and consciously imagined Matt and Aiden…and Shannon, holding hands, walking along the lake, talking and laughing. She decided she would use this vision to counteract the former one.

Matt woke up and lay in bed thinking. He too was thankful for Saturdays: no school, no obnoxious students who could not care less whether or not they were learning. He was thankful that Jillian was also off on Saturdays. He just knew she would want to make up for their not seeing each other this week and planned to invite her and the kids to go out with him and Aiden tonight. He loved Jillian and had missed being with her. Occasionally, Shannon's beautiful face would flash across the screen of his mind, and he would quickly say a prayer that her cancer treatment would be successful. His motivation was not pure; if she no longer had cancer, he would not feel guilty about refusing to take her back. In his way of thinking, once she was well, she wouldn't want him back anyway.

Shannon had slept surprisingly well at her mother's condo. Now she lounged in bed, picking from the breakfast tray the housekeeper had brought her. She sipped the pomegranate juice and smeared a tad of nonfat cream cheese on the whole wheat bagel. She was impressed that her mother had obviously instructed Lauren, the housekeeper, to prepare her meals from the dietary list Dr. Walker had provided. Her mother had never been one to express love physically, but when it came to practical or material ways, she did put forth an effort. Shannon had checked Dr. Walker's church out on its website and was eagerly looking forward to attending in the morning. She had decided not to tell her mother; instead she would use the excuse that she wanted to walk and get some fresh air. Dr. Walker had also recommended light exercise. She wasn't ready yet for her mother's inevitable ridicule.

Matt was elated and relieved when Jillian accepted his invitation for dinner. They agreed on a family-friendly Mexican restaurant. He and Aiden spent the day completing a few household chores and watching basketball on television.

Jillian knew she couldn't say no to Matt's invitation, but she felt uncomfortable continuing their previous involvement. She didn't want to but knew deep in her heart that inevitably they would have to alter their relationship. It was the middle of the afternoon and she had just finished folding a load of laundry when the doorbell sounded.

"Mrs. Wilson!" She knew her voice betrayed too much surprise, but this was the first time her Sunday school teacher had ever visited her at home. "Come in, please."

"I thought about calling first, Jillian, but to tell you the truth I was afraid you might say you were busy and I cannot put this off another day." Mrs. Wilson's voice betrayed an urgency that frightened Jillian.

"What's wrong, Mrs. Wilson?" she asked, expecting her to deliver some bad news.

"I need to talk to you, dear. I have been so unfair to you, even mean at times, and I need to make things right."

Jillian had no idea what was about to transpire and was unnerved by her teacher's bluntness. Yes, Mrs. Wilson had been rather inappropriate at times, but other than praying for her, Jillian had not given her words and actions a great deal of thought. Matters of greater importance were generally on her mind.

"Would you like some tea? We can sit at the table."

"No, thank you dear. This is not a social visit. But yes, let's sit at the table."

Jillian led the way to the eat-in kitchen and pulled out a chair for her guest. "Are you sure you wouldn't like something to drink?"

"A small glass of water will be fine…in case my mouth gets dry."

Wondering why Mrs. Wilson seemed uneasy, Jillian held a juice glass under the refrigerator dispenser. She sat the glass of water on a napkin in front of her unexpected guest. Mrs. Wilson took a sip, used the napkin to dab at her mouth, and then motioned Jillian to sit down. "I hope this is not too much of an inconvenience," she started. "But as I said, I just can't put this off."

Jillian tried to relax in the straight-backed wood chair, dreading whatever was about to transpire. *Well, maybe God is using her to show me what to do*, Jillian considered.

"I owe you an apology, oh I do, Jillian. I am so sorry for the way I have treated you and the awful things I have said. And that day I was praying for you and asked God out loud to keep you from adultery, I should have said that silently."

Jillian could only stare at her, mystified. Her base nature wanted to reply, "You shouldn't have prayed it at all," but she bit her tongue to stop the words. Before she could respond, her guest continued.

"I know there is no excuse for such actions, especially from your Sunday school teacher." She paused and lifted her eyes to

Jillian's face, attempting a strained smile. "But I do have an explanation, pitiful as it is. Would you like to hear it?"

Jillian was still confused. "Only if you want to tell me."

"It is not so much that I want to, but I have to so you will understand why I acted in such a deplorable manner. Not that it justifies me in any way, but maybe it will make it easier for you to forgive."

Jillian wanted to say she had not harbored ill feelings toward her but recognized that Mrs. Wilson's need to confess was authentic. "Go ahead."

"You know, my husband Charlie founded our church. We had only been married five years when we moved to Lakeview just to do that. Oh, he was a fine young minister, and I was so proud to be his wife. We had many happy years here, serving the people of this little community. There were a lot less people then of course. God gave us our two sons, and the church grew, and we were both so involved in ministry."

Jillian sat silently, still not understanding where Mrs. Wilson was going with this condensed life story. "Charlie loved the people, really loved them, and cared deeply about their needs. Zeb was one of our deacons, a wonderful man who supported Charlie without fail. He and his wife…his wife, Eunice…became our good friends and were always ready to lend a hand at the church. We became so close we even went on vacations together. Then Zeb was struck with Lou Gehrig's disease, a devastating illness, which took his life in less than a year. We always tried to be there for Zeb and Eunice, especially at the end when Zeb was in the hospital. They were about ten years younger than us, but Eunice, bless her heart, had always been doted on by Zeb and didn't even know how to drive. So Charlie would drive her back and forth to the hospital and help her with errands."

Uh-oh, Jillian thought. Her throat tightened, and she had a revelation of where Mrs. Wilson's story might be going.

"After Zeb died, Charlie continued to help out Eunice occasionally, and I did too. It just seemed the things she needed were things that Charlie could do, little repairs around the house and such, and she still didn't have her driver's license."

She paused and looked away as if recalling something from long ago. Jillian could not help but notice the tears forming in her eyes. Jillian sat, quietly waiting.

Mrs. Wilson sucked on her bottom lip, making a clucking noise when she stopped. She took a sip of water, and after a long, deep, sigh, she continued. "Charlie came home one Saturday night after spending a few hours at her house doing some chores. I wasn't completely naïve. I had occasional thoughts but never dwelled on them. Anyway, his confession was not a complete surprise. I just did not expect him to want to leave me for her. I thought he would tell me he was sorry for being unfaithful, and I would forgive him, and we would go on. Instead he told me to sit down because we needed to talk. I refused, probably the first time I had ever refused to do what he wanted. I stood there, facing him, with my arms crossed in front of me. I was ready to reach out and hug him as soon as he said he was sorry, but he didn't say he was sorry. He said he was in love with her and was going to divorce me and marry her. I was dumbfounded. I will never know how I was able to keep my wits about me. I didn't cry. I didn't yell. I didn't move. I thought for a minute, and then the words just came out. 'Charlie, you are a man of God, and if this is what God is leading you to do, then I will not stand in your way.' Of course I was being sarcastic. We both knew God's word forbids adultery and that he hates divorce. For a second, I thought Charlie would be convicted, realize how wrong he was, beg forgiveness. But he said nothing…just turned around and walked out the door. The next day he called together the church board and resigned. He told them the whole sordid affair as if he was proud of himself. Eunice was an elegant woman, not frumpy like me. It was almost as if he was brainwashed by that Jezebel.

He told the board members he felt that Eunice needed him more than I did. Zeb and Eunice never had any children. Charlie said that I had our boys—they were fifteen and seventeen at the time—to take care of me."

The tears that had been welling up in her eyes now trickled down her cheeks. Jillian responded with tears of her own. She gently placed her left hand on Mrs. Wilson's clasped ones.

"You don't have to go on," Jillian consoled.

The spurned woman dabbed at her eyes with a tissue she had pulled from her purse. She finished off the glass of water she had been sipping. Jillian reached for it to refill. Mrs. Wilson placed her hand over the glass and shook her head.

"Just a few more minutes and I will be through. As if two teenage sons could take the place of a husband and they were losing their father as well. Charlie and Eunice planned to move to Florida—that's where Eunice grew up——and get married. He was surprised when I contested the divorce. I guess he thought I was too meek and mild for that…well, when he had a massive heart attack two months later, he was living with her but married to me. That's why I can call myself a widow even though my husband deserted me before he died. I did not dare suggest that was God's judgment on him although a few people in the church made comments to that effect."

Jillian wanted to say the right thing. "I'm so sorry, I didn't know."

"The people that were in the church when it happened have been real good about not talking about it. Since Charlie resigned the pastorate before running off with that woman, it wasn't the scandal it could have been otherwise, but it still took a toll on the boys."

"I wasn't even aware you had two sons. I've never heard you mention them."

"Mostly I just mention them in my prayers. Charlie Junior moved to San Francisco and is living a lifestyle I can't approve. Mark was married once but divorced her and moved to Canada to live with some woman he met on his computer—what is it they call it?"

"The Internet."

"Yes, whoever heard of such a way to meet? Well, I haven't seen either one of my sons in over five years, but they do call me on Mother's Day and such.

Jillian hung her head in sorrow. She could think of no words to say; recalling the reason for Mrs. Wilson's visit, she assured her, "I do forgive you for anything you said or did that was out of place, but honestly, Mrs. Wilson, I did not harbor any ill feelings toward you."

"Well, I'm glad to hear that, but I'm not so sure about your young male friend. I think it would be better if you pass on my apology to him. Don't feel like you have to give him all the details unless he wants to know. You see, Jillian, I just did not want you to be the other woman and cause a sordid affair like Eunice did."

Whew! That stung. This scorned woman certainly did have a way with her words. Jillian chose to overlook what she felt was a cheap shot, even though from Mrs. Wilson's perspective, it was probably well intended; but she did feel justified in ending the conversation.

Standing from her chair, she smiled at Mrs. Wilson and spoke in a clear, unwavering voice. "Thank you for coming by to clear this up. Now can we consider this situation resolved?"

"If that's okay with you."

"It's okay with me." Jillian hugged her teacher gently, thinking that she looked much older than her sixty-five years. *A broken heart can age a person as much as a diseased one*, she reasoned.

Mrs. Wilson had been without a husband for almost twenty years and had lost her sons as well. Silently, Jillian accompanied her to the door. Just as the wounded widow started to step across the threshold, Jillian felt an urge she could not resist.

"Mrs. Wilson, I'd like to pray for you." Without waiting for permission, Jillian took the older woman's hands gently in her own. "Heavenly Father, please heal Mrs. Wilson's broken heart. Remove all sadness, regret, and bitterness, and replace it with your peace and love, and Lord, we ask that you speak to her sons, Charlie and Mark, and bring them back to you. In the precious name of Jesus, amen."

"Thank you, dear."

"God bless you, Mrs. Wilson."

Chapter 33

The Kiss

Father, help me know what to say to Matt tonight. He has been hurt, and I don't want to hurt him more, but I know you're speaking to my heart and directing me to end this relationship. I realize now the love you placed in my heart for him was not meant to be a romantic love, but a godly love that will allow me to encourage him to seek you and your will for his life, and I understand now why you have so often led me to pray for Shannon. Thank you, Lord, for saving her. Help her to grow spiritually, and be with her as she receives treatment for cancer. I pray that you will bring healing to her body. Tonight's going to be difficult. Give me your words, and help Matt be open to your leading, Jesus. I love you. Amen

Jillian didn't feel the need to redo her hair or makeup. She wasn't going on a date, just out to dinner with a very good friend. She didn't even bother to change from the casual jeans and shirt she had been wearing all day.

Matt didn't seem to notice that she had not attempted to make herself presentable for him, but she was immediately aware that he had taken time to look his best for her. His hair was perfectly disheveled; he skipped shaving that morning, displaying just a trace of dark stubble. On several occasions, she had confided to him that she thought he looked his most appealing when he avoided his razor on the weekend. His khaki pants were creased, and his pressed shirt tucked in neatly beneath his open sport coat, and his scent—the aroma of his cologne wafted in the air even before he walked around the van to open the door for her. Gently, he bent over to buss her forehead. She wanted to stiffen, to pull away, but she couldn't. Instead, when he tenderly caressed her face in his hands, she looked into those dark brown eyes and flashed a bright smile, reflecting his own.

"I have really been looking forward to tonight. I've missed you so much," he whispered with his lips against her cheek.

Jillian melted. *Maybe she was wrong. Maybe Mrs. Wilson's rebuke had invaded sound reasoning. Maybe this relationship was right in God's eyes. Maybe…*

Matt obviously mistook her smiling silence for permission to further express his affection. His lips met hers with an undeniable passion. The kiss wasn't long. After all, the kids were in the van, and Mrs. Cecil was sitting on her front porch, watching gleefully. But it was intense. Not a kiss between friends, even good friends.

Jillian slipped into the passenger seat feeling a little dazed and very confused. She was glad the kids were already involved in conversation and hadn't noticed their public display of affection. Mrs. Cecil waved buoyantly as Matt backed the van out of the driveway, indicating she *had* seen the kiss and approved.

"How was your day?" Thankfully, Matt seemed to be back in casual mode.

"Good. How about yours?" Jillian could feel her pulse still racing—a result of the kiss.

"Uneventful. Hey, didn't I see that old lady from church leaving your house earlier?"

His question brought her back to earth. She did not want to be reminded about Mrs. Wilson or her sermonette; even so, she defended her visitor. "She's not that old lady, she's my Sunday school teacher," Jillian replied with mock ire.

"So what did your old lady Sunday School teacher have to say today?"

Jillian knew Matt had never cared much for Mrs. Wilson. Her actions and less-than-kind words at church had put him off. She had planned to relay to Matt the whole account of Mrs. Wilson's wayward husband as well as her apology. But that was before *the kiss*.

"Just a friendly visit," Jillian fibbed, rationalizing this wasn't the time or place to open up that can of worms.

Dinner with Matt and the kids was a pleasure. The children behaved well, the food was delicious, and Jillian felt contented with Matt at her side. *Maybe I should reconsider my feelings about this relationship*, she contemplated. *It feels so right.*

Chapter 34

Worse than Expected

Father, it is never easy to give a patient grim news, but this young woman is so broken and so alone, and she has just given her heart to you. Help me as I explain to her about the cancer that is ravaging her body. Lord, help me give her hope, and if it be your will, Jesus, please bring healing to her body.

Dr. Walker was not only an exceptional physician, she was also a compassionate one. She believed God had led her into the medical field to minister to the soul as well as the body. Still, she dreaded these occasions when she had to deliver a diagnosis worse than the patient had expected and lay out the treatment options—none particularly pleasant—that might not succeed.

"Dr. Walker, your nine o'clock is here for follow-up—Shannon Stewart," her receptionist announced over the intercom.

"Thank you, Kendra. Have her come on back to my office." Dr. Walker waited just inside the slightly opened door. When she heard footsteps outside, she opened the door fully and greeted her patient warmly. "Good morning, Shannon. Are you by yourself today?"

"My only option was Mother…and really, I'd rather be by myself."

"Sure, no problem. Here, please make yourself comfortable, in one of the chairs or the sofa, either is fine," Dr. Walker invited as she motioned toward the sitting area.

Shannon chose the leather wing back chair, sinking into its deep-cushioned seat as she stretched out her legs, crossing them comfortably at her ankles. "Thanks for inviting me to your church. Wow, it's a big church, but I really liked it. The singing was great, almost like a concert, and I loved the theater chairs instead of pews, not so churchy."

"So you checked it out yesterday?"

"Yes, the eleven o'clock service yesterday morning. I'm not much for early morning services. I'm sure I'll go back again sometime."

"Did you find out about the Bible study for new Christians?"

"Not yet, but I will when I can find my way around better. It was a little intimidating…I mean everyone was nice and all. I'm just not used to going to church yet."

"I'm sure you'll feel more comfortable with each passing week. How did you feel about the sermon Pastor Troxler preached?"

Shannon bit her lip and giggled. "Umm…not really sure. I mean…I'm sure he's a good preacher, it's just that it was like…a little beyond me." Her last phrase sounded as if she was asking a question. "But he said one thing I thought was interesting."

"And what was that?" Dr. Walker's intention was to allow Shannon to talk as much as possible about yesterday's sermon before she delivered the bad news.

"He said when he prepared to preach, the rule he always kept in mind was to make Jesus the hero of each of his sermons."

"That's a good rule to follow because Jesus was and is and always will be our hero."

"You sort of sound like a preacher yourself." Shannon meant her words as a compliment.

As she gracefully slipped into the striped upholstered chair across from Shannon, Dr. Walker smiled her approval. "I believe addressing spiritual health is as important, if not more so, as physical ailments. After all, we will all die one day, but our souls will live forever."

"That's one way of looking at it," Shannon acknowledged. This forever stuff was still new to her.

Dr. Walker breathed a final silent prayer before beginning. "Shannon, we need to discuss the results of your tests and what your options are."

Shannon's smile turned into an expression of concern. "It's not bad, is it, Dr. Walker? I mean my mom had cancer when she was my age, and even back then, she made a full recovery. The doctor said I was in an early stage."

Dr. Walker really disliked this part. "Dear, the malignancy in your breast appears to be a rapidly growing type."

Shannon thought she was going to throw up; her entire body felt limp, and she had to grip the arms of the chair tightly to keep from falling forward. Her expression turned to one of disbelief. Her heart was beating out of her chest. "Am I going to die soon?" she asked, feeling as every breath was a struggle.

"Shannon, I did not say anything about your dying. I said you need treatment, and we need to discuss your options. But first I want to explain what is happening in your body."

Shannon looked faint.

"Are you sure you're okay? Do you want me to call your mother to be with you?"

"No...no...no..." Shannon closed her eyes and leaned backward, as far as she could, into the deep upholstery. Her hands tightly gripped the arms of the chair.

"How about some cold water? Would you like a sip?"

"I think it would be better if you threw a large glass of it in my face." Shannon was actually trying to lighten up the atmosphere. It was smothering her. She lowered her head, bending her neck from side to side, then placed her face in both hands with her elbows on her knees. She looked so vulnerable.

"We can wait, Shannon, if this is too much..."

"No, it's not too much. It's just what I deserve. I'm a whore. Why shouldn't God strike me with breast cancer and let me die?"

"Shannon, you do have a lot to learn about God. He loves you. He's forgiven you for your sins. You are a new creation in Christ, and don't let anyone tell you otherwise."

"You know, I didn't turn to God until I was diagnosed with cancer. It was a crutch, wasn't it?" Shannon's mascara, mixed with her tears, formed what look like dirty water running down her face.

Dr. Walker handed her a tissue. "God uses many different circumstances to encourage a sinner to turn to him. He doesn't want anyone—no matter her past—to be lost. And, Shannon, when you say you are sorry, he really does forgive."

"But he doesn't forget, does he?" Shannon had never read more than ten chapters of the Bible. She did indeed have a lot to learn.

"He forgets, too. The blood of Jesus has washed your sins away. The Bible says the repentant sinner is justified. That means *just as if you had never sinned*."

She shook her head, displacing her blonde strands, catching one of them in the stained tears on her cheek. Brushing it away with her left hand, she laughed pitifully. "Sure," she remarked unconvincingly. "But there are still consequences."

"Sometimes, there are natural consequences of sin." Dr. Walker spoke in a gentle yet assertive voice. "But breast cancer is not one of them."

Shannon had reached her saturation point. She couldn't take anymore. The tears spilled over her cheeks like a waterfall, and her cry was mournful.

Dr. Walker knelt in front of her and held her hands in her own. Softly she whispered the name, the only name that could help in this situation.

"Jesus, speak to Shannon's heart and let her know that even in this difficult time, you are with her."

As Dr. Walker prayed those hopeful words, she knew that Shannon was indeed about to endure the most difficult time of her young life.

Chapter 35

Breaking the News

Lord, I do love you so. You are so faithful. Thank you for my family—my family to be—and for Mom and Dad.

Oops! Jillian considered she shouldn't have mentioned her parents in prayer this morning. It reminded her she had to tell them soon. She wished she wasn't so apprehensive about sharing her good news. "Help me to explain…uh…tell…uh…oh, help Mom and Dad to understand that Matt and I are in love and that we belong together."

Why was it so hard to contemplate telling them? Hadn't she prayed and prayed about Matt's proposal and was convinced it was okay to accept—well not just okay—it's the right thing to do. *Maybe not God's perfect will, but surely his permissive will,* she had rationalized, knowing in her heart that God's will was God's will. Period. She had done a good job of convincing herself that marrying Matt was God's will for her.

She looked at the sparkling gem on her ring finger, holding up her hand to catch the rays of sunshine flowing through her bedroom window on this late winter morning. The ringing of the telephone called her from her reverie.

"Oood-de-shu," the female voice on the caller ID announced.

Who in the world? She asked herself as she reached for the receiver. She had hoped it was Matt, calling to wish her a good morning.

"Hello…hello…anyone there?" She thought she heard a voice, but it was overcome by static.

"Jillian—*static*—honey—*static*—is that you?"

The sound of her mom's voice alarmed her. They had agreed to make telephone calls only in the case of an emergency. "Mom! Mom, are you okay? Is Dad okay?"

It had been months since she had received a phone call from her parents. They kept in touch with weekly e-mails when her parents were able to travel to a village that provided Internet access.

"Yes, darling, we're fine. I just wanted to hear your voice. It's been so long."

"Yes, it has. Thank God for e-mail, or I don't think I could stand to be away from you and Dad."

"You're going to make me cry, Jillian. I miss you so much!"

"Mom, what's wrong with you? You're not usually like this."

"I don't know, Jillian. I've just been thinking about you a lot, and…well…I try not to, but I've been worried about you. Sometimes I feel your dad and I need to hop on the first jet out of Bhubaneswar and come home to you and our grandkids."

"Mom, are you crying?"

"Yes, dear, I am. Here's your dad."

"Hi, daughter!" At least her father sounded like his usual, cheerful self.

"Dad, is Mom really okay? What's wrong?"

"Actually, everything is going really well here with the ministry. The children in the orphanage are thriving. We keep busy. But we do miss you and our grandkids."

"Oh, Dad, I know, but God called you there. Do you doubt his call?" As much as she loved and missed her parents, now would not be the best time for them to return home.

"Not at all. But we still love and miss you."

"And we love and miss you…so much."

"It's been so long. If we had only known Bryan…"

"Dad, God knew Bryan was going to die, and he still directed you to go to India. God is taking care of the kids and me. Actually, we're doing very well."

"I'm so glad to hear that, honey. I've always believed that God would take care of you. Sometimes we get pretty sad when we look at the kids' pictures and read their letters, realizing they are growing up so quickly, and we've barely seen them."

"And what about those two hundred orphans you take care of? What would have happened to them? Dad, we'll have all eternity together. You always told me to put God first."

"Now who's preaching to whom?"

"I'm not preaching. I'm trying to reassure you. The children and I are getting along just fine. Our friends at church…and our neighbors"—Jillian considered adding neighbors would add honesty without specificity—"have been so good to us. You would be proud of your grandkids if you could see how well they have adjusted."

"I guess that's what your mother needs to hear. She's just had a heavy burden for you lately, and she's been praying for you and missing you."

"Dad…" Jillian had an idea of what may have sparked her mom's worry and this telephone call, "…has Mr. or Mrs. Hamilton contacted you?"

"We still receive donations from them every month, but no direct correspondence. Why?"

"Just wondering." Ever since the Christmas visit from her in-laws, Jillian had supposed it was just a matter of time until Elizabeth found a way to mention Joshua's *boyfriend* comment to her parents.

"Is there something you need to tell us, Jillian?" Her dad had always known when she was not revealing the rest of the story.

She wanted to wait to break the news. She was not prepared. She wanted Matt to be with her. "Put Mom back on the phone please." *Well, at least Matt will be pleased that I've finally told my parents about him.* She inhaled once, slowly and deliberately, then pursed her lips and blew out the carbon dioxide as if she were blowing out the candles on a birthday cake.

"Mom, I'm fine. I'm good. In fact, I'm great. I'm engaged."

"You're what! Oh Jillian, when did this happen?" Jillian couldn't read her mother's tone. Surprise? Happiness? Concern?

"Last month on Valentine's Day. He proposed to the kids and me. He's a Christian, our next-door neighbor, a teacher and coach at the kids' school. He loves me, and we want to spend the rest of our lives together."

"Why haven't you told me? You haven't even mentioned…oh my, what's his name?"

"His name is Matthew Morgan, and I was waiting to know for sure. You're so far away. I wanted to make sure before I told you."

"Are you planning to get married soon? Your Dad and I will want to be there."

"We haven't decided. Of course, we were going to talk to you first. If you were here, I'm sure he would have asked for your blessing, but since you're halfway around the world, he asked Joshua and Caleb and Molly for my hand in marriage. It was so sweet, and of course they said yes. They love him too."

"Well maybe that's why I've had a burden. Just praying that God would give you direction."

"And he has, Mom. I am so happy. Let me tell Dad the good news."

"Oh, he's listening. He wants to congratulate you. Here, I'll give him the phone." There was more static, and for a few seconds she could barely hear her dad.

"Jillian, honey, I do wish you had kept us informed. Why didn't you?"

"I'm sorry, Dad. Like I told Mom, I wanted to be sure, and Matt and I wanted to be together when we told you. We were making arrangements to Skype you one night soon."

"Well, I'm a little surprised…but very happy for you…as long as you know he's the right man for you."

"I do, Dad. He's amazing." She was feeling the anxiety build and suspected what was sure to come next.

"Well, tell us about our son-in-law to be. How old is he?"

Beginning to feel agitated at the inevitable interrogation, she considered answering, "About the same age as you," but with the possibility of a spontaneous disconnect, decided that was not a good idea. "Well, actually he's two years younger than me. That makes him thirty-three."

"How did you find an available thirty-three-year-old?" Jillian knew what her dad was really asking: "How did you find a single—as in never before married—thirty-three-year-old man?"

The tension that made her mouth dry and her palms perspire was increasing with each passing second. "God is good!" she exuded into the phone.

"I mean…" her father continued, "is he single?"

"No, Dad, I'm engaged to a married man!" She concluded her jesting remark with a forced laugh, knowing exactly what her dad meant, but she was willing to buy time even if it meant being cynical about a serious subject.

"Jillian, you know what I mean. Has he been married before?"

She could just imagine the look on her mother's face as she listened in on the conversation, all tensed up, waiting for her answer. She didn't dare envision the look of anguish she was sure was on her father's face at this moment. She wanted to declare, *I am not a teenager; I am a big girl. I have three kids. And I want to marry this man.* Instead, she dropped the D bomb.

"He's divorced, Dad. His wife committed adultery and left him. He has a son Caleb's age. And we love each other." She spit the words out in a tone that was sure, bordering on arrogance.

"Hey, Jillian, I'm not judging, hon. I just want you to make sure…"

"Oh, I understand, Dad. You would never judge anyone based on their marital status." *Dear Lord,* she gasped under her breath. She knew speaking those words to her dad were akin to stabbing a dagger in his heart.

Pause. Static. Pause. She prayed their conversation hadn't ended that way. From halfway around the world, she heard her mom's trembling voice.

"Oh, Jillian, honey, I love you and want what's best for you and the children. Just make sure it is what God wants.

"Of course I will, Mom. Of course I will…I mean, I already have, Mom." As burning tears trickled down her face, she tried to convince herself.

The still of the next few seconds was shrill. At last, Jillian gathered her courage.

"Is Dad okay? I didn't mean to…" She regretted being so… hateful. Yes, that was the word. She had been hateful to her father.

"Jillian, you know what your dad has gone through with *this.*"

She didn't want to talk about *this* anymore. "Tell Dad I'm sorry." And then, because she could no longer bear to be a part of this conversation, "Mom, I think we're losing signal," she lied. "E-mail me when you can. I love you both." She hung up the phone and flung herself backwards, missing her pillows and hitting her head hard against the bedpost.

Jillian had not planned to start her Saturday morning this way, nor was this the way she had wanted to announce her engagement to her parents. Emotionally, she was utterly drained. She could not recall ever having such a discordant exchange with her parents. *What am I going to do?* she asked herself despairingly.

"Mom, Matt's at the door!" Joshua called from the family room.

"Just a minute. Tell him I'll be right there."

It was a struggle to get out of bed and to the bathroom. One glance in the mirror told her she looked as distraught as she felt. She brushed her teeth and splashed cold water on her face. Rummaging through the top drawer of her vanity, she pulled out a ponytail holder and used it to corral her straying hair. Tossing her pajamas on the floor, she struggled into her sports bra, then pulled on the sweatshirt and pants she had worn last night. She pulled open the bedroom door and ambled down the hallway. Matt was waiting at the other end.

"Good morning, my lovely wife-to-be!"

"What's good about it?" Jillian's trickle of tears became a cloudburst as she crumpled into Matt's waiting arms.

"What did I do to deserve this?" he asked, dumbfounded by her actions.

"It's…not…you," she stuttered between gulping sobs. "My parents called this morning. I told them about us."

"Uh-oh. I take it they're not thrilled."

Chapter 36

Things Are Not Always as They Seem

Lord, thank you for guiding the surgeon's hands. Now Shannon is in your hands. Take good care of her.

Dr. Walker had asked the best surgeon she knew to perform the double mastectomy. When she asked his permission to observe, he gladly obliged. Dr. Walker stood unobtrusively at the end of the operating table, praying silently throughout the two-hour procedure.

"Okay, let's get the dressing on and move this young lady to recovery," the surgeon had directed as soon as he meticulously secured the last suture. Being a reconstructive as well as a general surgeon, he took great care to leave minimal scarring even when the patient's prognosis was dire.

Or Be Reconciled

Three months of chemotherapy had proven ineffective in stopping the rapidly growing malignancy. However, the treatments had been effective in causing Shannon to lose every strand of her golden hair and turn her perfect fingernails into thick, ugly, malodorous protuberances.

Dr. Walker had been impressed by Shannon's stamina and coping mechanisms. Mrs. Stewart had stood by her daughter, offering all the compassion of which she was capable. A few times, her father had even accompanied her to appointments, but his manner was aloof and offered minimal comfort. Shannon was bold in proclaiming that her newfound Friend was the one who had seen her through the unimaginable ordeal she was enduring.

She had not wanted to frighten Aiden; she did not want to be a nuisance to Matt. Out of concern for their well-being, she lied when she called to talk to Aiden the last Sunday afternoon of January. Matt had answered the phone.

"Hi, Matt, this is Shannon. Look, if you don't mind, would you take care of Aiden for a couple of months and give me a chance to recuperate from my treatments? My doctor thinks the rest will do me good…and I just don't think I could cope with taking care of him just now. As soon as all's well, we'll talk about shared custody."

Matt was surprised and relieved that Shannon had not once mentioned a word about reconciliation once she returned to Charlotte. He assumed she and her boss were back together. He also decided he must have been right about Shannon's conversion experience being a ploy to win him back.

I would have been such a fool to even consider going back to her, he had frequently reminded himself. Still, he was surprised at the gentleness in her voice when she asked him to keep Aiden.

Evidently, she had not lied about having cancer, but she seemed upbeat about her prognosis.

This apparent turn of events had cleared the way for Matt to propose to Jillian. Now they were excitedly planning a late summer wedding.

Jillian's parents' first reaction to her "good news" had been cautious, at best. She regretted telling them on the phone in such a callous way, especially since she had succeeded in hurting her dad's feelings in the process. When she told Matt about the phone conversation, he encouraged her to get back in touch with her parents as soon as possible. She had been quick to e-mail an apology, which her mom and dad readily accepted. Although Jillian and Matt had exchanged many pleasant e-mails with her parents since, Jillian still felt there was a chasm between them—and not just the physical distance of almost twelve thousand miles.

Neither of Jillian's parents had asked any more questions about Matt's marital status, which she assumed they had accepted. Her parents assumed they would offend her—even alienate her—if they pursued the subject. Instead, they agreed to take their concerns to God and intercede for Jillian and Matt. They even prayed for Matt's former wife although they knew nothing about her except that she had left Matt for another man.

Joshua, Caleb, and especially Molly were excited about the upcoming wedding. Molly could not believe she was going to be the flower girl at her mother's wedding. Aiden, at times, expressed happiness that he would have brothers and a sister; other times he was melancholy.

During these episodes, he tended to withdraw not only from the other children but from Matt and Jillian as well. Matt didn't seem to notice, even accusing Jillian of overreacting when she brought Aiden's moodiness to Matt's attention.

Stretched out on the sofa, Matt leaned his head against Jillian. He seemed to enjoy discussing their wedding plans as much as she did. Her kids were engrossed in the movie Matt had brought for them to watch. Aiden sat on the floor out of view of the television; his knees brought up to his chest and his arms hugging them in place. His chin was propped squarely on his knees, and he had a far-away look in his eyes.

"Aiden seems to be somewhere else tonight."

"Yeah, he probably misses his mom, but he needs to get used to it, Jillian. I hate to say it, but I don't think she is planning on having much to do with him. Do you realize she hasn't even called in over two months? And he hardly ever mentions her anymore." He kept his voice low so Aiden could not hear.

"Maybe he doesn't think he's supposed to."

"What's that suppose to mean?"

"Well, he hears us planning our wedding and talking about becoming a family. Maybe he thinks he's not suppose to talk about his mom."

"He didn't get that from me. I haven't even talked to him about her."

"Exactly. He takes his cues from you." Jillian tried not to sound as if she was scolding Matt, but it still sounded that way to him.

"So what do you want me to do? Call and invite her to visit for the weekend?"

Jillian considered that sometimes Matt could be harsh when Shannon was the subject of their conversation. She dreaded dealing with this matter now and in the future. In her heart, she knew it would always be a part of their family dynamic. "No, that's not what I had in mind. Just talk to Aiden about his mother sometime. I'm sure he has questions…wants to see her."

Matt groaned. "Can't we just pretend Shannon was a bad dream from which I've awakened?"

"I don't think it's that easy."

"You're right, as usual, wife-to-be. I'll mention her casually tonight when we get home and see what happens."

It was ten o'clock when Matt and Aiden returned home from Jillian's.

"Buddy, I thought you'd like the movie I took over for you guys to watch tonight. Why didn't you watch it?"

"Oh, it was okay. I just didn't…" Aiden's voice drifted off.

"Didn't what?" Matt would encourage him to talk; he had promised Jillian.

"Didn't feel like watching a movie."

"I'm sorry. If you had said something, I'm sure Caleb would have been glad to do something else with you, Legos or a video game."

"I didn't want to do that either."

"So what would have made you happy tonight? Putt-putt? Soccer in the backyard?"

"Seeing Mom…" Aiden's voice was barely audible.

"Say that again." Matt was pretty sure he knew what Aiden said but didn't want to go there if he didn't have to.

"Is Mom dead?"

"What? No, your mom's not dead. What gave you that idea?"

"She hasn't called. You never talk about her, and she was sick, and now you're gonna marry someone else." He began to sob.

Matt wanted to feel compassion, but annoyance was the emotion that overcame him. "Look, Aiden, your mom can call when-

Or Be Reconciled

ever she wants to. She just hasn't. Yes, she was sick, but she went to a doctor to get better. Remember, Aiden, your mom divorced me and went to live with another man."

"She didn't divorce me, did she? Isn't she still my mom?"

The always-just-under-the-surface feeling of loathing for Shannon tried to manifest itself, but for Aiden's sake, Matt defied it. Sometimes Matt forgot his life wasn't the only one devastated when Shannon ran off with her boss. Reaching his arms out to his son, he embraced him physically as well as emotionally.

"Come here, Aiden. I'm sorry. I don't mean to get angry when we talk about your mom."

"So she's okay…she's not dead?"

"I promise you she's not dead."

"Can we call her?"

"Sure, we'll call her tomorrow after church."

"Can't we call her tonight?"

"It's too late tonight."

"Please, Dad, please. I want to talk to her."

Matt almost gave in to Aiden's tearful pleas but opted for a stern but positive approach. "Tomorrow will be fine. As soon as we get home from church. You two can talk as long as you want. Now, it's bedtime."

Thankfully, Aiden gave in and went to sleep anticipating hearing his mother's voice. He rehearsed in his mind all the things he had been waiting to tell her. One thing he would not mention was that his dad was planning to marry Mrs. Hamilton. He thought that might make his mom sad, and he didn't want to see her cry like she had on New Year's Eve when he told her he had seen his dad kiss Caleb's mom.

Sunday was a delightful spring day. The dogwoods and Bradford pear trees were blooming in excess. Colorful azalea blossoms appeared in every front yard on their cul-de-sac, with Mrs. Cecil's bushes more abundant and beautiful than at any other house. Matt and Jillian and the kids went out for lunch together after church. As they were leaving the Park Restaurant, Matt finally had the opportunity to take Jillian aside and recount last night's conversation with Aiden. "So I'll give her a call when we get home."

Jillian smiled her approval without exposing any of the reservations she really felt.

Matt tried his best to keep his promise to Aiden, but the only phone number he had for Shannon—her cell phone—was no longer in service. Unconcerned at this revelation, Matt told Aiden there was no answer and they would try again later; then he spent the rest of the afternoon and evening attempting to redirect Aiden's thoughts. He succeeded. When he sent Aiden to bed at nine o'clock, he had gone seven hours without mentioning his mother.

Matt had been sleeping soundly when Aiden's cries rang out in the darkness. Hurrying to his room, Matt knelt by his son's bed. Aiden was sitting up, obviously not yet fully awake, but crying fretfully. "Mom, Mom, where are you?"

"It's okay, Aiden. I'm here. You must have had a bad dream."

"We didn't call her, Dad. You said you would call Mom."

"I tried, remember? No answer."

"You were suppose to try again…you forgot."

"Yes, son, I forgot. We'll do it tomorrow. Now get some sleep. It'll be time to get up soon."

The first words out of Aiden's mouth the next morning were, "Call Mom."

Matt dialed the disconnected number to appease Aiden, knowing he would not get an answer. "Still no answer. Guess I'll have to call her at work. I will tell her to call you tonight."

"I want to talk to her now."

"Well, Aiden, I can't make that happen. You'll just have to wait. Come on, we don't want to be late for school."

Matt was relieved when Aiden slung his book bag on his shoulder even though he stomped to the garage. At ten o'clock, Matt took a break in the teachers' lounge. He was a little concerned about how to keep his promise to Aiden. He had considered calling Maggie Stewart but recalled her number was unlisted. He hadn't telephoned her in almost two years and could only recall the first three digits of her home phone. Although it once annoyed him, he was now glad she had never given him her cell phone number. Deciding the easiest way to reach Shannon was at the law firm, he Googled Charlotte Law Firms. *Miller* popped up at the top of the list. He assumed she was back at work by now; if not, at least he could have someone give her a message that her son was trying to reach her. So what if the message embarrassed her? Then the ball would be in her court, and he could tell Aiden that.

"Good morning. Miller, Miller, and Wagoner. How may I direct your call?"

The voice on the other end sounded vaguely familiar. A vision of a plump but elegant middle-aged lady came to mind. *Moriah? Was that the name of the receptionist who worked at the law firm when Shannon and I were still married?* He wasn't sure.

"Hello, may I help you?"

"Good morning," he stammered. "Yes, could you please connect me with Shannon Mor—" Oops. Slip of the tongue. "With Shannon Stewart?"

No response. He could hear someone breathing on the other end.

"Matt...Matt Morgan...is that you?" came the reply.

"Yes, ma'am, this is Matt Morgan. With whom am I speaking?"

"Matt, oh my goodness gracious! It's been forever. This is Moriah!"

"I thought I recognized your voice, Moriah. How are you?"

"Good, good, better than ever."

Awkward silence.

"Is Shannon in this morning?"

There was puzzlement in her voice. "Matt, Shannon doesn't work here anymore."

"Oh really? Oh well, I just assumed that when she came back from her romp in Europe…" He just couldn't seem to talk about Shannon without adding an element of derision.

"Oh, Matt. I'm so sorry for all that's happened. You two were such a lovely couple…and your handsome little boy. How is Aiden taking all this?"

Matt thought she was referring to the divorce.

"He does okay most of the time, but when you go months without hearing from your mom…"

"Shannon hasn't been in touch with you?"

"I haven't heard from her in months. She dropped by New Year's Eve"—Matt shook his head as he recalled that dreadful night—"and she called in January to ask me to keep Aiden while she recovered from her treatments. I haven't heard a word from her since. I thought she was probably back at work by now. I'm calling for Aiden."

"Oh Matt, you haven't heard from Shannon since January?"

"Nope. Not one word. I guess she's enjoying her life with Mr. Miller and has forgotten about her son."

Moriah could not believe what she was hearing. "Oh Matt, Mr. Miller dumped Shannon as soon as he found out she had breast cancer. You know, they say he trades his women in every other year like some men do their cars." Moriah was bluntly honest; as she spoke, she looked around the office to make sure no one was listening.

"You're kidding!" Matt was confused.

"He found another." How should she put this? "He gave her job to…someone else. I know he did help her out a little at first, and she still has her insurance with the firm, thank goodness!"

"Moriah, I've been trying to call Shannon because Aiden wants to talk to her." He wanted to be perfectly clear that contacting Shannon was not his idea. "But her cell phone has been disconnected, and I don't have another number."

"So you haven't heard from Shannon since January?" She was incredulous.

"That was the last time. Moriah, is something going on I need to know about?" From her tone, he suspected there was. A sick feeling assailed the pit of his stomach. "She's still alive, isn't she?" *What if Aiden's fears were true?*

"Well, for now. I can't believe she didn't tell you about the cancer."

"She told me about the cancer...early stage, easily curable."

"That's not how it turned out. She's in the hospital right now. The chemo wasn't working for her, and they had to do surgery. She's not doing well."

Matt couldn't believe the news he had just received. *Why hadn't Shannon told him? How was Aiden going to react?* "I don't know what to say, Moriah. I had no idea."

"Well, bless her heart. That girl must have not wanted to trouble you after all she put you through."

Matt didn't believe Shannon cared at all about what she had put him through.

"I know how sorry she was. She told me about all her regrets. But she found the Lord, Matt! She's a Christian now."

Matt had not believed that either. "How do you know these things, Moriah?" Still in shock, he hoped this was all office gossip.

"Right after she tried to come back to work, just after she went to see you and Aiden for New Year's, I was the one who had to tell her someone else was working in her place. Well, we went out to lunch a few days later, and she broke down and told me everything...how sorry she was for hurting you and Aiden, about going into that little village church in Italy and finding Jesus. I could tell she had really changed, and I've been visiting her at the hospital."

Matt was speechless. The warning bell sounded just outside the lounge door; in three minutes he had to be back in a classroom full of seventh graders. "Moriah, I don't know what to say...I didn't know any of this."

"Of course, you didn't, baby. You would have been right here by her side if you had known."

Matt wasn't sure he agreed with that assumption. "Look, I'm at work, and I have to get back to class. Can I call you at your home tonight?"

"That will be fine. I'm sorry I was the one to have to tell you."

"Actually, Moriah, I'm glad it was you. You have a way about you that makes it easier." He was thinking that she didn't beat around the bush.

"That's sweet of you to say, Matt. I just hate to see what that ol' devil did to a fine couple like you and Shannon...and of course your little Aiden."

He ignored her comment about "that ol' devil." He had always credited Shannon with their breakup. "Little Aiden is eight years old now, Moriah, and he misses his mother."

"Of course, he does. Make sure he gets to see her soon."

Matt wrote Moriah's home phone number on a scrap of paper and stuck it in his pocket as he darted toward his third-period class.

God help me! Give me the strength to make it through this day. Please, Lord, help me! Throughout the rest of the school day, Matt's prayers were intense, and God answered him. How, he did not know, but he made it through the day without falling to pieces. The hardest task presented itself when Aiden climbed in the front seat of the van that afternoon. "Dad, let's call Mom as soon as we get home."

Matt had been so determined to make it through the school day that he had not even contemplated what to do next. He was going to have to tell Aiden about Shannon. Just not yet. He wanted to talk to Jillian first. She could help him decide what to do.

"Okay, it's going to take just a little while because your mother's phone number has changed, and I'm going to make a few calls to find out her new number."

Puzzled, Aiden looked as his dad. For a moment, Matt thought he was not going to be able to hold himself together. "Why don't we have her number?"

"Just a mix-up. You know, people are always changing their phone plans and getting new numbers." Matt tried to sound calm. "So how about let's stop at Krispy Kreme and get some donuts to take home. You can eat a couple with some milk while I'm looking for the number."

Aiden sighed. The thought of donuts didn't sound appealing just now. All he wanted was to talk to his mom to make sure she was okay. "Whatever."

Matt ordered a dozen of assorted donuts at the drive-thru, including several raspberry filled, Aiden's favorite.

Relieved to see Jillian's car in her driveway, Matt pulled the van into the garage, closing the door behind them. They both literally jumped out of the van. Aiden planned to eat the donuts quickly before his dad thought of another excuse to put off calling his mother. Matt needed to talk to Jillian.

Matt was in such a hurry, he spilled milk all over the counter. Aiden began to think something was really wrong with his dad or his mom, but he was afraid to ask.

"Darn. Oh well, don't cry over spilled milk," Matt muttered mostly to himself. "I have to run next door for a minute. As soon as I get back, we'll find that number."

Aiden had reached his limit. He threw the donut, oozing red jam on the floor, and stomped on it. "No! No! No! You just want to go see Caleb's mother instead of calling my mom. Call her now!" His demand was as menacing as any this suffering and fearful eight-year-old had ever delivered.

The confusion, the anger, the hurt, the fear—it all came together in one hideous raging barrage. "Who in the heck do you think you are to talk to your dad in that tone of voice?" he screamed at Aiden.

Aiden responded with howls of rage that had been brewing in a caldron of panic.

When she didn't see Matt's van in the driveway, Jillian decided to surprise him and Aiden and have their supper waiting on the table when they got home. Holding the covered dishes in one arm, she placed the key in the lock and turned it.

Matt was standing over Aiden, who was cowering under the overhang of the kitchen island. Jillian had not heard the angry voices, but now she heard clearly Aiden's loud, wounded yelps.

"What in the world?" she gasped. Almost dropping the dishes on the coffee table, she hurried to Matt's side, dreading the explanation she was about to receive.

Matt didn't even look up; he hung his head in shame. Aiden scooted out from his hiding place and ran toward his bedroom. When he knew he was well out of reach, he turned and shrieked at Jillian. "It's all your fault! I hate you!" His bedroom door slammed shut.

Only then did Matt reach out to her. He gently took her hand and led her to the sofa.

For a moment neither spoke.

"And again, I ask, what in the world?" Jillian could hardly believe what she had just witnessed, but somehow managed to maintain her composure. Never had she seen a confrontation even resembling this one between her husband-to-be and his son. In her mind, a conflict such as that was reserved for a debauched reality show on an off-limits cable station.

Matt loved that, even in the worst of circumstances, Jillian could usually exhibit a semblance of sanity. It was a good thing

Or Be Reconciled

that at this moment, he could not read her mind. "Well, it has nothing whatever to do with you, so please don't take Aiden's words personally."

"Okay." She did not believe that for a moment but decided to let Matt explain.

"Oh, Jillian…if God hadn't helped me through this day…"

Was this just an ugly argument between father and son? A bad day at school? Jillian's heart was pounding. She wasn't sure she wanted to know what had just transpired.

Matt inhaled and exhaled deeply twice. He held his forehead in his hands. This wasn't the first time she had seen Matt Morgan, a broken man. But at least the last time she knew what had transpired.

He decided to put the best spin he could on this hideous incident. "Aiden's upset because he wants to talk to his mom, but her cell phone number is no longer in service."

Jillian breathed a sigh of relief; maybe this wasn't about her. "That's odd."

"Well, I didn't think so at first because the last time she called, she did say she needed some time to recuperate, and I knew if she wanted to talk to Aiden, she would call. She was always hit-and-miss about contacting him."

Jillian waited patiently for Matt to continue. She sensed he wasn't looking forward to telling her the rest of the story.

"So today I called her at the law firm, except she doesn't work there anymore. I talked to the receptionist who's been there forever, Moriah—she recognized my voice. Anyway, Shannon's not doing well with the cancer. She's in the hospital, had surgery. It doesn't look good."

Jillian felt her heart skip a beat. She had to suppress a feeling of…was that a fleeting sensation of relief she felt? *No no no!* she scolded herself. She could not let herself feel good about bad news. "I'm so sorry, Matt. Why didn't Shannon tell you?"

"Moriah, the receptionist—Moriah thought she didn't want to trouble me or scare Aiden."

That was all Matt was willing to say. Whether or not Shannon was sorry for what she had done to him and Aiden or whether or not she was a Christian—he didn't need to discuss that with Jillian.

"Have you told Aiden?"

"No, I wanted to talk to you first, ask your advice."

"You have to tell him, Matt. You need to take him to see Shannon…as soon as possible."

"I knew you'd say that."

"You said you wanted my advice."

"Go with me, Jillian. Go with me and Aiden to see his mom."

"Oh, I don't think that's a good idea…especially after the way he just reacted to me."

"Man, I do not want to do this."

"I know you don't, but Aiden needs you to do it for him. God will help you."

Matt knew that Jillian was right. She always exhibited wisdom and understanding about matters dealing with Aiden and Shannon. But every fiber of his being was screaming, "No way!"

"When do you think I should go?"

"Considering what Moriah told you, as soon as possible."

"You mean tonight?"

She didn't want to send him away, but she knew she must encourage him to go. "You could probably use some rest first. Why don't you plan to leave in the morning? You can call out tonight, and that will give the secretary time to get a substitute. I'll tell Mr. Rogers that Aiden won't be at school tomorrow. I'll ask him to send Aiden's assignments home with Caleb."

"What would I do without you?" Matt reached over and kissed his fiancée tenderly. He wanted to linger, but she pulled away.

"I just don't want Aiden to come out and see us. He's so upset already."

Or Be Reconciled

"Aiden is going to have to get used to us—"

"But not tonight," she interrupted. Standing up, she took the dishes from the coffee table and carried them into the kitchen. Placing them on the island, she motioned toward them as she revealed the contents. "Meatloaf, mashed potatoes, and baby carrots. All ready."

"Yum." He smacked his lips. "I love you, Jillian. I can't wait until we're married."

"Me too. Is there anything I can do to help you get ready?"

"You've done enough already. Thanks for everything."

She blew a kiss as she opened the front door and headed home.

Matt called her as she was getting ready for bed. "I guess we'll leave early in the morning for Charlotte. As soon as I told Aiden I was taking him to see Shannon tomorrow, he appeared to forget our earlier confrontation. I still want him to apologize to you."

"Matt, that's not necessary. I would just as soon forget it ever happened. I'll be praying for you, guys. Have a safe trip."

"Okay, hon. I'll talk to you when we get back."

She wanted to ask when he planned to return but didn't want him to feel rushed or obligated. He would be back home to her when the time was right. "I love you."

"I love you too."

When he called Moriah, she warned him, "Now you're going to have to prepare that little boy to see his mama like this."

He couldn't bring himself to tell Aiden how sick his mom was. Matt imagined her in a high-tech hospital bed with numerous tubes and other strange medical paraphernalia. He had not actually considered how the cancer treatments may have ravaged the Shannon he met at the football game almost a decade earlier.

"She's at the Blumenthal Cancer Center. Do you want me to give you directions?"

"No, thanks, Moriah. I'll put it in my GPS."

"Oh yes, you men don't need us ladies to give you directions anymore now, do you?"

"Well, maybe in other areas, Moriah."

"That's true. You men will always need our input on the real important matters of life. I'll be praying for you and Shannon and little Aiden." Before ending their conversation, once again Moriah felt led to remind Matt of Shannon's repentant spirit. "She really is sorry about doing you wrong. Bless that girl's heart. I just pray it's not too late to make everything right again."

Even two Tylenol PMs couldn't induce a peaceful night's sleep. Matt set the alarm for six, hoping to get an early start to avoid rush-hour traffic but awoke from a fitful sleep at five-thirty and decided he might as well face his goliath. At the last minute, he told Aiden to pack a few things just in case they had to spend the night. His son reacted with excitement to this prospect. Matt threw together some essentials in his gym bag, and they were out the door just after six o'clock. Matt promised a stop at Biscuitville for breakfast once they were out of city traffic.

Chapter 37

Till Death Do Us Part

Jesus, be with Matt and Aiden. Comfort Aiden. And Lord, if it's your will, heal Shannon.

Jillian had gone to bed last night and woke up this morning, after a restless night's sleep, with that prayer on her lips.

While she was lying in bed praying, she heard Matt's van pull out onto the street. She could not help but wonder how this turn of events would affect their relationship. A random thought flashed in her mind: *Maybe even Mrs. Wilson will attend our wedding if Shannon dies.* Repulsed by her ability to contemplate the future in those terms, she tried, without success, to focus on the day at hand. While dressing and preparing breakfast for the kids, she chided herself for imagining what life would be like after

Shannon succumbed to cancer. *This is so complicated. How can I not think about the possibility?*

By hurrying the kids and leaving the breakfast dishes on the counter, they were able to leave a few minutes early. After dropping Molly and Joshua off at their buildings, Jillian walked with Caleb to his class. She informed Mr. Rogers that Aiden wouldn't be at school today. "Would you be so kind as to send his assignments home with Caleb this afternoon?"

"I saw on the roster that Matt called out today. Are they okay?"

Jillian knew that Mr. Rogers was expressing genuine concern, not being meddlesome. Still, she chose her words carefully. "Aiden's Mom is in the hospital, and he really wanted to go see her."

"Oh, I hope all goes well. I'll say a prayer for her."

"Thank you, Mr. Rogers. Just don't say it too loud. I wouldn't want you to get suspended," Jillian cautioned in jest.

Initially, Mr. Rogers didn't understand her awkward attempt at humor.

After a few seconds of contemplation, he replied, "Oh, yes, yes…no prayer in school…well, we can always pray silently," he reasoned.

I can't believe I said that, Jillian thought to herself as she returned to her car. *How could I be so flippant about such a serious situation?*

A slow morning in the emergency department allowed Jillian to conjure up continual imaginings of Shannon. Visualizing such a beautiful young woman as Shannon lying in a hospital bed, suffering from all the side effects of cancer's aggressive treatments, was heartbreaking to Jillian – even under their unusual circumstances. Knowing from her nursing experience what an ugly death that could be, she breathed a prayer for Shannon.

Matt was thankful that Aiden had fallen back to sleep almost as soon as he had merged the van on the highway; he needed some

Or Be Reconciled

quiet time to settle his thoughts. He wondered if Shannon and her mother had made any arrangements. Probably not. Still, they couldn't expect him to attend to any of those details. After all, he felt no responsibility, legal or otherwise.

Angst-ridden, Matt had no trouble staying awake. After a few hours, he did begin to feel hunger pangs gnawing at his stomach. At nine o'clock, he exited the interstate in Thomasville and pulled into the drive-thru at Biscuitville.

"Two bacon, egg and cheese biscuits, a large coffee, black, and an orange juice please," Matt ordered into the box with the human voice.

Aiden yawned himself awake. "Are we at Mom's?" he asked eagerly.

"Not yet. We're stopping for breakfast."

"Can we eat in the car?" Aiden did not want to waste any time.

"Yeah, I thought we would. Hey, do you need to go to the bathroom?"

"I think so."

Matt drove forward to the real-person window. "You guys have a great day!" the teenage girl offered as she handed the sack and drinks to Matt.

"Thank you," he replied cordially, all the while thinking, *Oh, if you only knew.*

Pulling the van into a parking space, Matt sent Aiden inside to the bathroom while he checked the information on the GPS. According to the calculations, they would arrive at their destination in two hours. Aiden stayed awake for the last portion of the trip, talking almost nonstop about his mother and asking over and over, "How much longer until we get there?"

As the voice on the GPS announced the exit that would lead them to the medical center, dread rose up in Matt in a palpable way. He knew that he had to do this for Aiden, but if there had been any gallant way he could have avoided it, he would have. *If only Jillian were with me!*

Once they were off the interstate, the GPS lead him out of the way, and he had to backtrack to find the parking garage. At one point, he thought he might vomit. When he finally pulled into a parking space, Aiden opened the van door before he had shifted into park.

"Whoa, son…not so fast. Your mom's not going anywhere." He knew he sounded too harsh; his nerves were working overtime, and his statement was definitely not composed with the best choice of words.

"Hurry, I want to see her." Aiden was almost dragging him through the enclosed bridge that led from the parking garage to the buildings that made up the medical complex.

With no GPS to navigate the medical center, Matt was forced to stop and ask directions twice. He had never liked the antiseptic smell of hospitals. Today he sensed something else in the air. As he and Aiden turned a corner after stepping off the elevator, two orderlies were pushing a gurney down the hallway. The patient was completely covered with a white sheet. Matt hurried Aiden in the other direction. Finally they stood outside the door of room 642. "Shannon Stewart – Dr. Walker" read the nameplate on the drab green wall beside the almost closed door.

Aiden started to rush in, but Matt grabbed his shoulders and held him back. "Let's knock first." Matt rapped his hand against the heavy door just as a nurse from inside pulled it slightly open; Matt and Aiden could not see inside.

"May I help you?" she asked cordially.

"Uh, yes. This is Mrs. Stewart's son, Aiden, and I'm…" Matt was trying to decide how to identify himself.

"Mom, Mom!" Aiden couldn't wait. Excitedly, he slipped between the nurse and the doorjamb. "Mom!" he called again as he caught his first glimpse of his mother, reclining in the hospital bed. The nurse swung around and extended her arm to stop him, but he had successfully scurried past her reach.

"Be careful, your mom's had surgery!" she called out, sounding more concerned than cross.

Aiden had already reached his mom's bedside. Heeding the nurse's warning, he carefully laid his head on the bed, beside Shannon, and enveloped her with both arms.

"Aiden!" Shannon was obviously stunned by the sight of her son. Although her voice conveyed surprise, it was weak and barely audible.

"Mom, I've missed you so much!" Aiden declared, gazing up into her face while being careful not to disturb her covers.

Cautiously, Shannon placed her left arm across Aiden's back, embracing him with all the strength she could muster.

The nurse paused at the end of the bed, observing this poignant reunion. She had a pleased smile on her face as she turned to Matt. "Come on in, sir."

Matt stopped in his tracks about two feet from the side of the bed in the diminutive, utilitarian room. Stunned, he could not take in the image confronting him. Shannon's face was pale and emaciated, her eyes sunken and lashless. Instead of long, sunlit tresses, spikey brown stubble covered her head. A drab hospital gown was draped around her shoulders. Medical paraphernalia took the place of fashionable accessories. Amber urine coursed through a transparent tube to a collection bag hanging on the bed rail. Matt was amazed that Aiden had recognized her.

"Mom, why haven't you called me?" Aiden inquired breathlessly, seemingly oblivious to his mom's pitiful appearance.

"I've been sick, and I didn't want you to worry about me," Shannon whispered graciously before closing her eyes as if taking a fleeting nap. She started coughing and grasped the pillow she was holding close to her chest, guarding her incisions.

"Are you okay, Ms. Stewart?" the nurse walked to the opposite side of the bed from where Aiden was reclining against his mother. "Can I get you anything?"

Shannon stroked Aiden's sandy hair. "I have everything I need now, thank you."

"Then I'll leave you alone with your visitors. Call if you need me," the nurse instructed before exiting the room.

Visitors? Shannon hadn't even looked past Aiden since he came in—until now. She grimaced when she saw Matt, obviously shaken, standing a few feet behind Aiden.

He was unable to speak.

"So you're the one who brought this precious gift to me," her voice sounded much stronger than it had just a few minutes earlier. "I thought maybe I was dreaming."

"Uh…yeah…we…I mean, Aiden…we…hadn't heard from you, and I thought by now you'd be back at work so I called yesterday…and…and Moriah told me…"

"It's so nice to see you," she sighed as she kissed the top of Aiden's head so Matt would understand she was addressing the comment to their son. In her heart, she wanted to express her joy at seeing both her former husband and her son, but she dared not. Aiden had barely moved since he first found this place of peaceful rest next to his mother's ailing body.

"Mom, when will you be able to come home?"

"That's up to the doctors…and God."

"I've been praying for you, every night in bed. I've been asking God to make you better so you can come home."

Shannon looked questioningly at Matt. He didn't want her to get any wrong ideas.

"Kids. I keep telling him that you have another home now. Wishful thinking, I guess." Matt immediately regretted being so blunt.

"But I want Mom to come home. I don't want a new mom." Aiden's tone had that reckless edge in it, akin to the one he had exhibited yesterday before going off on Jillian, and Matt was not about to let his son throw another tantrum.

"Aiden, your mom's sick. If you want to stay and visit her, you have to be very quiet and not throw a fit like you did yesterday. I'll take you right back home."

Aiden directed an angry stare at his father but knew it was in his best interest to keep his mouth closed. He wouldn't do anything that would jeopardize his being with his mother.

"I'm sorry, Shannon. Do you want us to go?"

"Oh please, no…don't go. I've been longing to see Aiden." She had been longing to see Matt too, but she knew it would not be fair to tell him that.

"Then why didn't you call?" Matt tried not to let his annoyance show. "Don't you think you owed Aiden that?"

"I wanted to make it easier on him and you. I've hurt you both so much already."

"Let's not talk about the past. What…don't you think we need to talk?" He tried to muster a little compassion.

Aiden still had his stare fixed on Matt. Shannon took the opportunity to gesture toward Matt, a motion he recognized as Shannon's way of saying, "Not in front of Aiden."

Matt nodded his head. "Okay, let me leave you two alone for a little while. I'm going to go get my parking ticket validated. Can I bring you anything?"

"No, I'm good," Shannon replied honestly because at that moment, she felt she had everything she could ever need.

"Aiden, you better behave yourself!"

His son knew that obeying his father's stern warning was necessary if he was going to remain with his mom. "Yes, Daddy," he murmured.

It had only taken a few minutes to validate the parking ticket. Wanting to gather his thoughts, Matt bypassed the chapel and found a comfortable chair in a waiting room where he sipped on a bitter cup of coffee from the vending machine. After an hour, his thoughts were still as jumbled as when he first sat down. Dreading facing Shannon again, he dutifully headed back toward her room. As he approached the door, an attractive middle-aged lady with a white lab coat was leaving. She smiled at him when he stopped in front of the door.

"Are you Matt?"

"Yes, ma'am, Matt Morgan." He extended his right hand to her.

"I'm so glad to meet you, and I'm so pleased that you and Aiden are here to visit Shannon."

"And you are…?"

"Oh, I'm sorry, Mr. Morgan. I feel like we know each other. Shannon has spoken of you so frequently. I'm her doctor, Leah Walker.

"So am I allowed to know what's going on with her…since… you know, we're divorced?

"Actually, Shannon put you at the top of her contact list."

"Probably because of Aiden…but, you know, she hadn't contacted us for over two months. The last I heard from her she said she had completed her treatments and was recuperating."

"Sometimes it's difficult to say why people with terminal illnesses react the way they do." Dr. Walker's voice expressed more understanding than Matt had been able to muster.

"Did you say terminal?"

"She hasn't told you, has she?"

"Like I said, she told me in January she was recuperating and wanted me to take care of Aiden until she could, and that was the last I heard from her until yesterday. I tried to call her at work, and the receptionist told me she had surgery and wasn't doing well."

"When she first came to me, her cancer was already serious… and aggressive. Neither the radiation or chemotherapy treatments were effective. We had no choice but to perform the mastectomy and try to remove the affected lymph nodes, but her prognosis is still not good. However, she looks better today than I have seen her in weeks."

Or Be Reconciled

Matt could not imagine Shannon looking any worse than how she appeared to him an hour earlier.

"I think you and Aiden are the best treatment she could receive at this stage."

"Well, I think it's Aiden...you know, we're divorced, and I'm engaged."

This announcement surprised Dr. Walker.

"Does Shannon know that you're engaged?"

"I haven't had a chance to tell her."

"Please, Mr. Morgan, unless you absolutely have to, don't tell her right now. You know, she's been praying that God would reconcile your marriage."

Matt shook his head and muttered something that sounded to Dr. Walker like, "Yeah, right."

"Well, Dr. Walker, that's not going to happen. Shannon made her choice several years ago. It's unfortunate that she's..." he started to say "going to die" but caught himself. "That she's terminally ill."

"Shannon's very sorry for her previous wrong actions. She knows she sinned against you and Aiden...and God."

Matt was incredulous to be having this conversation with Shannon's doctor.

Meticulously, Dr. Walker continued. "Like cancer, unforgiveness can be a very serious disease that spreads aggressively and destroys a life."

Matt balked at being preached at by Dr. Walker and wanted to turn and walk away. Something in his spirit said, *Listen*.

"Matt, are you a Christian?"

Feeling like a wounded little boy, he replied, "Not a great one, but I have asked Jesus to forgive my sins and come into my life."

"Did he forgive your sins?"

"I believe so."

"So what's your responsibility?"

Matt hung his head and stared at the floor for only a moment before attempting an answer. "Are you talking about forgiving others as he has forgiven us?"

"Yes, Matt. You know, in this old world in which we find ourselves, there are many people who will tell you that the Bible says it's okay to do some things, and another person will say that same action is wrong. But throughout God's word, there are some very clear truths he has given us to live by. One of those—and I know this without a doubt—is no matter the circumstances, we always have scriptural grounds for forgiveness."

At the sound of those words, Matt's head shot up, and he looked directly into Dr. Walker's eyes. "What did you say?"

"We always have scriptural grounds for forgiveness."

Those words sounded so familiar. He stood quietly, trying to remember where he had heard them, and as he did so, those words wrote themselves in his heart.

Dr. Walker thought she might have upset him. "Mr. Morgan, please know that I do not mean to offend you, but I am experienced in dealing with life-and-death situations every day. Sometimes there is no time to ponder. I tend not to mince words."

"No, it's okay." Matt was surprised that he had not been offended by Dr. Walker's words. But he was feeling a stirring in his spirit that he could not yet explain.

"I believe God wanted me to tell you that, Mr. Morgan, because God loves you and Aiden and Shannon."

"Yes, I know he does." Matt's reply was more than matter-of-fact. At that moment, God's love was flooding over him, breaking down the dam of unforgiveness he had harbored for such a long time.

Dr. Walker extended her hand, and Matt clasped it in his own. There was no need for additional words. The message had been boldly given and freely received. As Shannon's doctor's heels clicked down the hall, Matt quietly opened the door to Shannon's room. Aiden was stretched out on his mother's bed, his head gently cradled on the pillow beside her. Both appeared to be sleeping peacefully.

As Matt walked down the hall toward the medical center's chapel, he searched for local hotels on his phone and reserved a room for him and Aiden to stay in that night.

An older couple was sitting in a tender embrace on the very last pew. Holding hands, they appeared to be crying. Matt nodded as he walked past. When he reached the front of the chapel, he sat down and leaned forward, placing his head in his hands. "Father in heaven, thank you for forgiving my sins. Help me to forgive Shannon."

Chapter 38

Prayer Changes Things

Father, thank you for helping me make it through the day, and please, help tomorrow to be a better day. Give the kids a good night sleep and help them love and serve you. Give Matt and Aiden a safe trip home. And take care of Shannon.

Jillian's day in the emergency department had started slow but evolved into a torrent of patients with serious medical situations in the afternoon. An elderly gentleman arrived via ambulance from a local nursing home, obviously close to death. His orange Do Not Resuscitate bracelet alerted her to recheck the documents that had been sent with him. *No extraordinary measures. No life support.* Family members and his pastor gathered by his side. She was sure she saw a smile on his face as he breathed his last breath.

"Finally home," she had said out loud, eliciting a curious glance from the male nurse that had been assisting her and a knowing smile from the pastor.

A young husband rushed through the doors at one o'clock, pushing his wife in a wheel chair. "My wife is gushing blood, and she's only five months pregnant!" he almost screamed to the waiting staff.

Jillian directed the attendants to skip triage and take her to labor and delivery immediately; she asked God to intervene, realizing the probable outcome would not be a good one. Just before shift change, a little girl the same age as Molly was brought in by her stepfather. Crying hysterically and covered with bruises, the child readily left the man's grip and cuddled into Jillian's embrace. Jillian asked the man, dressed in dirty clothes and reeking of perspiration and whiskey, to take a seat in the waiting room. Reluctantly, he did so. As she carried the child to triage, she notified the hospital social worker.

Planning to wait up for Matt's return, she instead surrendered to her exhausted state and fell asleep on the sofa, an old and boring black-and-white movie playing in the background. At eleven o'clock, she stirred and, seeing the time, forced herself to go to bed. It seemed she had barely fallen back to sleep when the doorbell awakened her. She knew it had to be Matt. Not bothering to look at the clock, she ran to the door in her pajamas and opened the door wide for her husband-to-be. He took her in his arms, twirling her around again and again. His lips found her waiting ones. Passionately, she returned his kisses. "Soon, you'll be my husband…my husband…my husband."

"Stop it! Stop it! He's my dad! He doesn't belong to you. Let go of him!"

Not Aiden again. Oh yes, yanking on her pajama top, trying to get her to let go of his father. "It's all your fault! I hate you! Let go of him!"

She heard ringing in the background—the phone...she had to answer the phone.

"Hello?"

"Jillian, you were still sleeping, weren't you?"

"No...yes...I was dreaming. What time is it?"

Matt replied, "It's six-thirty. I'm sorry to call you so early. I meant to call last night to let you know we were staying over, but it was so late when we finally got to the hotel. Shannon's in really bad shape. The doctor said she was terminal."

Jillian was still groggy, coming out of her dreadful dream. "Yes, you told me the other night she wasn't doing well."

"I didn't know how badly until I talked to her doctor."

"So what do you plan to do?" The scene of Aiden from her dream was still reverberating in her mind.

"Could you tell Mr. Rogers that Aiden won't be back this week?"

Jillian rolled over and sat on the side of the bed; her feet hit the cool floor. "Sure. So you're staying all week?" Matt's words had deleted one awful vision from her mind, only to be replaced with another.

"No, I'm coming back today. Moriah has offered to take care of Aiden so he can be close to Shannon."

She felt a great sense of relief. "That's very nice of her. So you'll be back today?"

"I'm leaving after I get some breakfast for Aiden. I should be there before noon."

Jillian heard something in Matt's voice she could not precisely identify. "Jillian, do you think it would be a problem if you took the day off?"

She really didn't like the way that sounded...so solemn.

"If I have to, I could. I haven't called out since I've been at the hospital."

"I would really appreciate it. I'll come over when I get there. See you soon."

"Okay."

Jillian stood to her feet for just a moment before throwing herself back on the bed. Something was wrong. She knew it. No "I love you," no anticipation in Matt's voice. *Of course something is wrong! Aiden's mother is dying,* she told herself. She called Marie to tell her an unexpected situation had come up, and she would be unable to work today.

"You are hard to replace, but I am sure I can find someone to work for you," Marie assured. "Is everything okay?"

"Of course everything is not okay, or I would be there," Jillian responded, aware of the exasperation in her voice. "I can't talk about it right now, but please do say a prayer for me." She had almost asked Marie to pray for her and Matt but decided against that request.

"Of course, let me know if there's anything I can do."

"I'm sorry I'm so unpleasant, Marie. Thanks for understanding. I'll talk to you later."

Not wanting to have to explain to the children why she wasn't going to work, she slipped into her scrubs to drive them to school. She tried to act as if everything was okay. She knew, however, that was definitely not the case. As she was pulling into her driveway, the thought occurred to her that she had skipped her prayers this morning after being awakened from that horrible dream by Matt's phone call.

She plopped down on the sofa. The silence was deafening. She traipsed to the kitchen and selected a Christian music station on the under-counter radio. Once again falling back on the sofa, she closed her eyes. Not only could she see Aiden pulling on her pajama top, but she could also hear him yelling, "Let go of him!"

Determinedly, she opened her eyes to end that awful vision. As clear as the robin singing outside her dining room window, she heard a voice say, *Let go of him.*

She went to the kitchen and made herself a cup of tea. With her Bible in one hand and the hot tea in the other, she ambled outside to the porch. She sat in the wicker rocker facing Matt's driveway. She opened the Bible and began reading, then devouring, the words. The teacup was long empty, but she was still reading when the familiar navy-blue van turned into the cul-de-sac. She had cried a few tears, but for the most part, she was at peace.

Matt stepped out of his van slowly, not even looking up at her. He slowed his pace even more as he walked toward her front porch. Instead of bounding up the steps in his usual manner, he appeared to be struggling with each one. When he reached the top step, she stood up and smiled at him.

"Jillian, this is so hard…"

"It's okay. I know," she spoke clearly and distinctly; her voice was strong.

"You know?"

"I know what God wants us to do."

Matt shook his head in momentary disbelief, an arduous smile turning up the corners of his lips. "I should have known God would speak to both of us."

"Well, actually, Aiden told me first, in a dream, and then God spoke very clearly to me."

"God spoke very clearly to me too—well after Dr. Walker told me. They both said I had scriptural grounds for forgiveness."

"Therefore, I must let you go."

Simultaneously, each extended a hand to the other. Jillian's grip was gentle, almost limp; Matt's grip was strong.

"Not so hard, young man." She managed a forced grin, which he tentatively returned.

Simultaneously, and symbolically, they released each other's hands.

Jillian slipped the engagement ring off of her finger and held it out to him. Reluctantly, he held his hand open. Silently, she placed it in the palm of his hand. As if in slow motion, she gently closed his hand over the sphere of precious metal and stone that had held the promise of a new life together.

"Thank you, Jillian. I'll miss you and the kids." Tears were rolling down his unshaven cheeks.

Her efforts to keep from crying resulted in her almost being unable to speak, but somehow, she managed to say, "Thank you, Matt. We'll miss you too. God bless you and Aiden…and Shannon. I'll be praying for each of you."

"I know you will."

Epilogue

"Mommy! Hurry! It's time for the wedding!"

"The tea is almost ready. I'll be there."

Molly had looked forward to the royal wedding for weeks. Jillian planned a celebratory English tea with scones, tiny cheese biscuits, fruit, and of course dainty cups of steaming Earl Grey. She and Molly would share the delicacies as they watched William marry Catherine and turn her into a princess—every little girl's dream! Molly had even dressed up in her pink lace princess dress, the one Jillian had originally purchased for Molly to wear at another wedding…

Joshua and Caleb were sleeping in. They had no interest in weddings, princess or otherwise.

"Marriage is intended to be a way in which a man and a woman become what God wants them to be. Whatever the difficulty, we are committed to the way of generous love." Jillian was impressed by the minister's words.

"Are those little girls in white dresses the flower girls?"

"Yes, they're the flower girls. Aren't they pretty?" Jillian responded before addressing her own little flower girl, "But not as lovely as my Molly."

"Do you think I will ever get to be a flower girl?" Molly asked wistfully as she climbed into her mother's lap and embraced her with all the strength her six-year-old arms could muster.

"My baby girl is growing up," Jillian inhaled the fragrance of her daughter's long curls, "But you still have plenty of time to be a flower girl."

As the prince and princess shared their first kiss on the palace balcony, the boys were playing soccer in the backyard with friends from school. Molly was no longer enchanted and decided to change into her playclothes so she could go outside with her brothers. Jillian was pleased at how much her children's circle of friends had grown this past year. What had really surprised her was that Joshua and Caleb had become best buddies, and Joshua consistently set a good example for his little brother. They were doing well at school, and both were enjoying playing soccer. Molly loved school; she took gymnastic classes and had found a best friend forever at New Life Center, a seven-year-old named Gigi. It was spring break for the children, and Jillian had taken a week of vacation so she could spend time with them.

Two more days and back to work, she contemplated as she poured herself the last cup of tea from her fancy teapot. She carried the cup out to the front porch and sat in one of the wicker rockers. Once again, she frowned at the For Sale sign next door, wishing someone would buy her former neighbor's house and wondering why it hadn't yet sold. She waved to the mailman as he started to place some letters in her box. When he saw her, he jogged up the sidewalk and delivered them in person.

"Good morning, Mrs. Hamilton. It's a beautiful spring day."

"That it is," she responded, receiving the stack of letters from his outstretched hand. She scanned them quickly, looking for anything more interesting than the usual bills and advertisements. At first, she thought the legal-sized envelope was just another credit card offer. Then she saw the name on the return address: *Morgan.*

On the day Matt moved from Lakeview a year ago, he and Jillian had acknowledged it would be best not to contact each other unless there was a change in circumstances.

"Well, I guess this is good-by. If the situation ever…I mean if…" Matt had uttered those words as he climbed into the driver's seat of the moving van he had rented to return his and Aiden's belongings to Charlotte.

Jillian had only nodded in response, for she shared with Matt the inability to verbalize any plans contingent on Shannon's death.

Since that day, Jillian had kept her promise to pray for them. Daily she had interceded for Matt and Shannon and Aiden. Outside of her prayer time, she had tried not to think about them, but even now, so many daily activities reminded her of the times she had spent with Matt. The children, however, surprised her by quickly appearing to recover from loosing their friend and neighbor. Caleb spoke of Aiden occasionally, but it was usually just in recalling a pleasant memory. And although at first she had missed Matt terribly, God had helped her to once again overcome loss and loneliness. She had learned this time that it was not necessary to have another man in her life to make her happy and complete. God alone could meet her every need.

Now, her heart was beating out of her chest. She tapped the envelope on the porch railing. She caught a glimpse of Mrs. Cecil, eying her curiously from her front yard.

Just get it over with! she urged herself.

Anxiously, she slid her longest fingernail underneath the flap of the envelope and pulled out one handwritten page. The paper was shaking in her hand as she began to read:

Dearest Jillian,

You and your children have been in my thoughts and prayers. I know you've been praying for us as well. I'm sorry that I haven't written sooner. This has been quite a year for me.

In March, Dr. Walker gave me the good news that I am currently cancer free. She said it was a miracle! Of course, I know that without all the prayers, including yours, I would have not survived.

Matt and I were remarried last June when I was released from the hospital. In August, Matt started his new job as the assistant principal at Aiden's middle school, and both of them are enjoying that arrangement. I plan to stay home for now and try to be a good wife and mother. I am doing some volunteer work at the cancer center, however. Aiden is doing really well at home and at school. My mom has been attending church with us. That's another miracle! For the first time ever, Aiden has an attentive grandparent; that has been good for my son and my mom.

Most of all, I want to thank you—this may sound awkward—but thank you for letting Matt go. When you did that, it confirmed to him that it was God's will for us to reconcile. I'll always be grateful to you for giving him back to me.

Thanks again for everything, and please don't stop praying for us.

Love in Christ,

Shannon

Jillian pondered the letter for sometime before going inside to prepare lunch for the kids. Amazed at how God, with his perfect love, works in the imperfect lives of his children, she bowed her head and heart in sincere gratitude.

> Thank you, Lord, that you love us and that everything that happens in our lives has a purpose. We don't always understand, but we can know that you will be with us, that you will never leave or forsake us. Thank you for creating beauty from ashes. Thank you for my family—Joshua and Caleb and Molly, for Mom and Dad, for Grandma and Grandpa Hamilton. Thank you for my church family, especially Pastor Milkalski and Marie and Mrs. Wilson. Thank you for healing Shannon and reconciling her marriage to Matt. Bless Shannon and Matt and Aiden and his grandmother as they grow closer to you.

The *ding* alerted her to an incoming e-mail. Clicking on her inbox revealed a new message from her mom. She was so thankful for her parents and all they had taught her and especially how they had stood by her with their encouragement and prayers this past year. Several times they had even talked about returning to America. Recently, she had been contemplating how nice it would be to have them close.

> Hi, Jillian. Your dad and I need you to do us a favor. God has been speaking to our hearts that it is time for us to return home. The young man who has been serving with us as assistant director is quite capable of taking over the ministry. We will raise funds in America to send to provide the needs of the orphanage. If you don't mind, we would love to live close to you. We plan to return next month. Do you think you could check with a realtor about finding a house for us? Let me know what you think.
>
> Love you so much, Mom

Jillian immediately selected Reply and eagerly typed her return message.

Mom and Dad, I'm so excited! How about a house next door to us? I'll call the realtor right now. God is so good! Can't wait to tell the kids. Can't wait to see you!

Love, your daughter, Jillian

Study Questions

Chapter 1

Prayer is an integral part of Jillian's life. Read Psalm 5:3. How did Jillian begin each day? How do you begin each day?

How is Jillian dealing with her status as "single mom"?

Read Psalm 37:4. What is the desire of Jillian's heart? What does this scripture say we must do to receive the desires of our heart? What is the desire of your heart?

Chapter 2

In your opinion, what was Jillian's first impression of Matthew Morgan?

What was Matt's first impression of Jillian?

Read 1 Samuel 16:7. When you meet someone, on what is your first impression usually based?

Chapter 3

Does Mrs. Wilson remind you of someone you have known? If so, how did that person's behavior affect you? To what can you attribute Mrs. Wilson's curious demeanor?

Read 1 Corinthians 13:5. This verse states some characteristics of love. Which quality does not apply to Mrs. Wilson's actions? Which one describes Jillian's behavior?

Read Psalm 34:10. What is Jillian seeking? What does God promise to those who seek him? How do you understand the phrase "any good thing"?

Chapter 4

Read Proverbs 4:23. What new feeling is Jillian experiencing? If you were Jillian's friend, and she asked your advice, at this point what would you tell her?

Why did Jillian avoid walking past Mr. Morgan at the school?

Did this chapter remind you of a personal experience? If so, share your thoughts.

Chapter 5

How would you interpret Jillian's dream? Read Matthew 2:22. Throughout scripture, especially in the Old Testament, God speaks to people through dreams. Do you believe God still speaks through dreams today? Why or why not?

What was Jillian's reaction when Caleb told her that Mr. Morgan had a son?

Chapter 6

Why did cutting the anniversary card from Bryan cause Jillian to have such an emotional response? Read 1 Thessalonians 3:6. How do you deal with pleasant memories? With sad memories?

Chapter 7

What is going on in Joshua's life? Read Psalm 68:5. What resource does Joshua have? Is this enough?

Do you think widows and widowers should seek to remarry for the sake of their children? Explain your answer. (See 1 Corinthians 7:8-9; Romans 7:2-3)

Chapter 8

Read Romans 8:28. Jillian alludes to the idea presented in this scripture after Matt explains his situation. In your own life, have you experienced a fulfillment of this scriptural principle? Describe the event(s) that took place.

Why does Jillian's impression of Matt keep changing?

Chapter 9

What kinds of thoughts are running through Jillian's mind?

Read Proverbs 15:1. Was Matt's response to Mrs. Wilson appropriate? What effect did it have on Mrs. Wilson?

Chapter 10

Read Psalm 55:22. Paraphrase this verse. Why is Jillian trying to convince herself that her interest in Matt is only that of friendship? In your opinion, what are Matt's intentions?

Chapter 11

Read Hebrews 13:4. Do you think Rev. Brown's message was helpful? Was there anything with which you disagree? How is our society trying to redefine marriage?

Read Malachi 2:16. Mrs. Wilson was right with her fact, but not in her attitude. Why do you think God hates divorce? How should Christians feel about divorce?

Read 1 Chronicles 28:9. What was Jillian's motivation for taking the cookies to Matt?

Chapter 12

How did Jillian feel about the impromptu "performance" she and Matt executed at his house in front of Shannon and her mother? How did Matt respond? What do you think of their actions?

Read Matthew 19:6 and Mark 10:9. Who gave these directions? Write your own understanding of these two scriptures.

Chapter 13

Read Matthew 19:1-6. Does the Christian church teach this concept about marriage today? What does the command, "What then God has joined together let not man separate" mean to you?

Read Matthew 19:8. Why did Moses allow men to divorce their wives?

Read Matthew 19:9. According to Jesus, what is adultery? If you had been a member of Jillian's father's church, would you have stayed or left? Why?

Chapter 14

When Caleb suggested Ms. Caleche was "in love" with Matt, what was Jillian's response?

Read 1 Corinthians 13:4. Do you agree that love is not jealous? Is there ever a time when a spouse should be jealous? Explain.

Chapter 15

Read Romans 8:26. Jillian asked God to "speak to Shannon's heart" but had "no idea" what she wanted God to say to Shannon. If you were in Jillian's place, how would you have prayed for Shannon?

Chapter 16

Read Psalm 104:34. Jillian's thought life seems to be focused on Matt. Is this a problem? If so, what should she do?

Explain why Joshua has mixed feelings about Mr. Morgan.

Chapter 17

Read Song of Solomon 5:4. Do you think Jillian's heart was "thrilled" when she saw Matt?

Jillian had been telling herself that she and Matt could be no more than friends. Do you think she has changed her mind? Why?

When Jillian said "I have nothing to hide," was she being honest with herself? With Matt?

Chapter 18

Read 1 Timothy 5:11 and 14. Are Jillian's emotions normal for a young widow?

Make a list of difficulties a single mom faces; a single dad.

Chapter 19

As Matt and Jillian's feelings for each other escalate, what qualities in Matt attract Jillian? Which of Jillian's qualities attract Matt?

Read 1 Corinthians 7:39-40. What does "only in the Lord" mean to you? Is Jillian free to marry Matt? Is Matt free to marry Jillian?

What advice do you think the Apostle Paul, the writer of Corinthians, would have given her?

Chapter 20

What are some of the obstacles "blended" families face?

Read Ephesians 6:4 and Colossians 3:21. What qualities does Jillian admire in a father? List some qualities of a good father.

Chapter 21

Does Jillian still have reservations about her relationship with Matt? What actions convey this?

The chapter title, "Be Careful Not to Fall" could apply physically as well as emotionally. Read Proverbs 4:23. Is it too late for Jillian and Matt to guard their hearts? At what time in a relationship is in critical to guard your heart?

Chapter 22

What did you enjoy most about Jillian and Matt's family Christmas celebration? Describe your ideal celebration of Christmas Day.

Read Matthew 25: 35-40. How did Jillian's family's celebration honor Jesus? How did the celebration at New Life Center honor him?

Chapter 23

If you have lost a close family member, how did holiday celebrations change afterwards?

Read 1 Thessalonians 4:13. Was your loved one a Christian? How does this change the grieving process?

Chapter 24

Do you sense the tension between Jillian and Matt in this short chapter? What is the cause?

Read 1 Timothy 2:1. For whom are we to pray?

Read 1 Timothy 2:4. What does God desire?

Jillian struggles when she feels led to pray for Shannon. Why?

Chapter 25

As Jillian recalled the previous day's conversation with Matt, are there any remaining signs of tension between them? When did the tension ease?

Read Ephesians 6:2-3. Why was Jillian hesitant to tell her parents about her relationship with Matt?

Chapter 26

Do you agree with the directions Pastor Milkalski gave to Matt? If you had been the pastor, what would you have done?

Read 1 Peter 5:8-9. Whose voice did Jillian hear when she pulled in her driveway? Evidently, Satan thought she was vulnerable. Was she? Was her response effective? Why?

Chapter 27

Does Matt have any intentions of reconciling with Shannon? How does Jillian's revelation of Bryan's adultery and her willingness to forgive him affect Matt?

Read Luke 16:18, Matthew 19:9, and Mark 10:11-12. How are these verses the same? What *exception* is included in Matthew?

Chapter 28

Read 1 Corinthians 7:10-11. Paraphrase this scripture. How did Jillian respond to this scripture when her husband committed adultery? How should she respond now?

Chapter 29

How would you describe Jillian's attitude toward Shannon? Matt's?

Read Luke 6:27-28; 31. If Jillian is to follow this teaching, what should she do? What should Matt do?

Chapter 30

What is Matt learning about prayer?

Read James 5:16. Matt is praying for God's will. Is that what he really wants?

Do you agree with Jillian that she and Matt need to spend some time apart? Why?

Chapter 31

Read Psalm 37:4. What are the two desires of Shannon's heart? Do you think she knows what it means to "delight yourself in the Lord?" What does that phrase mean to you?

Chapter 32

Read Ephesians 4:31-32 and Hebrews 12:15. Mrs. Wilson's husband committed adultery against her; did she have the right to be bitter toward him? Why do you think her sons moved away and have little contact with their mother? If you could talk to Mrs. Wilson, what would you say to her?

Chapter 33

At the beginning of the chapter, what decision had Jillian made about her relationship with Matt? What happened to change her mind?

Read Titus 3:3. Which phrase in the verse could refer to "the kiss."

Read Galatians 5:24. Do you think Jillian has "crucified" her flesh?

Read 1 Corinthians 7:8-9. Does this verse give Jillian "permission" to pursue a romantic relationship with Matt? Explain your answer.

What happens when we follow our "feelings" instead of God's leading?

Chapter 34

Read Ezekiel 16:58 and Romans 3:23-24. Shannon knew she had sinned against God and Matt. Through Jesus, had she been justified?

Why was she having a difficult time accepting forgiveness? Do you sometimes find it difficult to believe you have been truly forgiven for a particular sin?

What was Dr. Walker's explanation of "justification"? Do you agree with this definition?

Chapter 35

Read Romans 12:2. Does this indicate that God has one will or that there are various degrees – good will, acceptable will, perfect will? Explain your answer.

Was Jillian being honest about her reason for waiting to tell her parents about Matt? Why do you think she had delayed telling them? What do you sense in Jillian's response to her father?

Chapter 36

Why did Shannon tell Matt she was recovering and just needed to rest?

Read Proverbs 16:2. What was her motive?

Write a paragraph describing what Aiden is experiencing. Throughout Jillian and Matt's relationship, her children appear to have accepted Matt, but Aiden has been resistant, at times, to Jillian. To what do you attribute the difference in their responses?

Chapter 37

Read Luke 6:37 and Matthew 6:14-15. Is there ever a circumstance, when as a Christian, it is legitimate to withhold forgiveness from someone who has sinned against you?

What if that sin is adultery?

What does Jesus say will happen to us if we do not forgive others?

Chapter 38

Read 1 Corinthians 7:10-11. Why was it appropriate for Jillian to "let Matt go"? Explain your answer.

Do you think that both Jillian and Matt "heard from God"? On what do you base your answer?

Epilogue

Read Romans 8:28

Do you see this scripture fulfilled in the lives of Jillian, Matt, and Shannon?

How might this story have ended differently if Jillian and Matt had not met?

Do you think it was God's will for Jillian and Matt to be more than friends?

Read 1 Corinthians 13. How did Jillian express God's love? How did Matt express God's love? How did Shannon express God's love?